LOVE REQUIRED

Book Three

The Real Love series

By Melanie Codina

Laura,
Jason loves you!
Thanks for reading
:)
Melanie
XOXO

The book you are about to enjoy is a work of fiction. A resemblance to any person, living or dead, events and/or location is purely coincidental. References to real locale have been allowed by the businesses and used in manner to create atmosphere the reader can relate to. All events, the characters and storylines have been created by the author's imagination and have been used fictitiously.

Cover design/art done by the awesome Regina Wamba over at Mae I Design and Photography. For more information visit her website at: http://www.maeidesign.com/

Or find her on Facebook at https://www.facebook.com/MaeIDesignandPhotography?fref=ts

Editing done by the fabulous Madison Seidler. For more information visit her website at:
http://www.madisonsays.com/
Or find her on Facebook at:
https://www.facebook.com/mseids
Published by Melanie Codina, San Diego, California.

ISBN: 978-1495957376

Dedication

In life, we make mistakes. It is hoped that we learn from them and the scars they leave behind. Our scars are there to remind us of where we've been, they tell our history. All of them are testaments of survival, and that is what makes them noteworthy. Scars don't define us or tell us where we're going ... they show us where we never want to be again.

This story is for anyone with scars of their own.

ACKNOWLEDGEMENTS

At any given time, there are at least a dozen different voices in my head, all with their own sets of opinions and demands. Even though the majority of them are fictional, there are few based in reality. Some are passerby's and some can be the supporting structure of my world. Whether you are the guy in line at Starbucks whose bad attitude caught my attention, or a permanent fixture in my life, all of you contribute.

And while I'm sure the jerk at the coffee shop has no idea his little tantrum just landed in a book, those of you who are important, know you have. To all of you, however trivial or vital your existence is in my world ... thank you for being a part of it. From my bitches who know how to Keep It Real, to my children who make me whole, I would be nothing without you. I hope that when you read my stories, you can see where your contributions have come through.

As I make another contribution to the world of fiction, I find it hard to acknowledge each and every person who has touched me along the way. The volume of words needed to do so would add chapters on this book. The insane amount of bloggers and readers who have voiced their love and support of my books is humbling. Without you, my books would just be words, waiting to be read. You have given them life, and for that I will be forever grateful.

Taking a step behind-the-scenes of Love Required, I have to give props to my Cover artist, Regina Wamba at MaelDesign.com. The covers you create find the readers for me, and for that, I thank you.

To my editor, Madison Seidler, you have once again taken my words and made them beautiful. Thank you for hearing what I say and making others want to hear them too. You are my super hero and I am currently working on your super hero name.

My beta readers and friends, Kristy, Jen, Marivett, Angie and Brenda, thank you for being brave enough to read the rough *rough* drafts. I never would have finished without you. To Casey, Starla, Debbie, Melinda and Trish, thank you for taking the time to read my unpolished work and wanting more.

To my children, you are the lights of my life, the pains in my neck and most certainly the foul odors in my day. Keep doing what you're doing.

And to my husband, Daniel, you are the love of my life, the thorn in my side and the hand that I love to hold. You know there are many songs I hear in my head when I think of you. A list I can sum up with one liners, song titles and quotes like: Me and You; The Only Exception; All I Need To Know; I Won't Give Up; Hard To Love; and You Had Me From Hello ... but I think I hear you the most when Jason Mraz says stuff like, "Maybe I annoy you, with my choices, well you annoy me sometimes too with your voice. But that ain't enough for me to move out and move on, I'm just gonna love you, like the woman I love." Thank you for making me laugh out loud, gasp in shock and smile every single day. I love you.

Table of Contents

Love Required 1
Dedication 3
ACKNOWLEDGEMENTS 4
Table of Contents 7
PROLOGUE 9
CHAPTER ONE 21
CHAPTER TWO 31
CHAPTER THREE 40
CHAPTER FOUR 53
CHAPTER FIVE 68
CHAPTER SIX 77
CHAPTER SEVEN 88
CHAPTER EIGHT 97
CHAPTER NINE 106
CHAPTER TEN 114
CHAPTER ELEVEN 122
CHAPTER TWELVE 130
CHAPTER THIRTEEN 139
CHAPTER FOURTEEN 150
CHAPTER FIFTEEN 160
CHAPTER SIXTEEN 167
CHAPTER SEVENTEEN 177
CHAPTER EIGHTEEN 186
CHAPTER NINETEEN 194

CHAPTER TWENTY 202
CHAPTER TWENTY-ONE 211
CHAPTER TWENTY-TWO 220
CHAPTER TWENTY-THREE 230
CHAPTER TWENTY-FOUR 237
CHAPTER TWENTY-FIVE 245
CHAPTER TWENTY-SIX 253
CHAPTER TWENTY-SEVEN 261
CHAPTER TWENTY-EIGHT 270
CHAPTER TWENTY-NINE 278
CHAPTER THIRTY 286
CHAPTER THIRTY-ONE 294
CHAPTER THIRTY-TWO 303
CHAPTER THIRTY-THREE 313
CHAPTER THIRTY-FOUR 321
CHAPTER THIRTY-FIVE 328
CHAPTER THIRTY-SIX 336
CHAPTER THIRTY-SEVEN 344
CHAPTER THIRTY-EIGHT 352
EPILOGUE 359
About the Author 362

PROLOGUE

Standing at the kitchen sink, Victoria rhythmically washed then snapped the ends off the fresh green beans, before tossing them in the nearby strainer. Recalling the events of her day, she couldn't help but smile. It wasn't every day a woman got her first look at her unborn child. After thoroughly drying her hands on her apron, she reached into her pocket and pulled out the paper the ultrasound technician had given her.

She could clearly identify the tiny spinal cord and head in the grainy black-and-white image, as well as the beginnings of what would be arms and legs. It was amazing what technology could produce, and the fact that she could carry around a picture of her developing child, blew her away. After one last look, she carefully folded it and slid it back into her pocket, making a mental note to pick up something from the store so she could protect the image. It's not like she could put it in a picture frame like the average mother-to-be did.

No. This precious little being needed to be, would be, protected, at all costs, and that meant not displaying his or her existence to her husband. Damien wouldn't be pleased to learn they'd conceived a child. A shiver ran over her body at the thought of what her husband would do if he ever found out. That was why he wouldn't—couldn't—ever find out. She knew time was of the essence, now more so than ever.

Glancing at the clock, she calculated how much time there was before Damien came home. He was nothing if not predictable; she knew that for certain. Which was why she was pushing to get dinner completed before he arrived, while also keeping in mind what could happen if she didn't. Reaching up, she ran her hand over the thin but raised scar that ran along her right cheek. He called it an 'everyday reminder' of why she should always tend to his needs first. It also served to remind her to always make fresh vegetables and avoid having cans in the house.

Victoria had learned to identify the things that Damien could use against or on her. She hadn't even considered him using the top to an opened can of green beans, which was a mistake she hadn't made since.

Rinsing the fresh vegetable mixture in her strainer, she dumped them in a pot before checking the chicken in the oven and giving the simmering Alfredo sauce a stir. Turning back to the pot of vegetables slowly filling with water, she closed her eyes and sighed. She smiled at the thought of her child again and placed her hand on her stomach. *My little miracle*, she thought as she turned the water off and placed the pot on a burner.

Once again at the sink, she washed the dishes she'd already used so as not to set Damien off. A clean house was part of her duty, part of the whole "tending to his needs first" routine. For her, a clean kitchen provided less weapons for him to threaten her with. After turning off the water, she reached for a towel to dry her hands when she felt a hand stroke down the length of her hair.

She stiffened as she looked at the clock to see that Damien had come home early. Panic began to bubble up at the thought that his dinner wasn't prepared yet since he hadn't been due home for another forty-five minutes. Not only was his meal not ready, she also hadn't changed or cleaned herself up for dinner, as per his instructions. Battling the sudden need to vomit, she tried to relax for him. Reactions that broadcast her fears had only triggered his need to torment her lately. Victoria wasn't sure why he had been more aggressive recently, but it was another reminder that time was short. Her plans to protect her child needed to be cemented in place, sooner rather than later.

Trying to find her voice, she cleared her throat and said, "Damien, you're home early. Is everything okay?"

Damien pressed his body into hers from behind as he swept her hair to one side, away from her face. She fought the urge to shiver as she felt his nose press against the side of her neck. He inhaled deeply before saying, "Can't a husband come home early to see his wife? Are you not happy to see me?"

Immediately recognizing his words as ones she needed to answer correctly, she said, "Of course I'm happy to see you. I was only expressing my concern for your needs."

A satisfied groan rumbled against her back. "Your words please me very much, Victoria."

Slightly relieved, she continued, "I apologize for your dinner not being on the table yet. Since I wasn't aware of your early arrival, your meal isn't quite ready. Would you like me to slice up some cheese and tomato for you to snack on while we wait?"

Knowing exactly how to speak and what to say to make him believe she was compliant was imperative. Patiently, she awaited his response as he slowly began to run his fingers through her long, thick hair. Momentarily cursing herself for not putting it up, she prayed that he didn't come along any tangles. Damien loved to stroke her hair, but despised when she allowed knots in it. Once his hand made the full sweep down the long length, she slowly let out a deep breath.

A moment later he finally answered, "Yes, I believe I would like you to prepare a snack for me. Since I have to wait."

He took a step back, allowing her to quickly retrieve what she would need. Placing the tomato and cheese on the cutting board, she cringed at having to take out a knife. Silently cursing herself, she resolved to the fact she had no choice. So she pulled it out and began to slice the cheese. After decoratively dressing the plate with it, she went to cut the tomato before realizing it hadn't been cleaned yet. She promptly washed it and returned to the cutting board—all the while knowing Damien stood somewhere behind her, watching.

Standing in front of the cutting board, she looked around but didn't see the knife. A quick glance to the sink told her she hadn't set it down over there. It was when she felt Damien press up against her that she caught sight of the knife. His body was firm against hers, and his hands boxed her in. His left hand rested along the edge of the counter on her one side, while his right hand had a firm grip around the handle of the knife.

Keeping her eye on his right hand, she fought the cauldron of fear that began bubbling over inside of her. Choosing her words carefully, she asked, "Damien? Have you changed your mind about a snack?"

He didn't answer her. Silence filled the room as her heart rate jumped from an accelerate rate to an outright gallop. The pounding of it made her ears buzz. The palms of her hands gathered moisture against the marble surface of the counter as he made her wait for his response. Knowing she couldn't do or say anything else at that moment, she focused on her breathing because the last thing she needed was to pass out from lack of oxygen.

After what seemed like hours, even though it was probably mere seconds, he finally spoke. Against the skin of her neck, she could feel his breath. "How are you feeling today, Victoria?"

Wondering why he would ask her that, and concerned that she wasn't sure how to answer it without causing a problem, she said, "Fine, thank you very much for asking." *Her practiced response*.

Damien waited a few moments before saying, "Don't you think it would be proper to ask me how *I'm* feeling today?"

Shit! "I'm sorry. I assumed you were well since I asked you if everything was okay," she said in a low, shaky voice. It was almost impossible to hide the fear and panic that were warring for top spot of emotions. She had no idea where Damien was going with the conversation, but experience told her it wasn't good.

"Oh, you assumed ..." he said, his voice moving a huge step away from calm and into the threatening category.

Realizing she still hadn't asked him how he was feeling, since that was apparently what he wanted, she rushed to say, "How are you feeling today, Damien?"

"I'm glad you asked, Victoria. I'm actually not feeling very well today." There was a pause as he lifted his left hand away from the countertop. Stiffening, she felt it once again run down the length of her hair before he continued, "It's a good thing I ran into Dr. Riley today."

At the mention of their general practitioner's name, she held her breath. Knowing that patient confidentiality was a law, she hoped the nice old man wouldn't have said anything to Damien about her referral to the obstetrician. Victoria also figured the doc probably assumed her husband knew about her pregnancy—since that would be the norm. She began to prepare herself for what he could say next, all the while knowing she might have just run out of time.

She knew she needed to continue the conversation he was forcing on her, so she said, "It's a good thing you ran into him if you weren't feeling well. Is there anything I can do for you?"

Hoping that directing her attention toward "taking care of his needs" would take the focus off her. She only had to wait a few seconds before she felt his hand begin to twist her hair, wrapping it around his fist, and yanking her head back. Hard.

Letting out a startled gasp, she tried desperately to clutch the countertop, giving herself an anchor. His lips were right against her ear as he whispered in a menacing tone, "Yes, there is something you can do for me, Victoria. How about you tell me why Dr. Riley would be congratulating me?"

She could almost hear the nails being hammered into her coffin with his words. A simple congratulation from a nice old man had promptly placed her life and the life of her unborn child in jeopardy. There was nothing to say that wouldn't be met with the same reaction from him, so she remained quiet. Thoughts of what she could do to protect her baby clouded her brain. She knew she was going to have to run, but she'd hoped there would be more time to make a plan. As it was, she was trapped between the counter and an angry Damien, who had one hand wrapped around the long length of her hair and the other clutching a knife.

He was stronger than her—she knew this well. Her lack of strength was used to his advantage most of the time, which was why she tried to play his mind games. It allowed her to come out the winner on the other side, sometimes. She feared this time was going to be different.

Damien yanked hard on her hair again, directing her face toward him in the process. The surprise of the move pulled her from her thoughts, as she felt her hands spread apart on the counter. This told her Damien's knife clutching hand was no longer on the counter.

She could feel his face in hers now. “Open your eyes, Victoria,” he demanded.

She had no choice, so she did. The rage she could see brewing in her husband’s eyes confirmed it—he knew there was a child growing inside her, and his hatred was evident. “Did you think I wasn’t going to notice?” he spit out.

Tightening his grip in her hair, he continued, “Did you think I wouldn’t see your body changing? It’s *my* body, Victoria! I know every inch of it, and I will not allow you to alter it into something disgusting and stretched out!”

As shocking as his words were, she’d heard them before. After they were married, he made sure she knew they would never have children—she would never be a mother. It was the first of many devastating blows he delivered in the early days of their marriage. But she could handle the shock of his words more than she could handle the feeling of his right hand, and knife, applying pressure on her abdomen.

Damien held the thick, flat part of the blade against her. There was two layers of fabric between it and her skin, but she could almost feel the metal, like a brand burning her. Tears welled up in her eyes and spilled over at the thought of what might happen next. He was forcing her gaze on him so she was unable to hide the reaction from him. An evil smile spread across his face as he watched her tears fall, but he didn’t say anything, only applied more pressure with the blade.

Victoria tried to get a grip on her thoughts as they spun like a tornado ripping through her head. She wasn't going to just let him harm her child, so she just needed to figure out how to get away from Damien and the knife. Still staring at him, tears blurring her vision, she blinked rapidly to clear them, causing more to fall. She felt them run down her upturned face and slip into her hair—the hair he gripped tightly in his hand. A sob began to rise up and escape as she fought the feeling of hopelessness that was becoming an overwhelming sensation. She had no way to fight him without a bigger threat being made to her child.

Damien broke the silence with his venom-filled voice. "Did you really think I would share you with someone else, Victoria?" He gave her hair another yank to prove he had control of her. She spread her hands wider on the counter and made contact with the hot surface of the stovetop. On reflex she pulled back, but then her mind caught up and she realized she had just found her weapon. Knowing Damien was going to hurt her regardless, she really had nothing to lose.

She needed to get her hand a little closer to the sauce simmering on the stove, but without causing him to notice. She slowly closed her eyes in an attempt to make him yank on her head one more time, which would allow her to shift her arms in reflex. Sending a silent prayer up to whatever God would listen, time slowed down as she waited for his reaction. Thankful for the predictable yank, she extended her arm just enough to come into contact with the handle of the pan.

With his focus directly on her face, he must not have noticed. "How do you suppose we handle this little problem? Is it something *you* will take care of? Or should I?"

Anger, rage, nausea, and desperation filled her. *Take care of it*, she thought with disgust as her hand formed a tight grip around the handle. Bracing herself, she knew it was her only chance, even if she injured herself. It was far better than what Damien was threatening to do. Sucking in a shaky breath, she said, "I'll take care of it, Damien."

That evil smile was back on his face again. She took a moment to remember exactly how evil her husband really was just before she lifted the pot full of sauce and flung it in the direction of his face. His scream of pain was the first thing she registered, seconds before she felt the sting of the sauce scalding the skin of her shoulder and upper back. His hand released her hair as she felt the swift slide of the knife blade across her abdomen, immediately followed by sharp pain. Ignoring the pain, knowing this was her only chance, she braced her left hand on the countertop for leverage and spun herself around, letting the heavy weight of the pot in her hand guide her.

When the satisfying sound of her cookware making contact with Damien's head reached her ears, she finally opened her eyes and watched. In slow motion, Damien fell into the counter opposite her, screaming in pain while trying to clear the thick white sauce from his face. Taking one more swing at his head with the pot, she almost slipped in the mess on the floor before righting herself.

Her second swing didn't make as satisfying contact as the first, but still had him stumbling backward.

Flinging the pot to the kitchen floor, Victoria took off at full speed toward the front of the house. She could hear Damien moaning in agony as the kitchen faucet came to life. Fumbling with the chain on the front door, it took her two tries before successfully swinging the door wide open. Darting out the front door, she wasn't sure where she was going to go, but the sight of her neighbor across the street pulling into his garage caught her eye.

Not looking back, she started yelling in his direction, "Help! Please help me!" After getting out of his car, he came around to the back of it. She had caught his attention and he must have seen the urgency on her face as he dropped his briefcase and moved quickly toward her. She heard Damien yell her name, but she didn't turn to look. When her neighbor reached her, she pleaded, "Please ... help me. He'll kill me ..."

Feeling the strong arm of the man helping her wrap around her waist, she leaned into him as he pulled her quickly up his driveway and into his open garage. Her breath caught in her throat as she heard Damien's voice again; he was getting closer. Looking back this time, she could see him running across the street toward the closing garage door she was trying to hide behind. Her savior gripped her tightly as they watched the door descend, blocking their view of her husband's pursuit. The door met the ground seconds before a loud bang echoed through the garage, causing her to jump, and the other man to hold her tightly. "Don't worry, he can't get to you now."

Damien began pounding and yelling as the man whose name she didn't know began speaking into his phone. "We need help. I'm with a woman who was being attacked. We're trapped in my garage, and her attacker is trying to get to us through the door. Yes, she's injured, but I don't know how badly. There appears to be blood on her front, but I don't know if it's hers or not."

Blood? Her hand quickly went to her stomach as she looked down. When she registered the wetness of her clothes against her body, she pulled her hand back to see it was covered in blood. Shock began to overwhelm her as her body finally registered the pain from an injury she had forgotten she received. Shaking, she let her weight pull her to the ground. The man guided her as he continued to talk into the phone, coming down on the cold cement next to her.

His face swam in her vision as blackness began to fill the edges and cloud over him. She whispered, "No, not my baby ... please ..." before everything went black.

CHAPTER ONE

JASON scanned the crowd of people slowly filling the reception hall. Jake and Gillian had put together a great looking party, and he was looking forward to having a good night with his family. Spotting his friend, Mike, escorting Allie to a table near the front of the room, Jason made his way toward them. Wasn't the wedding party supposed to sit together? Feeling confident that was the case, he followed them.

Stepping up alongside Allie, one of his oldest friends, he slipped his arm around her waist and squeezed just where he knew she was ticklish. He smiled as Allie jerked to the side and let out a squeal. He was still smiling when she turned and looked up at him. "Dammit, Jason! Never make a girl move like that when she's been squeezed into a dress like this and is balancing on four-inch heels."

Allie shoved him in the chest, but he didn't move much. Leaning forward, he kissed her cheek, "Sorry, Al. Did I mention how great you look tonight?"

"Oh, you're smooth. Direct me away from my annoyance by offering compliments," she said with a smirk.

He shrugged. "It would only be wrong to do something like that if I were lying, and I'm not, so it's a smart move on my part."

"I would have to agree," Mike said as he moved in close to Allie and pulled her softly against him. Jason watched when Allie leaned against Mike's chest, sighing as he kissed the top of her head.

Jason was happy Allie had found a man like Mike to fill the empty spot in her life. When they all lost Marc almost six years ago, he never thought it was something he would see happen. But seeing how it had, he couldn't be happier with the choice Allie made. Mike Lawson was one of the good guys—the kind you could easily get approval from big-brother types like himself.

Earlier in the day, he was with the two of them as Allie took a big step in her life and passed her late husband's 1968 Camaro off to their nephew, Jonathan. It was a huge deal for her, and Jason was glad he got to be a part of it. Shaking off the nostalgia of the morning events, he moved on to the nostalgia of the events of the evening. His little brother's wedding.

Accepting Mike's offered hand, Jason shook it, saying, "Looks like it's going to be a great party."

Allie shook her head. "It's a reception you nimrod, not a party. There's a difference you know."

Jason gave her questioning look. "Uh, it's a group of people gathered together to celebrate an event. That sounds like a party to me," he said jokingly.

Mike pulled out a chair for Allie and then took the seat next to her. Jason followed suit and sat opposite him while Allie continued, "Just remember: whenever you get married, you never want to call it that around your fiancé. It just makes you sound like you're discounting the importance of it."

Jason looked to Mike, who was smiling indulgently at Allie, love evident in his gaze. "Help me out here, Mike."

Mike snorted a laugh as he picked up a glass of water and took a sip. "I don't think so, man. Don't try and toss me in the dog house tonight. I'll pick Allie's side anytime she's wearing four-inch heels. Hell, I'll even start a petition to help her prove her point."

Jason shook his head. "Damn, man, whipped much?"

Mike smiled and nodded his head. "Hell yeah I am. Have you seen those shoes?"

Jason looked back to Allie's knowing grin, then down to where her legs were crossed and one foot was bouncing in front of her. Taking in the shoes, Jason would have to concede. They *were* hot shoes. Not that he thought Allie was hot in them, because he didn't view her that way, but he knew a sexy pair of shoes when he saw them.

Looking back up at Mike, he said, "I see your point. You get a pass today."

Allie scooted her chair closer to Mike as he swung his arm around the back of it. Jason watched as she snuggled in closer to him, getting comfortable. Well, Mike might have a pass today, but Jason didn't. "I still stand by my words—it's a party."

"Ask any chick in here if this is considered a 'party' and you will get a resounding *hell no*," Allie said with confidence.

"All right half-pint," Jason said with a smirk. He knew using her nickname would irritate her. It worked, so he continued, "I'm sure there's at least one woman in here who will agree with my view. Care to make a wager?"

Allie's eyebrow went up as she looked sideways at Jason. Mike huffed a laugh in Jason's direction. "Hey man, remember what happened the last time Allie made a wager? You ended up singing karaoke."

Jason waved off Mike's warning, but didn't take his eyes off Allie as she continued to smirk and give him a considering look. "I'm not worried. There's no way she would let something like that go down at Gillian's wedding."

Allie scowled. "Damn, you're right, I wouldn't. But I didn't think you would know that. Now I need to up my game."

"Bring it on, half-pint," he said, taunting her. She only smirked before leaning up and whispering in Mike's ear. He smiled as she pulled away and looked up at him. Mike nodded at her, and then she turned her gaze on Jason.

"Okay, so here's how it's gonna go down. The terms are this: You can ask as many women you can find if this is a reception or a party. If you can find one who agrees with you, you win. If you don't, I win," she said.

"Okay. What are the stakes?" Jason said as he began to look around for the first woman he would approach.

"If I win, you have to be our table bitch for the night. If you win, I'll be it."

"What the hell is a table bitch?" Jason asked as he looked back at her.

"A bitch, plain and simple. We say jump, you ask how high. We want more champagne, you go fetch it. You know, the crap we normally make the kids do," she said with a smirk.

"I really should know better than to make bets with you. Your ability to come up with some seriously creative terms is a bit diabolical." Shaking his head once again, he added, "I agree to your terms, but I have one condition. No dancing. I don't do dancing." Putting his hand out, they shook before standing.

"You pick 'em, gigantor. I can't have you blaming my choice in women for your loss." Jason only nodded his head as he made his way to the first woman he was going to ask, Allie close on his heels.

TORI was pleased with how smoothly things were moving in the kitchen. The salad plates had all been prepped and ready to go on time, and the wait staff had efficiently delivered them to all the tables. Now it was time to start serving the main courses. Without even looking up, she called out, "Main courses ready to drop. I need everyone front and center, please."

The crew knew the drill and, after working together for the past six months, they all responded quickly. Just the way she expected. Looking up from the tray she was putting together, she addressed the staff. "You know what to do. The trays are marked with names and choice of entrée. It shouldn't be too hard, just make sure you confirm the choice as you serve them. If you get a difficult one who claims to want something else, move along to the next one and let me know when you bring the tray back. I have extras. When you pick up the salad plates, please don't stack them with the entrée covers, it only makes cleaning them more annoying."

Giving everyone a quick glance. "Yes?" She received a few knowing looks, a few nods and few who seemed embarrassed since they were the culprits from the last job. Individual humiliation was never something she would do—addressing them as a group worked just fine. "Okay, grab your trays, and let's get this show on the road. The sooner these people are fed, the sooner they eat cake, and the sooner your jobs will be done for the night. Nimble feet and steady hands please."

Bringing her attention back to what she was working on, she could hear the staff moving about and collecting their trays. She felt her friend, Tessa, sidle up next to her before giving her a little hip check. "You know what? You are the nicest drill instructor out there."

Tori didn't have to look at her to know she was just giving her a hard time. Tessa thought she was too nice for being the team leader, but she wasn't someone who thought being boss meant being mean. "I only said 'please' once. What more do you want?"

Tessa began placing the lids on the plates in front of them before they both started to stack them two high on the large tray to be carried out. "Personally, I think you should increase the volume of your voice and add some snapping. That would really get them fired up."

Tori laughed and looked at Tessa, who gave her an evil grin and nod, encouraging her to go along with her suggestions. Shaking her head, she looked back down to make sure she had the tray ready before loading it at the bottom of the cart. Standing back up, she turned to Tessa and said, "Don't you have a tray to offload? Go on, get to it." She made sure to raise her voice a little and snap her fingers a time or two.

Tessa smiled as she moved away. Looking back over her shoulder she gave Tori a seductive look. "I think bossy Tori is *hot*." Then she winked and walked away with her tray.

Her wait staff was beginning to come back in with empty trays. Tori stood there, assessing the activity—monitoring. Grabbing a rag, she wiped down the surface she had just finished using when a deep voice startled her. "Excuse me, can you help me?"

Looking up, Tori was taken aback by the giant of a man standing before her. Well over six feet tall, with broad shoulders that made the tuxedo he was wearing almost look painted on. His brown hair was longer on top and tapered closer to the head as it reached his neck. His hair trailed seamlessly into a tightly trimmed beard that cleanly outlined his strong jawline before ending at his thick, corded neck.

Her eyes made the circuit back up to his face and found a set of bright hazel eyes taking her in. As if she couldn't help it, she dropped her gaze to a one-sided smirk that changed his expression from intense to playful. Moments later, his full lips pulled back to reveal a hypnotizing smile that threatened her ability to breathe and had her heart picking up its pace just a bit. The smile said something, but she didn't hear it. Snapping herself out an apparent trance, she brought her gaze back to his eyes, which were also smiling at her.

"Hi," the tux said.

Literally giving her head a shake, she slipped her professional demeanor back on and responded, "Can I help you with something?"

Again with his smile, he said, "I sure hope so." Motioning with his thumb over his shoulder to the main room where the reception was being held, he added, "The people at my table are being a bit difficult and have asked me to come back and retrieve some salad dressing. Can I get some from you?"

She thought it was a bit odd, and she gave him a questioning look. "Difficult? Did my staff not give you any with your salad?" While awaiting his answer, she mentally tried to come up with another way to double check that the salads had dressing next time.

"No, the salads all had dressing on them," he replied.

"Oh, okay. So then you just need more?" she asked as she moved to the side to open the refrigerator for the dressing.

"Yes, please. Can I have a few small cups? I'm sure that after I come back with one, Allie will send me back for more," he said as he shook his head and then mumbled, "It's going to be a long night."

Tori huffed a laugh at him, "It can't be all that bad. You're at a party after all." Returning to the counter, she pulled a plate out and lined it with small serving cups for the dressing.

"What did you just say?" the tux asked, almost hopefully.

She stopped what she was doing and looked up at him, trying not to get lost in those bright hazel eyes of his. "I said, it can't be all that bad?"

"No, the other part," he insisted, his tone laced with excitement.

"I think I said, you're at a party after all," she replied in a questioning tone, not sure what he was getting at.

"Exactly! Thank you," he declared as his arms stretched out to his sides, giving her a glimpse of his impressive wingspan.

Still not quite sure what was going on, she raised her eyebrows as she said, "Glad I could help?"

Dropping her attention back to the dressing cups, she proceeded to fill them. A moment later he was around the counter and in her personal space. Momentarily startled by his size, she stepped back and looked up at him as he said, "Come with me, I need you."

Tori choked on her words before clearing her throat. "Excuse me?"

He gave his head a shake and then smiled down at her with a laugh, "I'm sorry. Can you come out to our table? I need you to say that to my friend."

"Okaaay," she said as she moved over to rinse her hands off in the sink. "So long as it only takes a minute, and I'm not causing anyone any trouble."

The tux smiled and nodded. "It will be quick, and you won't be causing any trouble. In fact, you'll be helping me."

Drying her hands off on a towel, she slipped off her apron and set it on the counter before turning to follow the tux out of the kitchen. She almost ran into him as he stayed rooted in place. Looking up at his face, he was still smiling as he said, "My name's Jason, by the way."

She dropped her gaze to his outstretched hand. It was a large, strong-looking hand. The type of hand that could inflict a lot of pain and damage if it were attached to the wrong kind of man. Hesitantly, she slipped her smaller hand into his, preparing herself for his strength. What she felt instead was the warm, gentle touch of his fingers wrap around hers before he gave it a small shake.

Staring at their joined hands, she was surprised that she didn't feel any hesitation or fear. Just warmth. He was still holding her hand when she looked back up at him in question, but his own questioning stare forced her to realize she hadn't responded to him. She spoke up, "Oh, sorry. Tori ... my name is Tori."

He gave her hand another gentle squeeze before letting go. "Nice to meet you, Tori."

CHAPTER TWO

JASON made his way out of the kitchen toward his table of family and friends. He shortened his long stride so Tori didn't have to chase after him. *She was a tiny thing*, he thought. Smiling to himself, he glanced back as they weaved between tables and chairs on their way to the front of the room. He noticed she stopped to speak with one of the waiters before she resumed following him. He felt rude having her trail behind him, but there was no way to make it between the obstacles without going single file.

When they made it through the first group of tables and came to the dance floor, Jason paused and allowed her to come up next to him. She looked up at him in question. He could only give her a smile as he gestured for her to follow the path around the dance floor. She did, allowing him to place his hand on her lower back to guide her. Tori flinched when his hand made contact, but she relaxed a moment later. He wasn't sure if he should be worried about that reaction, but he convinced himself this was the gentlemanly thing to do. Plus, he wanted to touch her.

It was selfish, he knew, but that didn't change his mind. Getting closer to his table, he knew the second Allie caught sight of his approach. Her face took on a knowing glint as she turned and whispered something to Mike before looking back at Jason.

Jason extended his hand forward, showing Tori they'd arrived. "Here we are."

Tori looked up at him and asked, "What exactly is it you need from me?"

He just smiled as he moved to her other side, positioning himself between Allie and Tori. "I just need you to say what you said in the kitchen."

Tori gave him an adorable shrug as she turned her attention toward the table. Standing on her right side, he caught sight of a long scar that ran from the corner of her mouth at an upward angle toward her ear. It was clear she had used something to cover it up, but his height over her afforded him a view. It was so precise, which told him it was not an accidental injury; it was intentional. The thought of someone deliberately hurting her stole his ability to speak, and they were left standing at his table in awkward silence.

Allie spoke up, "What's going on, Jason? Did you get in trouble in the kitchen?"

Shaking his head at Allie's sarcasm, he distanced himself from the vision in his head. He looked at Allie as Tori leaned forward, placing the plate of dressing on the table. She let out a small laugh as she defended him, "He was no trouble at all in the kitchen. In fact, he asked me to make sure we brought out extra dressing for you so you wouldn't have to go without. He was very insistent."

Tori looked back up at him and winked before turning back to the table, waiting for whatever it was he brought her out there for. *She winked at him.* He thought that was one of the hottest things a woman could do. It showed she was flirty, confident, and comfortable. He really liked that. Not to mention the vibrant green eyes she was winking at him with were like emeralds set in ivory cream surrounded by a crown of deep auburn hair. Her hair was in such vibrant contrast to her eyes, it made both features stand out more. He had to fight the urge to reach out and touch her. It was a strangely hard thing for him to do.

When she turned back to look at him, she had that questioning look on her face again, and he realized he was making a fool of himself by only staring at her and not speaking to the table of people looking up at them. He could care less what his family and friends thought; it was her he didn't want thinking he was an idiot. Finally finding his voice, he said, "Everyone, this is Tori. She was helping me in the kitchen when she said something I thought you should hear."

Jason could see Mike smirking behind Allie. Jonathan and Zane were also sporting matching grins. Allie's narrowed eyes and raised eyebrow showed she knew he was up to something. He loved knowing he was about to take her down. A smile spread across his face as he thought of his plans once she became the table bitch. Looking back over to Tori, he asked, "Could you please repeat our conversation in the kitchen for my family here?"

"Um, okay. Well, first you complained that it was going to be a long night. Then I said, it can't be all that bad, you're at a party after all." She said to the table before turning to look at him again. He smiled and gave her an encouraging nod. Her answering smile was like a punch to the gut, and he had no idea why this little woman had such a visceral effect on him. Taking a deep breath to calm himself down, he broke eye contact and looked to Allie, who was watching him intently. He was certain she picked up on his reactions to Tori, but he focused on how he was now the one on the winning side of their wager.

"There you go, half-pint. A woman who has the same opinion as me," he gloated. Sure, only jerks gloated, but the fact was that Allie would definitely gloat, so why shouldn't he?

"Whatever, gigantor," Allie said to him before turning her attention to Tori. "He didn't tell you to say that, did he?"

Tori asked, "Say what? He only asked me to repeat what I said in the kitchen."

"So he didn't tell you to say this was a party and not a reception?" Allie asked again, clearly trying to avoid the fact that she was about to be bossed around. Jason couldn't help but huff a laugh at her.

Tori glanced over at him before answering Allie, "No, he didn't, but this *is* a party. Sure, it's a wedding reception, but that's just the description of the *type* of party. The actual definition for reception is a social gathering to celebrate something or to welcome someone. Party is a synonym of reception." She finished with a smile like she had just solved a puzzle. Jason couldn't have said that any better himself, and he was pretty amused by her ability to quote the actual definition. He wasn't sure if it was weird or not, but he was a little turned on by it.

Turning back to Allie, Jason relished in the shocked look on her face. Which was quickly followed by an amused one. Allie was never quiet, but now she was stunned silent. The silence must have made Tori uncomfortable because she quickly began to babble, “I’m sorry, did I say something wrong? I only know the definition because I’m in the catering business and it helps us determine what we wear for the job. Parties get black and white attire. Business luncheons get polo shirts and kakis, and sometimes we do jobs on the beach and we wear Hawaiian shirts and leis. When the schedules are posted, party is the word used to describe the event ...”

Jason watched as Tori continued to chatter on in her own defense. He felt bad that she had become uncomfortable, and he suddenly felt the need to protect her. Whether it was appropriate or not, he stepped closer to her and wrapped his arm around her waist, and interrupted her chatter, he glared down at Allie and said, “Oh, come on, half-pint, your silence is making the poor woman feel she needs to defend herself.”

Tori didn’t stiffen when he touched her that time, but she did look up at him. He didn’t look down at her because he knew her face would be very close to his, and he wasn’t sure what her proximity would make him want to do. More so than what he already wanted to do that was. Allie smiled. “Sorry, I wasn’t trying to make you uncomfortable, Tori. I was in shock that you delivered that definition without an ounce of sarcasm, and I was trying to come up with a way to get out of what I know is going to happen when you leave our table. Oh, and I can’t stop staring at your hair.”

TORI watched as the very pretty Allie stood and rounded the table in her direction. When she reached her, Tori wasn't sure what to do. Allie's eyes were round as she gently picked up the thick braid that rested on Tori's left shoulder. She couldn't help but think how this was a touchy feely group of people but that it didn't seem to bother her as it normally would.

Allie was playing with the end of her braid and examining it closely as she ran her hand gently down the bumps of it. "The coloring is beautiful," she said.

Tori smiled and was about to speak when the man who was seated next to Allie said something, "Allie, sweetheart, it's not polite to randomly stroke people's hair when you don't know them." His amusement was evident in his tone. "Apparently we've found Allie's kryptonite: Tori's hair."

Allie snorted a laugh next to Tori and said, "Oh, be quiet. I'm a hairdresser; I stroke people's hair all day long. But I've yet to see a color this stunning except in pictures." Allie stepped back and said, "I'm sorry, it's rude to ask, but I have to know who does your hair so I can find out what color that is. It's stunning. You can't say it's brown, and you can't say its red."

Tori and Allie stood close to the same height, which Tori loved because she was usually the short one in the crowd. She also couldn't help but take in Allie's beauty, and with that acknowledgement, came the insecurity of standing next to a woman who looked flawless, when Tori herself was flawed.

Reaching up, she unconsciously touched her right cheek, feeling the scar. She quickly moved her hand up to push a bit of hair behind her ear, hoping she hadn't drawn attention to the scar itself. She could feel Jason's eyes on her and she didn't want him to see her imperfection. Covering up her scar was routine for her, if only to avoid questions or sympathetic looks. But for some reason, allowing him to see it felt like she was exposing too much.

His hand was still resting at her waist and as comfortable as it felt, her need to hide her flaw was greater. Turning her body to face Allie more, and away from Jason's assessing gaze, she answered Allie's question, "Oh, I don't have a hairdresser, this is my natural color."

Allie looked at her like she was crazy. "Shut the front door. No way! That beautiful coloring is all yours?" She picked up the braid again and marveled at it.

On more than one occasion, Tori had been asked who did her hair because the color was so beautiful. But it was one hundred percent hers. A slight feeling of sadness welled up inside when she admitted, "My mother had the same color, too." She really missed her mom lately.

When Tori felt a hand on her shoulder, she looked up and saw Allie smiling at her before she said, "What a beautiful reminder."

Tori wasn't sure how Allie picked up on the past tense in her sentence so easily, but it was nice of her to acknowledge it. Realizing she had spent far too much time away from the kitchen, she cleared the small lump in her throat and looked to the table of people in front of her. "Well, it was nice chatting with all of you, but I really should get back to the kitchen. Lord only knows what trouble could be happening without my direction. Please, let me know if there is anything you need tonight."

Allie took a step away, and Tori turned back to look up at Jason. The movement disengaged his hand from her waist and a slight bit of disappointment swelled up inside her. Masking the feeling, she smiled and said, "I hope I was able to help. Let me know if you need me for anything else."

She extended her hand to him, and he quickly took it in his own. Once again, she enjoyed the warmth his touch brought to her—even more so when he used both of his big hands to surround her small one. When he gave her that hypnotizing smile again, she fought her desire to stare at it. "You more than helped me, Tori. And believe me, I will definitely find you later."

Her body's reaction to his touch was almost foreign to her. Given the past few years where the thought of being with a man was of little concern for her. Sure, she'd seen men who she thought were attractive, and she'd even been asked out a time or two, but none had that palpable of an effect on her. It was refreshing to know that she wasn't completely damaged.

Giving his hand a squeeze, she smiled and winked at him before turning and heading back to the kitchen. She fought the desire to look back at him over her shoulder. Even though she thought it was possible he was watching her leave, she didn't want to risk the disappointment if he wasn't. There hadn't been anything other than a great smile and some friendly gestures, so she had no reason to think he was attracted to her. But a girl could dream, and if she were to be completely honest, that man was what dreams were made of.

CHAPTER THREE

TORI was still smiling as she walked into the kitchen and found Tessa snapping her fingers and pointing at a tray as she gave orders to one of the waitresses. Huffing a laugh, she shook her head and picked up her apron, wrapping it around her waist. Tessa was a crack-up, and her blatant display of what she believed to be authoritative, but truthfully came across as annoyingly bossy, always made her smile. Friends who you could trust were few and far between for a woman who left behind a life that had taken away all of the people she held close. At some point, she hoped it would be possible to repair those relationships—the ones destroyed by her marriage. For now, though, she had Tessa, and the other stuff remained on her list of things to do.

Coming up alongside Tessa, Tori said, "Go ahead, Melody, you can take your tray out now." The young woman nodded and quickly removed herself and her tray of food.

"Trying out a new bossy voice again?" Tori asked as she gauged where they were in serving the meal. Her kitchen was organized and ran smoothly, her staff respected her, and she loved doing this. Creating meals was one of her favorite things to do, and she was grateful that her evil husband didn't take that away from her, too. *Kiss my ass, Damien,* she thought with a smile as she leaned against the counter and watched the activity around her.

"Well one of us needs to be bossy around here. You just smile and *ask* them to do things. What's the fun of being a boss if you don't get to boss people around?" Tessa asked.

"Does it look like my staff needs me to yell at them?" Tori asked with amusement. This had been the topic of conversation at least once at every event they worked together. It was apparently their thing.

Tessa gave her a confused look, "No, they don't. That's what I don't understand. How do you get them to do whatever you ask without being mean?"

"The only person who doesn't do what they're told to do is you, Tess. Maybe they want to please me, and you … maybe you just like being bossed around? Is there some underlying need to be dominated or something? Oh, maybe you want to be bossed around by a chick?" Tori added with humor.

Tessa looked like she was considering the idea before saying, "That's a possibility. I did think you were hot when you told me what to do. How about we make out and see where it goes?"

A loud clattering sound behind them got Tori's attention. Whirling around, she found two young men from her staff staring at them with wide eyes. One of them cleared his throat and smiled. "I wouldn't mind watching that."

Tori threw a towel at the young man, hitting him in the chest. "I'd move along, guys. You know what Tessa's like when she gets ideas in her head. She might think it'll be a good idea to watch the two of you make out."

The silent one made a choking sound before saying, "I'm outta here."

The other young man only smiled bigger and said, "I'm game if I get to see you two make out."

Giving him a stern look, she made a shooing motion with her hands. "Get back to work, Joel. Nobody is going to be making out here."

He looked disappointed, but made sure to add before turning away, "Make sure you find me if things change, though."

Shaking her head, she turned back to Tessa who was smiling big as she watched Joel walk away. When she looked back to Tori she said, "I wouldn't mind making out with that." She motioned her head in his direction, as if Tori didn't know who she was talking about.

"You are at least ten years older than him, Tess. And you need to stop talking like that at work. I don't need someone complaining about sexual harassment."

"There would be nothing harassing about you and me making out, just sayin'. And ten years is no big deal; he's at least twenty-one, and that's plenty old to know what to do with his working parts. Besides, I'm sure I could teach him a thing or two," Tessa added as she leaned on the counter facing Tori.

"You really need to look up the definition of sexual harassment in the work place."

"I will, but only if there are pictures." Tori found herself once again trying to stifle a laugh at her friend. She was totally comfortable in her skin, and Tori was so glad to have found her.

Together, they watched as the wait staff started to bring in empty dinner plates. The cleanup process had begun, and soon the bride and groom would be cutting the cake. Thankfully Tori was able to delegate the cake cutting to someone else; she hated doing that part. Glancing over at Tess, she said, "I'm putting my bossy voice on for you." Clearing her throat and scowling, she said, "You're cutting the cake tonight, so make sure you don't screw this up."

Tessa smirked. "That totally just gave me a lady boner over here. Bossy Tori is definitely hot."

Of course, Joel was walking by as Tessa said that. His smile and obvious glance down to look for Tessa's "lady boner" was almost too much to handle. Taking her apron off and tossing it on the counter, she said, "For crying out loud, Tessa, you have got to stop saying crap like that here."

Tori began to leave the kitchen in search of the bride or groom when she heard Tessa say, "Hey, Joel, find me after work and I'll show you what a lady boner looks like." Shaking her head, she thought to herself that poor Joel didn't know what he was getting himself into; Tessa would swallow him whole.

Once back in the main dining area, Tori sought out the people she needed so she could keep things flowing properly for the wedding festivities. As she walked around the room, she couldn't help but let her eyes drift back toward the table where she knew Jason might be. When she found him, her breath hitched at the sight of him. He was relaxing back in his seat, long legs forward, holding a sleeping baby on his chest. The feeling of longing that erupted in her chest was almost overwhelming, but the disappointment at the possibility he was unavailable tampered that longing. Again, he never gave her an indication that he liked her, but she had been looking forward to the daydreams about him wanting her, like she apparently wanted him.

JASON was content sitting there holding his niece, Ella. He knew he would need to thank Mike for occupying Allie, thus preventing her from stealing the sleeping child. He also made sure to point out that he didn't need to share Ella with her because Allie was now the table bitch and had to do what Jason said. As fun as it would've been to boss her around, he knew he could inflict the most damage by keeping her from the baby. He smiled, remembering her pouty face when Mike convinced her to dance with him instead of glaring at Jason.

Of course he would share Ella with Allie in a little bit, preferably when it was time to change her diaper, but that was still sharing. He also knew that would be when he made his way back to the kitchen area to talk to Tori again. The only reason he wasn't lurking back there trying to find a reason to talk with her now was because he knew exactly how creepy that would be. Plus, he did enjoy being able to torture Allie by hoarding Ella.

He was watching his older niece, Madison, dance with Zane when Mike came back to the table to take his seat, sans Allie. Under normal circumstances, Jason would assume that Allie was preparing a sneak attack to steal the baby, but not tonight. Tonight, he was safe. Mike was also watching his son dance with Madison, and Jason couldn't help but wonder if there was something going on there. "Does your son have good intentions where my niece is concerned?"

Mike smiled at Jason's question. "I have no idea about my son's intentions, but I assure you that whatever they are, they are honorable. He would never do anything inappropriate with Madison. You have my word on that." Mike finished his statement by giving Jason a confident, yet pointed, look.

Jason nodded. "I accept that." Zane was two years older than Madison and seemed to be a mature young man for his age. Jason admired that Mike had raised him alone for most of his life, and he had never seen the boy act any way but appropriate. But that didn't mean he wasn't going to keep an eye on him when he was dancing closely with Madison.

"Where's Allie?" Jason asked.

"She's helping Gillian use the facilities. Apparently when there's a bride involved, it's at least a two-woman job," Mike said with a small laugh. Jason couldn't help but laugh at the thought of how difficult it might be for Gillian to use the bathroom in her wedding gown.

Picking up his beer, his raised it up toward Mike. "Here's to being a man and possessing the ability to pee standing up."

Mike clinked his beer with Jason's. "I'll drink to that." And they both took a drink.

A few moments later, Mike spoke up again, "So, that woman you brought to the table earlier was quite beautiful."

Jason's scowl was firmly in place when he glared over at his new friend. Yes, she was beautiful, but Mike had no business looking at her. When Mike just smiled big at him and continued, Jason knew he had walked into a trap. "That's what I thought. Why don't you ask her out? You're not getting any younger, man, and take it from me, when they make you work for it, the time really adds up."

Mike was no doubt referring to the months that he basically chased Allie until her dare backfired on her, forcing her to accept a date with him. It was genius on Mike's part, and Jason couldn't be more pleased with the outcome. Jason just smiled. "I plan on asking her out, but I just figured I'd wait until a little later to do it. She's working, after all, and it's rude to put her on the spot like that in front of all her coworkers."

"Agreed." Mike took a slug of his beer before adding, "But, in the meantime, if you want to stare at her, she's over there by your brother."

Jason's gaze immediately went to where he had last seen his brother chatting with someone and landed on Tori. She had a smile on her pretty face as she spoke with Jake, and Jason immediately wondered what they were talking about and wished he were part of the conversation. Like Mike knew what he was thinking, he said, "There's nothing wrong with a man walking over to speak with his brother. Especially when he's holding said brother's daughter. And if the beautiful woman you want to speak with just *happens* to be there, without any coworkers around her, it's a win-win situation."

Jason smiled at Mike as he shrugged his shoulders and took another sip of his beer. Even though Jason knew that it was the perfect opportunity to talk to her, he couldn't help but give Mike shit. "You've been hanging around Allie too much; she's turning you into a chick."

Mike only smiled as he stood and clapped Jason on the shoulder, saying, "Think what you want, man, but I'm not going to bed alone tonight." Watching him walk away, he couldn't help but think Mike had him on that one.

Jason *was* going to bed alone that night. Not that he was planning on picking up a chick at his brother's wedding and taking her home with him seeing as he was in charge of Dylan and Ryan tonight anyway. But the days of spending one night with a woman had long ago left him with a bad taste in his mouth. He was done with feeling that way, and if he had learned anything from his group of friends lately, it was that it was never too late to find what you needed in life.

Deciding he was going to talk to Tori, he stood and turned in the direction he had last seen her when he almost ran right into Gillian. He smiled down at her as he took her in. He'd heard people describe a woman as "glowing" at one point or another in his adult life, but he didn't fully get it until this moment. She smiled back at him before saying, "I figured you'd be the one to have Ella. Allie was a little bitter about losing her own bet. I love it when her wagers backfire on her." She leaned forward and kissed her daughter on the cheek before adding, "Are you okay with her?"

"Of course I am, so don't worry about her. She's perfectly fine," Jason assured her. Gillian seemed to be having a little separation anxiety. She was a great mother, but today was about being in love with Jake, not being a mom. "Go enjoy yourself. She's in good hands with all of us, and you know it."

She heaved a big sigh. "I know she is, but it's crazy hard being away from her. I'm not sure how I'm going to handle the coming nights without her."

Jason smiled. "I'm sure your husband will find plenty of things to occupy your mind, Gilly."

Gillian blushed and quickly leaned in to kiss her daughter again. He assumed she was hiding her embarrassment at his comment, but it wasn't like everyone there didn't know what Jake and Gillian were going to be doing for the next few days. So he couldn't bring himself to feel bad for saying it. She smiled up at him. "I love you for being such a good uncle."

"It's not a hard thing to do." She smiled bigger before turning to go and enjoy herself.

It took Jason a moment to remember where he was heading before Gillian found him. When he did, he looked for Jake but found he was no longer talking to Tori. Disappointed that he had missed his opportunity, he sat back down and scanned the room. He hoped another opportunity would present itself, and sooner rather than later since the anticipation of talking to her seemed to be making him restless now.

There was a possessive side of him that wanted to find her and tell her she was going to spend time with him. Thankfully he had a rational side too that reminded him that this woman was worth taking his time with, and he needed to make sure he approached with utmost care. Missing the chance at getting to know her was not something he was going to tolerate. He was a little surprised that his possessive nature was rearing its head over a woman he knew nothing about but she seemed to draw him in. It had been a long time since he had felt something like that, and for it to be as strong as it was unsettled him a bit.

As the evening rolled on, the duties as best man continued to drag Jason in different directions. He was beginning to wonder if he would ever find the opportunity to seek out Tori. Once the cake was cut, the dances were done, Ella had been handed over to his parents, and he had happily seen his brother and Gillian off, he made his way to the kitchen to find her. Walking in, he found a tall woman with dark hair piled on top of head. When she realized he was there, she gave him a saucy smile and said, "Is there something I can do for you?"

Disappointed that Tori wasn't anywhere as he glanced around, he gave the other woman a hesitant smile. "No thanks. I just wanted to make sure your staff didn't need anything else from us."

As much as he wanted to ask Tori out, he didn't want to get her in trouble by mentioning her to this woman. For all he knew, there could be a policy preventing them from dating people they met while working. He quickly decided that he would just get more information on who she was from his brother if he couldn't find her. The woman told him, "We've wrapped up in here, and the staff has gone home, so no, there's nothing else needed."

Glad he had a backup plan, he nodded and left the kitchen. Now he'd have to text his brother tomorrow and hope Jake took a few moments away from his new wife to answer his questions. Jason held on to the hope that he would, but only because Ryan was with him. He smiled to himself as he thought he could use that to his advantage, and he wasn't going to feel the least bit bad about that.

TORI took a last look around the walk-in freezer to make sure everything was in its place. There was nothing that bothered her more than getting a call from one of the other teams asking where something was. If she was the last one out, then there was no reason she couldn't tell someone where to find something if necessary.

Walking out into the kitchen, she found Tessa waiting for her. Unlocking the drawer they stored their purses in, she pulled them out and handed Tessa hers. "All set?" Tori asked.

"Well, I was thinking of climbing up that wall of a man that just left, but that might be frowned upon since he just got married," Tessa said as she slung her bag over her shoulder while digging out her keys.

"The groom was here in the kitchen?" Tori asked as they began shutting off lights and heading for the exit.

"Yeah, he said he wanted to make sure we didn't need anything from them. I told him all was good."

"Okay, great. He *was* quite the looker, wasn't he? The bride was beautiful, too, and they were so nice," Tori added as they crossed the nearly empty parking lot to the section where the staff parked. It was located near the offices on the opposite side of the reception hall. Since they usually left when it was late, they encouraged the employees to leave in pairs. Tessa had designated herself to protect Tori from 'unspeakable acts of violence, unless the man was hot, in which case, she promised she wouldn't interrupt.'

"Of course they were nice and gorgeous. It wouldn't be a week in our life if we didn't have to witness couples like that living happily ever after," Tessa said in a voice that was a cross between sarcasm and bitterness. Tori didn't add to the comment. It would only get Tessa riled up, and then she'd launch into a bitter conversation questioning why they didn't have men like that in their lives. Tori knew the reason she didn't, but tonight she'd be fine avoiding that topic. She just wanted to go home, snuggle in bed, and go to sleep. When they reached their cars, Tori walked up behind hers and noticed that it was leaning. Rounding to the driver's side, she saw that her rear tire was flat. "Well, shit!"

Tessa had made it a few steps past Tori, but thankfully hadn't gotten far. "What's up?"

"I have a flat tire. Shit! I don't have time to change it tonight. Can you give me ride?"

“Sure thing, hop in. Just kick whatever’s on the seat to the floor,” Tessa said as she unlocked her doors. Looking back to her car, Tori just shook her head. She would just have to deal with that in the morning. *So much for an easy day off,* she thought as Tessa peeled out of the parking lot.

CHAPTER FOUR

JASON shook his head as he led his nephews, Dylan and Ryan, from the reception hall office. "Do you have any idea how lucky you are someone turned it in, Dylan?"

His nephew didn't respond as his attention was completely devoted to his newly recovered iPod. The nine year old had saved all of his good grade and birthday money for months and then bought it for himself. So when he woke up that morning and realized he had left it at the wedding reception the night before, saying he panicked would be an understatement. Even though this was his nephew, he knew if Gillian or Logan were there, they would take the opportunity to turn what happened into a lesson. So he tried.

"Dylan? Did you hear what I said?" he asked with a little more sternness to get Dylan's attention.

It worked. "Huh, what Uncle Jason?" Dylan stammered as he looked up at him.

He couldn't help but smirk at him. "I said, do you have any idea how lucky you are that someone turned that in? That usually isn't the case at all." He momentarily thought about reinforcing his words with an experience of his own then thought better. It wasn't his job to do that; he'd leave that kind of crap to their parents. All of them, step-parents included. He smiled at the thought that Gillian was now his sister, officially. Not that they weren't already family in his mind, but he was happy Jake finally got his girl. His brother deserved his happy ever after, and marrying Gillian was just another layer that linked them all together.

Dylan let out a big sigh next to him as they walked toward the car. “I know, Uncle Jason. Do you have to tell my parents? I learned my lesson, I did, and it was my money that was used to buy it. If we didn’t find it, then it was only my money wasted. Please?”

Reaching into his pocket for his keys, he looked to his nephew. Shaking his head once again, he said, “I’m not telling your parents anything, buddy, that’s not my job. But if I’m asked, I will not lie for you. Understood?”

He watched Dylan’s face light up at his words. “Thanks Uncle Jason. You’re the best!”

Jason snorted. “Of course I am.” Unlocking the car so the boys could climb in, he said, “Make sure there’s nothing on your feet before you rub them all over my upholstery. I just had the car detailed.”

There was some noise of agreement from both of them before they loaded themselves into the back seat. Jason had just opened his door when he heard someone heave an aggravated sound, followed by a few colorful words. He smiled as he moved away from his car to investigate. Following the noise two cars down from his, he couldn’t help but smile bigger when he caught sight of the source. There was Tori from last night, hunched over a tire iron, attempting to remove a flat tire and grumbling obscenities. It was adorable.

He stood for a second, waiting for her to notice him, not wanting to startle her. But he wasn’t able to maintain his silence when he heard her say, "I can do this, really I can. I do *not* need a *stupid* man to do this."

Huffing a laugh, he said, "Of course you don't need a stupid man, but we can be fun to have around sometimes."

She let out a startled squeak at the sound of his words and lost her grip on the tire iron. It fell to the ground in front of her, as she landed with a thud on the asphalt behind her.

"Oh shit, I'm sorry," he said as he moved to help her up. Not bothering to put his hand out to offer assistance, he moved behind her, slipped his hands under her arms, and lifted her to her feet. Her hands immediately went to her backside as she moaned her discomfort. His mind was instantly filled with thoughts of doing that for her. *Mind, meet your old friend, gutter,* he thought as he quickly let go of her.

Moving around to face her, he said, "I'm so sorry, I didn't mean to startle you."

Her sunglasses had slid down her nose from the not so subtle collision with the asphalt, and she had yet to correct them. She was still rubbing her rear, with eyes closed and a look of discomfort on her face. Reaching up, he removed her awkwardly angled shades. "Are you okay?"

She opened her eyes, showing him that vibrant green that reminded him of the night before and her sexy wink. Giving him a crooked smile that conveyed her slight embarrassment, she said, "Nothing like a small dose of humiliation in the morning to add to the events of my day." She shook her head as she accepted her sunglasses from him. "I'm fine, thank you."

Jason gave her a nod. "Can I help you with the tire? It's the least this stupid man could do after essentially knocking you on your ass."

She gave him a hesitant smile. "Great. Of course you had to hear the *stupid* part of my pity-party."

He shrugged and smiled big. "It sounded more like a pep-talk than a pity-party."

She put her hands on her hips and tossed another sigh in his direction. "Good, we'll call it that then." She stared down at the flat tire, then the tire iron on the ground before looking back to him. "Sure, I'd appreciate the help. It *is* the least you could do, after all. I'm pretty sure I'll be sporting a bruised ego to match my butt for a few days so I think I want to avoid trying that again."

Jason winced at the thought of her skin being marked, which was quickly followed by a tightening of his body as the visual of her bare skin came to mind. Needing to hide the red-blooded-male reaction he was beginning to have, he bent down to retrieve the tire iron. Getting into position, he moved to the small jack propping the car up, and released it, bringing the car back down to the ground with a gentle thud.

Tori was standing to his left, but moved to the other side of the car with urgency and another muttered curse when he did this. Standing up, he glanced in her direction as she stood, having retrieved something—no someone—from the backseat. It wasn't until he saw that head full of brownish-red curls that he realized why she moved so quickly.

He watched as she soothed the baby girl, who had that bottom lip extended as if she was still deciding whether or not she wanted to cry. It was a face he had seen on his nieces plenty of times, and it always filled him with the need to give them whatever would make them happy. Toys, money, food, a pony. He was a big sucker for babies, and he knew it. Allie never hesitated to give him shit over it, but he didn't care.

Tori bounced the little one as she nestled into the crook of her neck, snuggling in to go back to sleep. Jason watched, waiting to make sure she was okay. Not that she could've been hurt or anything, but she was obviously startled by the car's movements. When Tori looked up at him, he said, "Sorry again. I didn't know you had a baby in the car. Is she okay?"

She gave him a small smile as she continued her movements, soothing the baby. "Yeah, she's fine. I think she's teething, and she didn't sleep well, so she seems oversensitive today." Leaning down, she pressed her lips to the now calm and possibly sleeping child.

Jason got a little irritated at the fact that this woman, and her child, were out there trying to change a flat tire—alone. He didn't care if she didn't *need* a man, there had to be one somewhere considering she had a child. Not wanting to pry, or come across as a total asshole, he reined in his irritation and asked, "Why isn't your husband here changing the tire for you?"

She stilled her rocking and gave him an odd look, one he couldn't figure out before she covered it up and began her gentle swaying again. "My husband is no longer around, that's why. If it's a problem, I'm sure I can do it myself."

Realizing that even though he didn't want to sound like an asshole, he did. Giving his head a shake, he found himself once again apologizing to this redheaded beauty. I guess third times the charm, or would it be three strikes and you're out?

"No, of course it's not a problem. I just figured if there's a child, there should be a man nearby. And call me old-fashioned, but there are just some things a man should make sure are done for his woman." He finished the statement with a shrug before squatting back down to complete the job at hand, all the while crossing his fingers he could get it done without shoving his giant shoe in his mouth. Again.

TORI watched as the man who had a starring role in last night's dreams disappeared from her view. She could hear the noise of metal on metal as he got to work on changing her tire. Her defensive tone when he asked about her husband was uncalled for—she knew this—but for some reason he had her on edge. Maybe it was the combination of Lexi being up multiple times last night, or the fact she couldn't get back to sleep because when she closed her eyes, her dreams repeated getting her worked up in ways she hadn't been in a while. Regardless of why, she knew it was her turn to apologize.

Making her way back to the other side of the car, she struggled to maintain a groan as she caught sight of

Jason's broad shoulders flexing beneath the tightly pulled fabric of his shirt. He certainly was a sight to behold, and a little distracting, too. Deciding to move over by the driver's door so she could avoid the distraction of his strong back and shoulder muscles hard at work, she said, "I'm sorry for sounding so snappy. It's not like you're the first person to assume there was a father or husband around. You're doing me a favor, and I was rude, so I apologize."

She watched as his corded arms deftly loosened the lug nuts that she was unable to budge. When he looked up and smirked at her, her pulse sped up. He was so damn masculine and sexy it brought out the lonely female who had been hiding inside for almost two years. She could only hope her reaction to his presence wasn't written all over her face.

"There's nothing for you to apologize about. I asked a question that was none of my business, and you responded appropriately," he said as his smirk turned into a smile, and he returned his attention to the tire. She was about to say something when she heard a little boy's voice call out.

"Uncle Jason?"

Jason responded, "Over here, guys, I'm two cars down." But he never stopped doing what he was doing. When two of the little boys she remembered from last night appeared at the back of her car with questioning looks on their faces, it made her wonder why he was there to rescue her from her flat tire that morning.

"Boys, I know you have manners, so introduce yourself to the ladies," Jason instructed them. They both smiled up at her before moving in her direction.

The first one held his hand out. "Hi, I'm Dylan."

Then the second one followed suit. "Hi, I'm Ryan." She shook both of their hands before responding, "Nice to meet you. My name's Tori."

"Your baby's cute. What's her name? She looks like she's the same age as our sister," Dylan said before Ryan confirmed his statement with a smile. "That's what I was going to say. She's the same size as Ladybug."

Ladybug? What a strange name, she thought. They were cute boys, and since they had a baby sister, she assumed they were brothers. Since they looked to be the same age, she had to wonder if they were fraternal twins.

"Thanks, her name is Alexis, but I call her Lexi. And she's ten months old. How old is your sister?" Tori asked, wanting to keep up the conversation with these boys instead of ogling their Uncle Jason.

"Oh, she's older. Ella is only nine months old, right Uncle Jason?" Dylan answered. And he called his sister Ella, which meant that Ladybug was a nickname. Thank God. She would never understand why people sometimes named their kids such weird names.

Jason responded, "That's right, she's nine months old."

The quieter of the two boys, Ryan, reached up and rubbed Lexi's back in a soothing fashion. Clearly, he was a good big brother. Smiling down at him she said, "You must be a great big brother, you know just how to do that."

He smiled proudly and said, "Mom says that I have the magic touch with Ella."

How sweet, she thought a second before she was saddened that Lexi didn't have a big brother like him to look after her. Shaking that thought off, she asked, "So, why are you guys here today? You don't look like you partied here all night?"

Ryan giggled and Dylan sported an embarrassed look. Jason was the one to answer. "Nope, we didn't party all night. But one of the knucklehead twins over there," he started as he gestured to Dylan while making his way to her trunk to pull out the spare tire. When he brought it back to the area he was working in, he continued, "He was careless and forgot his iPod last night. So we came back looking for it today."

She remembered one of her crew finding it, and she told them to turn it in to the office, so she was glad that they did. She was about to say so when Ryan spoke up, "Hey, I thought we were the goofball twins?"

Jason chuckled. "You were both demoted when knucklehead number one there forgot his iPod. You'll have to work to gain the goofball title back."

They both groaned at their new title, while Tori just laughed. "So, you *are* twins. I was wondering about that."

When they both looked at her and shook their heads, Dylan spoke up and said, "No, we're cousins."

And then Ryan said, “But we’re brothers now, too.”

Confused, Tori looked to Jason who had just stood up from his task. He was dusting his hands off when he laughed and looked lovingly at his nephews. “I’m confused,” she said.

Jason leaned against her car and explained. “Ryan is my brother’s boy, and Dylan is Logan and Gillian’s son. The two of them grew up together and have been practically inseparable. In fact, we are pretty sure they share the same brain.” He laughed before continuing, “They have always called each other cousins, but yesterday, they became brothers by marriage when my brother, Jake, married Gillian.”

“Okay, I think I get it, and Ella is whose sister?” she asked.

“She’s both of ours,” they said together. Jason chuckled again and clarified. “Ella is Jake and Gillian’s daughter. So she is half-sister to both boys.”

Dylan added, “Yeah, and I have a whole sister and brother, too.”

Ryan defended, “They said they’re my brother and sister, too, Dylan.”

Jason moved away from the car and put his hand on Ryan’s back. “Of course they are, big guy. Dylan didn’t mean they weren’t. He was only adding them to the equation to confuse Tori a little more.”

Tori responded, “Well, he did. But I think I got it figured out. It’s like a modern-day Brady Bunch.”

Jason smiled big. "That about sums it up. But we don't have an Alice."

Ryan said proudly, "We have an Allie, though."

Jason said, "Yeah, we do, but let's not overwhelm Tori here."

"Oh, Allie. I remember her from last night. She's the pretty one with the purple streak who had a thing for my hair."

Jason nodded. "That's her."

"Okay, I think I got it figured out. Sort of," she said with amusement.

"It usually takes more than one lesson and possibly a diagram to figure it all out," Jason said.

She just gave him a laugh before her gaze met his, and they stared at each other silently for a few moments. Jason cleared his throat and broke the trance that seemed to be settling over them. "Okay, so I have some good news and some bad news. Which do you want first?"

Tori groaned. Of course there was bad news. "Okay, give me the bad news first."

"All right, the bad news is that your spare is also flat."

"Seriously?" she asked as she looked at the offending tire lying on the ground before looking back up at him.

Jason nodded. "Afraid so. But the good news is that your flat tire just looks to be a nail, which can be repaired easily. Did the flat happen today or do you have another car here?"

She grumbled inwardly at how things could go from fine to complicated at warp speed. “No, I found the flat last night. My landlord dropped me off this morning on his way to the store.”

Jason sounded irritated when he said, “What kind of man drops a woman off to take care of a flat tire on her own with an infant in the backseat?”

She wanted to laugh and cry at the same time. Chivalrous men were few and far between, but clearly Jason was one of them. Why couldn’t he be the kind of man she had found instead of Damien? Shaking her head at the direction of her thoughts, she responded, “My landlord is a seventy year old, cane-wielding man with terrible arthritis. I’m quite certain if he was physically capable to fix it for me, he would have.”

Jason dropped his shoulders and gave her a nod. “Okay, he gets a pass then.”

“Good, he deserves it,” she said with affection as she thought of how lucky she was to have found her landlord, Hal. She wasn’t sure how she would’ve made it without him. He didn’t charge her rent, but rather she helped him prepare meals and did some small household tasks he couldn’t perform. Hal was like having a grandfather around, and that was something she never had the luxury of. She cherished the experience now. For her, it felt like two people who needed one another found each other at just the right time.

Jason interrupted her thoughts. “Okay then, how about we take you to get this repaired?”

"Oh, I couldn't interrupt your day like that. I'll figure something out. Surely you boys have plans today," Tori said quickly, feeling bad for his time she had already wasted.

"Nonsense. This is the kind of stuff we stupid men like to do," he replied with a smirk.

"You're gonna keep reminding me of that, aren't you?" she asked with feigned annoyance.

"Sure am," he assured with humor before adding, "Besides, there's a crew of women in my family who would totally kick my ass if I didn't help a lady in distress out."

"Lady in distress?" she scoffed as she rubbed the sore spot on her butt. "I don't think I was in distress until you knocked me on my ass."

Jason barked out a laugh and said, "Good point. And it only reinforces my requirement to assist you."

"Maybe, but you're basically a stranger to me. What kind of lesson would we be teaching these impressionable boys if I were to just get in a car with you?" Even though what she was saying was true, she hoped he caught the humor she added. Considering her options, she was going to have to accept his offer, but she wasn't an ignorant person. He was a stranger, but the fact that she met him last night and he had two young boys with him made her much less worried.

He smiled brightly. "Very good response, Tori. You're right, I am a stranger. So ..." He paused and pulled his wallet out and retrieved a business card from it. Holding his hand out, he continued, "Here is my business card, which has all my information on it. Bring it inside to the receptionist and tell her that I'm helping you with your flat tire."

Taking the card from his hand, her fingers brushed his, and she smiled when she could see the muscles in his arm tighten. It was good to know she wasn't the only one affected by their proximity. Lifting the card up to examine it, she gave him a questioning look. "And telling them in the office that you're fixing my flat tire will accomplish?"

"Two things actually. First, it will help prevent them from towing your car while we're gone. Second, it will leave a trail if something were to happen to you—someone knows who you were with. Therefore, proving that you have nothing to worry about when you get in my car." He gave her a smug smile as if he was so smart. *Nothing to worry about? Yeah right.* She had a feeling that being near this man was a dangerous thing, and not for the *Silence of the Lambs* kind of reason, but more like the *Love Potion No.9* kind of problem.

Even though she had already decided she would accept his help, she made it look like she was still considering it. She wasn't sure if this was her way of playing hard to get with the first man who evoked a reaction from her in a long time, but she had a feeling he would appreciate that she was thinking about it. His praise a few minutes ago, and the fact that he seemed irritated that she was doing this alone with her daughter in tow, told her that he was *that* kind of guy who cared about people in general.

She turned and leaned into the car, lifting and shouldering her purse as she turned back to him. "Would you mind grabbing the car seat for me while I run your business card inside?"

His smile spread wide as he nodded. "Sure thing."

The smile he was wearing transformed his face from a strong masculine man to a carefree young man. It wasn't as though he hadn't given her a smile already, but that one, it was different. It was mesmerizing. Shaking her head to break the spell she was falling under, she said, "I'll be right back."

"We'll be waiting for you, Tori."

CHAPTER FIVE

JASON watched as Tori walked away, taking in the subtle sway of her curved hips. He couldn't look away from the heavenly sight, and he felt his body tighten as he imagined what it would feel like to run his hands over those curves. Taking a deep breath, he absorbed the vision and let the euphoric sensation that came with it spread through his body. He wasn't sure what it was about this woman that had him reacting this way, but he knew he wanted to feel a whole lot more of it. When she finally disappeared into the same office he and the boys had visited earlier, he managed to pull his gaze from the closed door.

As he looked down at his nephews, he willed his body to calm down. "Okay, boys, looks like we get to take two ladies out to eat this morning." He said as he walked toward his car with the flat tire. Loading one and then the other in his trunk before moving to the back seat of Tori's car, where he retrieved the infant seat and base to move into his. Closing the door, he made sure to grab her keys and what looked like a diaper bag sitting on the front seat before locking the rest of the doors.

Dylan asked, "I thought we were taking her to fix her tire? Do they have food there too?"

Jason laughed. "No knucklehead, they don't. But it'll take a little time to get the tire fixed so what better thing to do then escort the ladies to an early lunch." He motioned to his car, telling the boys to head that way. Once there, he secured the base and seat in the middle, thankful he recently got a lesson from Jake on how to do it properly. Not that he was an idiot or anything, but since Jake was a paramedic, he helped at the firehouse when they held open houses allowing parents to have their car seat installation checked to make sure it was done properly. Prior to that, Jason had no idea how important it was to make sure a seat was level.

After he finished, the boys climbed in on either side of the seat, and Jason drove his car around the lot. Pulling up in front of the doors Tori had gone into with the baby, he got out and positioned himself on the passenger side of the car to wait for her. No way was he gonna just wait in the car and not open her door for her. His mother raised him to be a gentleman, so he made sure to always act the part.

It was natural for him to open doors for a woman, escort her through rooms, pull out her chair, and stand when she left the table. He never hesitated to act on those instincts. He not only wanted to open doors for Tori, he wanted to carry her through those doors so she wouldn't have to worry about tripping or stubbing her toe.

Jason knew these feelings were completely irrational and would have to be examined more closely. But for now, he was going to gather information on the green-eyed beauty who'd cast a spell over him. Nope, no need to track her down since she managed to fall on her butt right in front of him today.

TORI chatted with Darlene, the office receptionist, for a moment as she tried to slow the excitement that was making a circuit through her body. The sudden warmth she was feeling had nothing to do with the temperature outside. The older woman smiled and talked the customary baby talk that seemed to take over composed adults when a baby was in their company. There was just something about little ones that brought out the best side of people, and Tori loved having a front row seat to it.

Once Lexi was hoisted into Darlene's arms, Tori realized that coming into the office might have been a bad idea. Jason may have suggested it, but he neglected to take into account that when there was a baby in your arms, everyone wanted a piece of the baby love.

Smiling to herself, she watched Lexi stare at the older woman with a strange expression on her face. She didn't want to be rude but she needed to get out of there. Didn't Darlene understand there was a man who was the pure definition of masculinity waiting outside for them? After a few moments, and figuring it was as good an excuse as any, she said, "Well, we better get going. I have a ride waiting for us to take me to get my flat fixed."

Reaching for the baby, Darlene reluctantly handed her over with the standard look of disappointment people had when their "baby time" was done. Tori smiled in understanding as she pulled Lexi against her chest. Leaning forward, she kissed her daughter on the head before readjusting her on to her hip. Darlene waggled her fingers at Lexi in an exaggerated fashion as she said good-bye in her baby-talk voice before looking back up to Tori and asking, "Didn't you work the wedding reception last night?"

Tori nodded as she shifted the baby to her other hip and re-shouldered her purse, making a mental note that she needed to grab the diaper bag from the car before they left. She nodded, "Was there a problem or a complaint about last night?"

"Oh no, not at all," Darlene reassured her. "I was just going to ask you if all the men there looked as good as the one who was just in here. Quite a looker, if you know what I mean."

Tori couldn't help but laugh a little. Darlene might have been in her late sixties, but she clearly had great taste in men. "Yes, there were quite a few good looking men there last night." She didn't want to come off as inappropriate with her response, but she wasn't the one who brought up handsome men. Dropping her voice to a whisper, she leaned forward like she had a secret. Darlene was instantly intrigued and mirrored Tori's posture. "But the one who just left was the best looking one for sure. And as it turns out, he's more than just good looks; he's the one taking me to get my tire fixed."

Darlene's eyebrows shot up as she stood straight. For a second Tori thought that maybe she had crossed a line, but then Darlene smiled big. A second later, she was around the desk and looking out the window by the door. Tori knew when Jason must have come into view because Darlene sighed. She actually sighed. Turning back to Tori, she said, "Mmm, mmm, mmm … if I was thirty years younger."

Dropping back down in the seat behind her desk, she fanned herself. "I sure hope you shaved your legs today, young lady."

Now who was saying inappropriate things? "Darlene! I can't believe you just said that."

"What? It's true. You wouldn't want to make a terrible first impression by rubbing sandpaper legs up against him when you're wrapped around him. Things might end before they even get started."

"Oh my God, I take it back. I can't believe you said *that*!" Tori exclaimed in shock as she tried not to blush at the image of her beneath that big body of his as she wrapped her legs around his waist.

The older woman shrugged. "I may be old, but I'm not dead, sweetie. I know how these things work."

Shaking her head and moving toward the door, Tori said, "It doesn't matter if I shaved my legs today because they won't be wrapped around or rubbing up against anyone later. He's just being a gentleman and helping me with my tire."

When she turned to open the door, Darlene said, "Honey, a gentleman calls a tow truck. A man who's interested finds a reason to be in your presence longer." Looking back over her shoulder at Darlene, she realized she didn't have a response. He could've just called a tow truck, but instead he was personally making sure her tire was fixed. Suddenly she was very happy that she did, in fact, shave her legs that morning.

Stepping out into the late morning sun, Tori pulled her sunglasses from the top of her head to shield her eyes. It was a bright, clear blue sky and a lovely day to be outside. Too bad she had a car to take care of instead ... her thoughts trailed off when she caught sight of Jason. He was talking on the phone while leaning against his car, in his tight t-shirt with jeans, slung low on his waist. A waist that she had imagined squeezing between her legs a few moments ago. *Apparently she had no control over her recently revived libido any longer.*

He had pulled the shiny black car up to the curb, and it gave her a little thrill to know that he did that for her. He was certainly polite. Then she recalled Darlene's comment from a few moments ago and wondered if he was acting as a gentleman or was an interested man finding a reason to be in her company. Her rational mind warred with her heart. Her girlie parts kicked both her mind's and heart's asses when it declared that the second option was the only one, and a small tremor worked its way from between her legs and vibrated outward.

Pausing for a moment, she squeezed her legs together to help dispel the sensation. She was unsuccessful. She moved toward him as he ended his call and gave her a breath-taking grin. She'd heard of such smiles existing, but had yet to find one in person. But she had a feeling that Jason would be able to elicit a whole mess of sensations that she was unfamiliar with. *Stop it,* she scolded herself before she could catalog all the possibilities.

Jason opened the back door, and one of his nephews hopped out before he reached in and lifted Lexi's seat out. His basic familiarity with moving the car seat around reminded her of the baby she had seen him with last night. Clearly this man had experience being around children.

"Here you go," he said as he held the seat up in a position where she could belt Lexi in.

"Thanks," Tori said as she shifted Lexi into the seat and began to buckle her in. "You could've put the seat on the ground. I hate making you do more than necessary."

Lexi was staring up at the hulk of a man holding her car seat. She didn't appear bothered in the least. It was obvious that his attractiveness was acknowledged by all ages. Taking ahold of her daughter's hand, she lifted it to her mouth and kissed it, but Lexi was still looking at Jason.

"Of course I *could* have, but then you'd have had to get down on the ground to load her in. This way is easier for you," he said and then looked down at Lexi. When her daughter and Jason made eye contact, Tori watched as a big, mostly toothless, drool-dripping smile spread across her face. When Tori followed Lexi's gaze, she saw Jason had puffed out his cheeks and crossed his eyes to make a funny face. Then he let out a big breath and made a raspberry sound which had Lexi giggling immediately.

Hiding behind her sunglasses, Tori watched as Jason made silly faces and noises to entertain Lexi. A deep sense of longing began to swell in her chest as she let Jason move the car seat into the car, where he efficiently snapped it into the base. He definitely knew his way around baby equipment.

When Jason motioned for his nephew to get back in the car, he closed the back door before opening the front door for her. Smiling again, she stepped up to get in and said, "You sure are good at that."

"It's really not that hard to make a baby laugh."

"No. I mean, you're right it's not. But I was talking about how you know your way around a car seat." She stumbled through her words as she dropped into the passenger seat. Looking back up at him, he gave her a half smile and one-shouldered shrug.

"I have eight nieces and nephews of varying ages. Not to mention a brother who insisted I knew how to load an infant seat before he allowed his daughter to ride in my car."

So no children of his own, she thought as he closed her door and walked around the front of the vehicle, allowing her to view his confident stride. She marveled at how he moved so smoothly for being such a tall, broad man. He moved with agility and purpose. Turning her head toward the driver's door, she was graced with a front seat view of his tight backend as he folded himself into his seat. Tori had never been much for men's butts, but now she saw what all the fuss was about.

Her cheeks warmed below her sunglasses, and she found herself once again needing to redirect her thoughts. This was Darlene's fault for bringing up the differences between a gentleman and a man who was seeking a way to spend time a woman.

To take her mind off Jason's tight ass, she asked, "Only nieces and nephews? No kids of your own?"

He started the car before giving her a sideways glance. Maybe it was more of a cocky smirk, as he said, "Only nieces and nephews so far. Haven't found the woman meant to have my children yet."

He winked at her, turned his attention to driving, and pulled the car away from the curb. He didn't even notice the fire he just lit in the seat next to him.

CHAPTER SIX

JASON parked the car opposite the large open garage doors of the tire shop, glad he'd called his buddy ahead of time to make sure he was working. Looking toward Tori, he said, "I'll just bring the tire in and see how long it'll be."

"Oh. Is it something that takes a long time to do?" Tori asked. "I really hate keeping you from whatever your plans were for today."

"No worries, Tori. I rather like how the day has turned out." Opening his door, he stood to see his friend, Garrett, stroll from the garage. Moving to the trunk, he popped it and hoisted the flat tire out and to the ground. When Garrett reached him, he looked up and said, "Good to see you, man."

Jason grabbed his friend's outstretched hand before giving a one-armed guy hug. "Yeah, you too. Thanks for taking my call earlier. You got these in stock?"

"Yeah, you said you needed two. Where's the other rim?" Garrett asked.

"It's still on the car, so I'll bring that one back later," Jason told him. "This is the spare, and it was flat, too."

"Okay, but since when do you drive late model imports that sport these kind of wheels?"

Before Jason could answer, Tori stepped out of the car. It didn't take Garrett but a few seconds to figure out why Jason was bringing him a wheel that belonged to a car he would never drive.

Garrett nodded to Tori. “Morning. We’ll get this tire patched up for you as quickly as possible, ma’am.”

Tori smiled and made her way toward them. Jason caught the not-so-subtle perusal his friend made of Tori when she came into view. “Great, thanks so much. Do I take care of paying now or when you’re done?”

“When we finish is fine.”

“How long do you think it’ll take?” she asked.

Garrett made eye contact with him, giving him a considering look before turning back to Tori. For whatever reason, Jason wasn’t too pleased with his friend’s wandering eyes. He was proud of his ability to resist throwing something at Garrett’s head. Although that probably had more to do with the fact that he had nothing to throw, but he’d gladly accept credit for his restraint.

“Not too long. About an hour or two. It should be enough time for you all to grab a bite to eat.” Garrett then looked back at him, flashing a cocky smile—like he thought Jason now owed him one. “I can just text Jason when we’re all done.”

Yep. He was going to owe him one all right. Jason held back his urge to smirk. An hour or two of time where Tori couldn’t escape him was just fine. Something told him this woman was strong-willed and didn’t usually make herself completely dependent on another person. Especially a man. A momentary flash of guilt for feeling like he manipulated the situation in his favor came and went. He wasn’t doing anything harmful, and if she wanted to go, she could. He would just make sure he was accommodating enough so she wouldn't want to.

When Tori looked at him, he gave her his best can't-say-no-to-this-face kind of smile and said, "Are you hungry? 'Cause I know a place not too far from here that has great burgers."

There was a pause as she once again considered what he was saying. Jason only hoped she was contemplating saying yes to food and not how to grab her daughter and make a quick break for it. After a few seconds she said, "Are you *sure* this isn't completely ruining your plans for the day?"

"Are you kidding?" Jason said, making his way toward her. As he opened the passenger door and gestured for her to get in, he continued, "My day is turning out better than expected."

TORI dropped into the front seat, shaking her head and smiling as Jason closed the door. She had seen the look that passed between the two men. That *knowing* look telling her she had been set up, or at least she played right along with whatever plans were orchestrated. The funny thing was she kinda liked that she did. It made her think Jason had an interest in her beyond the whole 'helping a lady in distress' thing. Looking in the rearview mirror, she could see Jason talking with his friend before they shook hands, and he made his way to the driver's seat.

When he went to get in, Tori made sure to pay attention. She watched as he bent and tucked his large frame through the open door and dropped into his seat. Her gaze followed the motion of his thick arms as he easily turned the key and started the engine. Why hadn't anyone told her starting a car was so sexy to watch? When she brought her gaze back up to his face, they locked eyes.

He graced her with one of the sexiest, most confident smiles she had ever seen, and all the girlie parts of her body perked up and paid attention. He seemed to be very pleased with himself. She huffed a little laugh and decided that she was also pleased with the way her day was turning out. That dangerous feeling of hope began to form, and she relished in the sensation of it.

Answering his smile with what she hoped was a sexy one of her own, she said, "Burgers, huh? What if I was a vegetarian?"

She smiled bigger and laughed a little at how his eyes widened and a slight look of panic crossed his face. "Uh, I'm sorry. Are you? Because I'm pretty sure they have salads, too. I know I've seen Allie and Gillian eating something green." He pulled out his phone and started scrolling through as he continued to back pedal. "Madison, too. She only eats salads, and she eats there. Let me call and see if they do."

She let out a full laugh this time and placed her hand on his arm. "Sorry, I couldn't help but tease you. You'll see I'm a bit of a smartass. And don't worry, Jason, I totally eat meat. Find me a great burger, and we'll be friends forever."

Jason paused his rapid search on his phone and moved his gaze to her hand on his arm. For a split second she thought maybe she had overstepped her bounds with an unwanted touch. But when he lifted his eyes to hers, unleashing that mesmerizing smile on her again, she knew there had been no overstepping. In fact, the look was so inviting she considered climbing across the center console of his car, straddling his lap, tunneling her hands in his hair, and finding out what that sexy beard would feel like against her skin.

His words momentarily brought her out of her fantasy. "Just when I didn't think you could get more attractive, I find out you're a teasing smartass. This day just keeps getting better and better."

The visual in her head shifted and now had him pulling her across the center console, tunneling his hands into her hair, and feasting on her lips. It was a stunningly erotic image that she could almost feel as if it were happening. Her heart rate picked up, and she took a slow, somewhat steady breath as he watched her reaction. When his hand slipped over hers, which was still resting on his arm for no apparent reason, she shivered. A warm tingling sensation slowly spread through her hand, which he now had trapped against his skin. The desire to move was strong. Not move it away, but move it around and absorb more of his touch.

Tori let a few beats pass, enjoying the sensation of touching a man after so long. Taking in a measured breath, she gave Jason a sultry smile. "It looks like I'm not the only one around here who likes to tease."

She winked and then slowly slid her hand out from beneath his, placing it in her lap.

JASON had never been a love-at-first-sight kind of guy, and he still didn't think he was. Lust-at-first-sight was something he could certainly understand. But whatever was going on with Tori was off-the-charts intoxicating. The pull he felt to touch her bordered on inappropriate, because he'd always made sure to act respectful around women, with the exception of a few years in his early twenties where youth and stupidity dominated his environment. But what was running through his head now was anything but respectable.

Knowing he needed to focus on driving instead of openly lusting at the woman sitting beside him, he put the car in gear and pulled out of the parking lot. It was a short drive to Brody's Burgers, so it didn't take long to get there. Jason couldn't help but take notice of how comfortable he felt having her in his car. When they pulled into a parking space, she was engaged in a conversation with the boys, instigated by Dylan, about which superhero was coolest.

He was intent on opening her door for her, but settled for helping lift the baby out of the backseat once he saw she was already getting out on her side. He couldn't help but smile when he saw the look of surprise on her face at him helping with the baby seat. "I'll carry the seat if you get the diaper bag. While I have no problem sporting the whole brown and pink polka-dot print, it does nothing for my complexion."

Tori laughed as she slung the bag over her shoulder. "You're probably right. I'd have you pegged as more of blues and greens kind of guy."

"Blues and greens are good, but I'm told that blacks and grays really bring out my eyes." He finished with a wink before turning toward the door. Holding it open, he watched as she motioned for Dylan and Ryan to head in before her, and he followed. Glancing down, he couldn't help but smile at the beautiful baby girl he was carrying. When she saw him look at her, a big smile appeared, and her little body began to squirm as she reached up for him.

Yep, he was a goner for baby girls, he thought as he lifted her seat up higher in his arms. Looking toward the bar, he held up his hand to show how many were in their group. The young man motioned toward a table in the corner and they migrated that way.

"Where would you like me to put the baby?" Jason asked. Tori moved to grab the carrier from his grip, but he held tight, saying, "I got it. Just tell me where you want her."

"Oh, on the bench is a good spot for it. I'm going to take her out of it anyway," Tori said as she sat down next to where he had just placed the seat.

Jason took the seat across from Tori as he watched her lift Lexi out of the carrier. Lexi's hands went directly to Tori's hair as she grabbed onto her and cuddled into her neck. When Tori hugged her back and leaned down to kiss her head, Jason felt a twinge of jealousy. He wasn't sure who he was more jealous of—Tori cuddling Lexi ... or Lexi snuggling Tori? Probably both if he were being honest with himself.

Him not being a father yet had come up plenty of times in the past, more so as he got older. But it was always something he brushed off as nobody's business but his own—though he was more considerate with his parents because they *were* his parents.

Up until recently, he was content with his current situation, even though he wanted more. But he was patient. Now, though, he could feel his patience slipping away as longing set up camp in his chest while he watched this woman he didn't know mothering her child.

He was grateful when the waitress approached for their drink orders, which he happily gave for him and the boys. Once she got Tori's order and promised to return to take their orders, Jason turned to his nephews. "Go wash your hands, boys."

Both of them did as they were told, which left him sitting alone with Tori and Lexi. Wanting to avoid any awkward silence, he mentioned the conversation he'd overheard in the car. "So, you think Spiderman is the coolest superhero, huh? I thought all woman liked Superman the best."

She giggled as she turned Lexi in her lap to face the table and Jason. "I'd have to say Superman would probably come in second, but that's only because I'm afraid of flying. Scaling the side of a building is more appealing—less distance to fall."

"That's a valid method of determining," he said with a smirk.

"Glad you approve," Tori said with a nod as the boys returned to the table. The waitress brought their drinks, took their food order, and they all chatted very casually.

But Jason's primary focus was to stare at the new objects of his desire, without being caught.

TORI couldn't get over how much she was enjoying her conversation with Dylan and Ryan. The two boys seemed much older than their nine or ten years. She smiled as she noticed that they almost constantly finished each other's sentences. Looking up at Jason, she asked, "Do they always do that?"

He huffed a laugh as his gaze moved from Lexi to her. "What, share the same brain? All the time. It's always been funny to watch." Jason then continued his game of peek-a-boo with the baby. Lexi giggled and watched as Jason did it again. When he dropped his hands down and smiled at Lexi, Tori's heart melted a little bit. He really was good with little ones, making it sad that he didn't have any of his own.

His gaze finally lifted away from Lexi and met hers. "Their relationship is pretty cool, but you should really see how Gillian is with Allie. I'm pretty sure those two can communicate without talking. My brother jokes that they are two halves of a whole, and it sure seems that way."

She remembered the two women from the night before, but she hadn't been around them together. It must be amazing to be so close to someone like that. Tori and her mother were close—so much so that her mother worried too much about what Tori would do without her. When her mother was diagnosed with cancer, she had made it her mission to make sure Tori wasn't alone after she was gone. It was also this closeness that Damien used to his benefit, taking advantage of Tori in her grief.

Not wanting to let that evil infiltrate the good time she was having, she gave herself a mental shake before standing. "I better go wash up before our food comes," she said as she moved Lexi to her hip and reached for the seat.

Jason stood and moved to her side of the table. "You can just leave her with me when you go to the bathroom. I don't mind."

Tori considered it, reminding herself that she didn't know him and shouldn't be leaving her daughter with him. She shook her head and was about to say no thank you when Jason continued, "I know you don't know me, so will it make you feel better to take my car keys with you. I can't very well steal your child without my car, now can I?"

Shaking her head, she said, "You really do have an answer for everything, don't you?"

He shrugged before reaching for the baby. When Lexi leaned toward him, Tori let him lift her into his arms. Pulling his keys from his pocket, he handed them to her without moving his gaze from Lexi's face. "What can I say, I'm a problem solver. I could let you have my wallet, too, if it would help."

Taking the keys from his hand, she answered, "That won't be necessary. I'll be right back."

She heard him say, "Take your time," as she walked away. Looking back over her shoulder, she gasped at Lexi clinging to Jason as he hugged her to him with his eyes closed. Like a father holding his child, it was a perfect sight, which made her both elated but also so sad. Her daughter's father was a monster, incapable of what she was witnessing at that moment. Dashing away the tears that had quickly filled her eyes and spilled over, she made her way to the bathroom.

Tori quickly washed her hands and then looked at her reflection as she turned off the water. Grabbing a towel, she took a deep breath and got her emotions in check. Jason was a friendly man helping her out with her tire, not someone signing up for the vacant father position in Lexi's life. She needed to make sure she remembered that before she made a fool of herself. Squaring her shoulders, she gave herself a nod of agreement and left the bathroom. All the way back to the table she couldn't help but think of Jason filling the vacant position in her daughter's life, as well as her own.

CHAPTER SEVEN

JASON gathered all the restraint he could muster and held onto it when Tori insisted on paying for their meal. Her determination was so great, he feared if he fought her on it, the likelihood he'd be able to get her on a date with him would be slim. And damn, he really wanted to take her on a date. After subduing his alpha tendencies and a few minutes of negotiation, he allowed her to pay for his and her food, but drew the line at paying the whole bill since his nephews were not her responsibility.

He grumbled a bit, and she smiled her victory at him over the roof of his car before getting in. They picked up the new tire, which she believed was just a repaired version of the flat, and made their way to her work. He positioned his car behind hers and, before climbing out, told Ryan and Dylan to entertain the baby.

When Tori followed him, she said, "They're really great kids. You can tell they have a lot of experience with babies."

Jason smiled as he thought of his niece, Ella. As he pulled the tire from his trunk, he made sure to grab a work blanket he had in there, too. "I might be a little biased, but I have to say that all of my nieces and nephews are pretty great kids." He dropped the blanket to the ground before lying on it and positioning the jack under the car. "I even like the teenaged ones."

He felt her squat down next to him, but he didn't take his attention off what he was doing. "Wow, even the teenagers? You really are biased."

Letting out a laugh, he sat up so he could jack up the car. "Don't get me wrong," he said as he continued with changing the tire, "Madison is sixteen, and to say she hasn't been a handful at times would be a lie." He stopped talking as he hoisted the flat tire off and then replaced it before continuing, "There were times during Gillian and Logan's divorce that I wanted to shake that girl. But she was forced to come around in the end. She's much easier to get along with now."

"That bad, huh?" Tori said when she held out her hand full of lug nuts. He smiled at how she was helping him and grabbed one from the palm of her hand. "Yeah, she was, but it was understandable at the time."

One by one, he replaced the lug nuts and tightened them. When he got to the last one, he paused as his fingers made contact with her skin and looked up at her. There was slight hitch in her breathing, which was the only indication that she was affected by him. Grabbing the last one, he closed his fist around it and dropped his arm to rest on one of his knees. Squatting for so long was making his feet ache, but he didn't want to move. She was at the same level, in a similar position. The fact that their time together was almost up didn't escape him. He thought, *There's no time like the present*.

"Hey, Tori?" he asked in a low, deceptively calm voice.

"Yeah, Jason," she replied in a soft, shaky one of her own.

"I know you said your husband wasn't around anymore ... I was just wondering if he was still a husband, or if he was an ex-husband?" Jason asked.

Her jaw clenched for a moment before she released it, saying, "Oh, he's definitely an ex-husband."

Before he could respond, she stood and slipped her hands into the pockets of her jeans and sighed. She looked anywhere but at him. He slowly released the jack and lowered the car before also standing. Lifting the tire that still needed repair, he hauled it to his trunk. When she saw what he was doing, she asked, "Did you mean to put my other tire in your trunk?"

Closing the trunk, he dusted off his hands as he looked at her. "Sure did."

Confused, she asked, "Okay ... why?"

He smiled confidently and shrugged as he leaned back against his car. "Gives me an excuse to have to see you again."

Her hands slipped from her front pockets and into her back ones as she shifted from one foot to the other. This movement caused her shirt to tighten across her chest, giving him a perfect image of what was lying beneath. He was certain the vision before him would be relived repeatedly over the next few days. Or at least until she gave him another one. Tori brought him back to the conversation, asking, "Did you really need an *excuse*?"

"No, but it helps in case you have one."

"An excuse for what?" she asked, looking both confused and curious.

"To tell me no when I ask if I can see you again." He knew he was smirking, but he couldn't help it. He was really enjoying watching her squirm—every emotion possible crossing her face. There was surprise, followed by a little excitement, then topped by apprehension. When she didn't answer him, he feared apprehension was going to win, so he added, "So Tori, do you need an excuse to see me again? 'Cause you have three more tires that might need some attention. I could easily just keeping swapping the new ones out until you finally say yes."

She let out a laugh and dropped her head down to stare at the ground. Using her foot to play with a rock on the pavement, he let her think for a moment. Jason knew he had it in him to be more convincing, and he could definitely up his game if necessary. But he wanted her to say yes without needing an excuse.

When she looked up at him and gave him a shy smile, he knew he was in. "You want to see me again, for like ... a date?"

"Yes, a date. But to be honest, I'd accept appointments for any and all car problems, maybe to carry some heavy boxes. Oh, I'm pretty good with yard work, too. You know, all that stuff that makes it worth having us *stupid* men around." He winked at her and waited for her response.

As hoped, she smiled and said, "Well, as you can see, my tires have seen better days. And my yard really could use some attention."

She was playing with him. And he loved it. “Great. Just tell me when, and I’ll be there. Then afterward, maybe you’ll let me take you somewhere so you can thank me for all of my hard work.”

With an unbelieving look she said, “You really would do something like that, wouldn’t you?”

Jason shrugged. “I’m thinking you’d be worth it, Tori. So yes, I probably would.”

“I work a lot of weekends,” she added.

He replied, “I’m my own boss and can work around your schedule.”

“I’m not the type of mom who would give up spending time with her daughter for anyone.”

“Do I come across as the type of man who would have a problem spending time with you *and* your daughter?”

“I have baggage,” she said abruptly in what appeared to be a last ditch effort to deter him.

She would have to accept that he was not a man who was easily deterred. “Like I said before, I’m really good with the heavy lifting.

TORI couldn’t help but smile at Jason. “You weren’t kidding when you said you had an answer for everything, huh?”

He only smiled as he stood leaning against his car. Strong arms crossed over his broad chest as he waited for her to respond to his original question.

She straightened her face and said, “No.”

His confident posture faltered, and he stood up, so she felt a little bad for attempting to tease him. Apparently he was a sensitive guy, so she continued, "No, I don't need an excuse."

And just like that, his face lit up with a smile. He raked a hand through his short dark hair before dropping it down and slipping it back into his pocket. His shoulders rose as he straightened his arms and asked in a seemingly happy tone, "When is your next day off?"

"Wednesday, but I'm off on Friday, too."

"Wednesday works better for me," he said. "It's sooner than Friday."

And just like that, the hope she had been holding at bay blossomed a little more. "Wednesday it is then."

"Wednesday," he agreed with that same happy tone and a smile to match.

They stood there quietly staring at each other for a few moments before their attention was redirected toward the backseat of his car.

"Uncle Jason," one of his nephews called out. "The baby is waking up, and I think she wants her mom."

Tori quickly moved to the open car door, feeling a little bad that she seemed to be in her own little world, practically forgetting about her daughter. Okay, she didn't forget her daughter, since she was within ten feet of her and until two minutes ago was sound asleep. She needed to give herself a break, but it was odd for her to be feeling these emotions. It was foreign for her to be thinking of anyone but Lexi, even if it was just about herself. Shaking that off, she reached in and lifted the car seat out of the car. Before she even had her fully out of the car, Lexi gave up whining and started smiling, easing some of her tension.

Smiling back at her, she moved to get her purse and the diaper bag from the front seat. When she closed the door, she could see Jason removing the base for her. He quietly moved to Tori's car and strapped it in before taking the seat from her hands. When he started talking to Lexi, Tori found herself once again being drawn to him.

"Now you're going to be a good girl for Mommy, aren't you? Yes, you are. You're always a good girl, aren't you?"

Tori just smiled and watched as he bent over and snapped the seat into place as Lexi just smiled and giggled at him in answer. She dropped her bags into the front seat and turned back to him as he stood up and closed the back door. "She says she's going to be a good girl for you. Just so you know."

She smiled up at him. Her life had been nothing but complicated over the past few years, so she couldn't help but marvel at how content she felt at the moment. The only light in her life had been Lexi. She was her strength and courage all balled up into one beautiful little package. Dating a man was not something she worried about, at all, and she was fine with that. But that didn't seem to be the case anymore. Even with all her baggage, she wanted to take the risk. And something told her Jason could carry it without a problem.

Without hesitation, she stepped into his space and stood on her tiptoes. Leaning in, she placed a soft kiss on his cheek. His hands went to her waist, steadying her since he was at least a foot taller, and his beard tickled her chin a little, but she noticed how soft it felt against her skin. Fighting the urge to feel more of it, she dropped back down, "Thank you, for everything."

His hands were still on her waist as he smiled down at her. "It was my pleasure, Tori."

"Wednesday," she said.

He nodded. "Wednesday."

Jason moved and opened the driver's door for her. As she slipped into the seat, he asked, "Are you going to give me your number? Or are you going to drive off and leave me hanging in hope that I can figure out where you live on Wednesday?"

She laughed and said, "I've got your business card still. I'll text you."

"You didn't give it to the lady in the office earlier?"

Tori shook her head. "No, something told me you were one of those guys a girl could trust."

If it was even possible, his smiled grew bigger. "I'll be waiting for that text then."

"Bye, Jason. Thanks again for everything."

"Bye, Tori. You call if you need any more flats fixed. Especially since I have your spare." He winked at her and closed the door.

She watched as he walked to his car and gave her one last glance before getting in. When he pulled away, she sighed and said, “Well, Lexi, it’s nice to see that not all men are monsters.”

CHAPTER EIGHT

JASON looked at his cell phone for what seemed like the hundredth time. He quickly opened his text messages to make sure he hadn't missed something. Again, he'd done this every time he turned his phone on. Sighing in a mixture of disappointment and anxiety, he slipped the currently useless electronic back into his pocket.

"You expecting that phone to do tricks or something?" his friend and business partner, Logan, asked as he made his way over to where Jason was working—trying to work was more like it. His concentration had been shit all morning, and he wasn't sure how to get himself back on track. Double checking his calculations would probably be a good idea.

"Bite me," Jason grumbled, hoping Logan would drop it.

"Are you expecting an important call?" Logan asked. He should've known better than to hope, and since Logan was capable of driving a saint mad with his persistence, Jason confessed.

"Yeah, I'm expecting an important call," he said as he tried to jot down some notes for the job they were working on. After a few moments passed, and Logan hadn't pushed further, Jason resisted looking up. If he had indeed dropped it, he didn't want to rehash it. Directing his gaze toward the opposite side of the large room, Jason took in the amount of work their crew had completed yesterday. It was more than expected, for a Monday, and he was happy knowing they might just finish ahead of schedule.

Slipping his pencil behind his ear, he moved to take a closer look at the archway they would be working on tomorrow. Wednesday. The day he had a date with Tori. His phone vibrated against his leg.

Quickly shoving his hand in his pocket to pull it out, he was not the least bit surprised at his anxiousness. When he finally got the phone out and saw the screen, his disappointment grew exponentially. Logan's caller ID glared up at him, the profile picture of him flipping the camera off. The image only added irritation to his already growing pile of emotions.

Turning to Logan, he could see he still had his phone to his ear, like Jason was actually going to answer the call. Jason pulled the pencil from behind his ear and threw it at Logan. "I'm not going to answer it, douchebag."

Logan let out a laugh as he dodged the pencil and put his phone away. "So what you're saying is that a phone call from me isn't an important thing."

Jason shook his head as a small smirk graced his face, grateful for the banter to distract him. "That's exactly what I'm saying. Don't we have employees you could be harassing?"

"Already done. I know my duties, big guy," Logan said as he moved up next to Jason again, handing him his stupid pencil. "Now, you gonna tell me whose phone call you're waiting for?"

Jason walked over to a nearby table and, leaning against it, he dropped his pad of paper down before crossing his arms and looking back at Logan. "Sorry man, guess I'm a bit tense this morning."

Huffing a laugh in agreement, Logan said, "I'd say so. You want tell me what's got you tied in knots?"

Logan and Jason had been friends since high school, and even though Jason wasn't a talkative guy, if he were going to talk, it'd be to Logan. Well, and Jake. Pinching the bridge of his nose, Jason closed his eyes and sighed, trying to relax. When he opened his eyes, he found his friend patiently waiting.

"I'm waiting for a call from a woman, okay. And before you say something like 'just call her,' the answer to that is, I can't. She has my number, but I didn't get hers."

"Well, that was your first mistake. Since when do you give out your number, instead of the other way around?" Logan asked with sincere interest. "And when did you meet this woman? It's the first I've heard about it."

Jason shrugged. "I met her at the wedding, and I haven't seen you since then."

Tension rolled off Logan at the mention of Gillian and Jake's wedding, and he dropped his gaze from Jason's. Jason wanted to be sensitive to Logan's feelings about it, but he wouldn't sugarcoat the truth either. Logan had been a bit tough to be around the week prior to the wedding—understandably so. Even though he and Logan were best friends, Jake was his brother, and he was truly happy for him. Logan was the one who screwed things up; he would have to suck it up.

After a few moments, Logan asked, “Someone from the wedding who you hooked up with? Wait, didn’t you have my son with you that night?”

“I’m going to pretend that you didn’t just say something as asinine as that. Seriously, man? Come the hell on.” Jason glared at him. When Logan just raised his eyebrows, as if he really wanted an answer to his question, Jason glared harder and damn near growled through a clenched jaw. “No, I did not *hook-up* with some random chick while I was watching my two nine year old nephews. You can be such an asshole sometimes, you know that?”

Logan’s shoulders slumped. “Sorry man, not really sure why I thought that.”

“I could take one guess why.” Jason shook his head and continued, “Time to get the hell over her and move on ... she has.”

Logan’s eyes took on that far-away look, which was customary when he thought about his ex-wife. Jason pitied the guy, but it was his own damn fault. Nodding, Logan moved to lean against the table next to him, his expression now exhausted. It only took him a moment to recover as he asked, “So, who is this woman who has you all anxious?”

Thankful they were back on track, Jason smiled as an image of Tori popped in his head, “A red-headed beauty named Tori.”

Logan snorted a laugh. “Dude, did you just say ‘red-headed beauty’?”

Totally comfortable with what he said, Jason nodded and let a big smirk cross his face. "I sure as hell did. Logan, my man," he said as he patted his friend on the shoulder, "she has this amazing set of green eyes, pale creamy skin, and dark reddish-brown hair. Her hair is such a unique color, even your sister was shocked silent by it."

Logan looked at him like he was crazy. "Allie was silent? Holy shit ... that must've been some hair."

Jason added, "Aside from the obvious attractiveness, she's got a great sense of humor. Totally sarcastic and funny. She was great with the boys, and my favorite part ..." He paused for dramatic effect as his best friend waited for it. "... she winked at me."

"Well, hell, why didn't you just start with that?" Logan said with a laugh. "I know what a hard-on you get for a chick who winks at you. I think it's weird, but I know it's your *thing*."

He shrugged, once again comfortable with himself, "Hey, some guys have a thing for asses, some for breasts. Me? I love all of those, too, but damn, give me a woman with a witty sense of humor and a fun, sarcastic side, and I'm a goner."

"Okay, so you're a goner for this woman. Is that how you let her get away without getting her number?" Logan asked. Sighing, Logan's words killed the buzz Jason had gotten from telling him about her.

"She had my business card, and I figured it was a closed deal. I'm thinking of calling her work and possibly leaving a message there for her if I can. Hell, I have her damn spare tire in my truck."

"Not sure how you ended up with her spare tire in your truck when you met at a wedding," Logan said.

"It's a long story," he said as he looked at his watch. "Let's grab some lunch, and I can tell you all about it."

~*~*~*~

Jason and Logan had just sat down at a patio table at their favorite taco shop when his phone rang. He was once again met with disappointment when he saw his brother's name flashing on the screen. Answering it, he said, "Don't you have anything better to be doing than calling me?" He made sure he was cautious about ribbing his brother in front of Logan. That would just be all kinds of fucked up to talk about Jake and Gillian having sex in front of him.

"I sure do, bro." Jason could hear the smile in Jake's voice as he spoke. "But I had to call and ask why the head caterer from my wedding would be leaving me a message asking for *your* phone number."

Jason paused mid-bite at Jake's words, the chip in his hand forgotten. "You got a message from Tori?" he asked with obvious excitement.

"Yeah, I did. She rambled on about how she had your number in her pants but washed them and now she can't read the card. I figured I'd call you first and make sure you wanted her to have your number."

"Hell yeah, I want her to have my number. We have a date scheduled for tomorrow, and she was supposed to text me her info. I was worried she had changed her mind," Jason confessed.

"She sounded a little desperate to get your number," Jake offered before Jason heard him defending himself to Gillian. "Okay, maybe desperate is the wrong word to describe her," Jake clarified a second before his phone was overtaken.

"Jay?" Gillian's voice made him smile.

"Hey, Gilly. Did I just hear you assault my brother?"

"I have no idea what you're talking about, but if he says stupid crap like that again, he's gonna be awfully lonely the rest of his honeymoon," she said with mock offense. Jake's voice in the background was pleading his defense. Apparently the thought of being "lonely" on your honeymoon was enough to make Jake beg for understanding.

"Anyway," Gillian said after she told Jake to be quiet, "why is my caterer calling and looking for you? You didn't have a one-night-stand with her and then give her a shit number, did you?"

"Jesus. What the hell is it with you *Baxters* assuming crap like that about me today?" Jason asked with irritation.

After a moment of silence, Gillian said, "I'm sorry. I know you're not that kind of guy, Jay. I just got worried because I loved what she did for the wedding, and she does catering on the side, so I wanted to use her again. So, ugh, I'm sorry ... forgive me?"

His irritation dissipated. "You're forgiven."

"You said 'Baxters.' Did Logan say something like that, too?" she asked. "Tell him to apologize to you as well."

Even though Logan kind of did earlier, he knew the guy would still do whatever Gillian said. "Gillian says you have to apologize to me, too."

Logan rolled his eyes as he shoved a rolled taco into his mouth and mumbled, "I already said sorry, and you know it. Now tell her that."

Obviously overhearing Logan's response, Gillian laughed before saying, "Good, now do we give her your number?"

"No," Jason said. "I want hers now. I'm all anxious waiting for her to call me."

Gillian let out a small laugh. "I bet you are, big guy. I'll text you as soon as we get off the phone."

Jason hung up and set it next to his food. Digging in to his now slightly chilled burrito, he tried to patiently wait for the text to arrive. Once he got it, he quickly saved the info to his contacts, like it was going to disappear or something. Then he took a few moments to come up with what he wanted to say to her. He wanted to be playful, hoping he could make her laugh.

When they finished eating, Logan excused himself to the restroom, and Jason promptly dialed her number. After two rings he heard her voice—soft and sweet—come across the line.

"Hello."

"So I heard you were trying to get ahold of me. Something about losing me in your pants ..." he said with humor.

"Oh God, I hope this is Jason Michaels, because he's the only person I recall losing in my pants this week."

Jason laughed out loud, and the anxiety that had taken up residence in his shoulders dissolved.

CHAPTER NINE

TORI sighed as she rolled over and looked at her clock. Even if she was grateful for having the day off, it hadn't been her intention to start it so damn early. And she couldn't even blame it on her daughter. Between the vivid dreams and her aching hands from the night before, well rested she was not.

Her crew had a standing job with a church one Tuesday a month, and it always exhausted her. She didn't really understand how the church managed to have so many people show up to their weekly dinner events.

Rolling back over, she glanced through the doorway into Lexi's room and saw her sleeping still. Living in a small place worked out perfectly fine for the two of them, and it gave her peace of mind to have Lexi so close. She looked quite comfortable, snuggled up with her bear, her blanket tangled around her feet. With a soft sigh and matching smile, she flipped the covers back and made her way to the bathroom for a shower before Lexi woke.

As soon as Tori turned off the shower, she could hear the demanding wail coming from the bedroom. Shaking her head, she quickly popped her head out and grabbed a towel as she tried comforting her daughter from a distance. "Hang on baby girl, Mommy's coming." Wrapping her head in the towel, she grabbed her robe off the door and flung it on. Once Lexi spotted her, her cry turned to more of an excited whimper as she held her hands out to Tori.

“Good morning, sweetheart,” Tori said with a kiss and hug before she made her way into the kitchen. Or maybe kitchenette was a better description. Since she lived in what was now classified as a one-bedroom apartment, with attached office space, it was originally a garage. Her landlord, Hal, had converted the garage for his disabled son. He wanted him to have the luxury of independence, but still be nearby. Unfortunately, his son got ill and passed away unexpectedly, leaving Hal alone.

Tori poured herself a glass of orange juice and padded over to her favorite spot on the couch. Reading to Lexi while nursing her every morning had become their new routine. Since the rest of the day she took a bottle, it made her time in the morning with her more precious. It was a closeness neither shared with another.

It also made her think of her mother and how she wished she’d met Lexi. A small part of her liked to believe that her mother protected and guided her after she fled from Damien. She definitely knew someone had been watching over her.

Shaking off the darker thoughts, she picked up the book of children’s stories and began reading to her daughter, mentally mapping out what the rest of her day would be like. Wednesday was when she helped Hal with groceries and prepared individual meals for him. Since she loved cooking, and was quite accustomed to making large portions, it was no hardship to do this for him.

When she was done with all of that, she hoped she’d be able to find something worth wearing for her date that night. Her desire to look good for Jason had kept her awake late last night. Certain that she was going to need at least an hour to pick her wardrobe, she would have to make sure not to fall behind on her tasks that day. She smiled as she once again let the anticipation of going on a first date flutter through her chest. It was an excitement she hadn't thought she would ever feel again. Knowing that Damien hadn't stolen that from her permanently, had her smiling even bigger. That sense of satisfaction was immeasurable.

JASON checked the inventory list his foreman handed him. Placing a work order for the upcoming job was his goal for the morning, and he was thankful his head wasn't nearly as far up his ass as it was the day before. It was a little baffling how anxious he was waiting for Tori to call him. Looking forward to the evening ahead, he thanked his foreman and made his way to the onsite office he and Logan shared.

Dropping down into the seat at his desk, he put his phone next to the laptop and got to work. Logan strolled in a few minutes later with their lunch. He took the offered bag with his sandwich in it without even looking up from the screen. Mumbling his thanks, he blindly pulled the food out and began eating while he finished his work. A few minutes and half a sandwich later, Logan asked, "So, you know where you're taking your date tonight?"

Leaning back in his chair, Jason finished the food in his mouth before answering, "I have a few places in mind, but was thinking of asking her where she felt like going." He shrugged.

“Not a bad idea. Nothing worse than making plans only to find out you were totally off base with your choice. Shit like that on a first date could probably derail the second date before dinner even hits the table,” Logan said as he took another bite of his sandwich.

Jason smirked at his friend. “You speaking from experience? Didn’t know you were an authority on first dates.”

“Not on first dates, but I’m definitely an expert on being totally off base. Been there done that, even with my wife of seventeen years. Problem was, Gillian was always quiet about things when she was bothered. I used to think that was her being weak.” He paused and seemed to be reflecting on something before adding, “Now I know that was just her trying to make me happy.”

Logan shook his head and shoved more food in his mouth. Jason hated seeing his friend like that, but was glad it didn’t happen all the time. It seemed to be only when he realized he had screwed everything up all by himself. Wanting to lighten the mood, Jason said, “I don’t know too much about her, but I can tell you she’s not a vegetarian. She tried to make me think she was, then confessed, saying ‘I totally eat meat.’”

Logan started choking on his soda. Jason laughed, happy he succeeded in lightening the mood, as Logan’s feet hit the ground, and he proceeded to cough. Taking another bite of his own food, Jason waited for him to recover.

When Logan had found his voice, he said, "You're an asshole. You had to say that when I had a mouth full of soda?"

Jason shrugged and smiled bigger. "Didn't plan it that way, but I enjoyed the outcome."

Logan was cut off from responding further when Jason's phone rang. When he saw Tori's name on the screen, he felt a shot of excitement course through him at her unexpected call. Then it quickly turned to concern at the thought that maybe she was calling to cancel. If he needed to give her another reason to go out with him, he would, but there was only one way to find out, so he answered.

"Hello."

There was no response, so he pulled the phone from his ear and looked at the screen. The connection was still there, but *she* didn't seem to be. Listening closer, he could hear noise in the background and then a high-pitched baby squeal, followed by a slurping, sucking sound. It was so loud in his ear, he had to pull it away for a moment. He could hear Tori talking in the background but couldn't make out the words. For a split second he felt like he was eavesdropping, but squashed that down because she was the one who called him. Well, maybe not intentionally, but it was still true.

He said hello again, a little louder, and was met by a baby giggle. Looking up at Logan, he laughed. "I'm pretty sure I got butt-dialed by an infant."

Logan stood from his chair to discard his trash. "Smart kid. They keep learning younger and younger nowadays."

Jason snorted. "Quit using words like 'nowadays;' it makes you sound old."

Resuming his listening, he started talking to Lexi, "It sounds like Lexi is playing with Mommy's phone, isn't she?" He knew she wasn't going to answer, but he paused anyway before saying, "I'm going to hang up the phone now baby girl and call you back, so if the ring scares you, I'm sorry."

Hanging up, he waited a beat before calling the number back. After three rings, a laughing Tori answered, "Hello?"

"Hi, did she get scared when the phone rang?" he asked.

"Actually, you startled her. The look on her face before she got excited about it was hilarious. How did you know?" Tori asked.

"Because I'm calling you back. She had somehow called me, and there was no other way to get your attention."

"Ha! Ten months old and already calling guys. I should be very afraid." Tori laughed, and Jason could hear her talking to Lexi. It brought a smile to his face as he listened. A moment later, she was back. "Sorry about that. I hope she wasn't interrupting anything important."

"No, just having lunch. It was a pleasant distraction."

"Then I'm glad she called you. I have to tell you, though, I was worried you were calling to cancel on me," she admitted.

"Funny, 'cause that's what I was worried about when I saw *you* calling *me*."

"Nope, not me. Besides, you have my spare tire," she said with exasperation.

Smiling even bigger than he already was, he said, "I knew that tire would come in handy."

He loved the banter between them. She was funny and fun to be around. Add in all the sexy parts, and Jason almost groaned at how much he was looking forward to their evening together.

"Yes, handy indeed. I will have to make sure I add that to my list of things to do when I want to hold someone hostage. Steal something of theirs so they have no choice but to submit."

With that, his body's physical anticipation heightened. He wanted to keep talking to her, but knew he needed to get his shit done or there would be hell to pay in the morning when his men didn't have what they needed to get their jobs completed. "It mainly only works with objects of significant need or large ticket items. You know, like cell phones, cars, prosthetic limbs. Any of those would work."

She barked out a laugh, louder than he'd heard from her yet, and Jason couldn't help but laugh with her. "All good stuff to know! I will have to make a list of people I know with prosthetic limbs and determine if they have something I want."

"Sounds like a great plan." He paused, a moment of insecurity passing through him. "So ... does six-thirty still work for you?"

After a few moments of silence, in a soft voice, Tori answered, "Yes. See you later, Jason."

"Later, Tori," he answered before she hung up. When he set his phone down on the desk, he took in a deep breath and let it out, enjoying how content he felt after talking to her. When he felt a crumpled up piece of paper hit him in the forehead, he glared over at Logan.

Logan put his hands up in mock surrender. "Sorry, man, couldn't help it. I was afraid you might start spouting poetry with that dreamy look on your face."

Shaking his head but holding in a laugh, Jason said, "Did you really just say 'dreamy look'?"

Logan smiled confidently. "I have a teenage daughter. What's your excuse for sounding like a chick?"

"Hey, if sounding like a chick, gets me the chick, then I'm all for it." Logan looked to be considering what he said, and they both got back to work. He focused on the task at hand, telling himself that the sooner he got it done, the sooner he'd be out of there, and the sooner he'd be on his way to Tori's. Thoughts of his evening were put on the backburner, but his anticipation remained on a low simmer.

CHAPTER TEN

TORI took another deep breath—in through the nose, out through the mouth. That was what they said to do to help calm down, right? Her nerves were getting the best of her, and Tessa wasn't helping. Friends were for moral support, or so she thought. Shaking her head, she listened to her best friend tell Lexi about how important it was for Mommy to go on a date with the hot hunk because Mommy needed orgasms to survive. While she absolutely agreed that orgasms with hot hunks were desired, Tori knew that her evening wasn't going to end that way. There would be no sex. Sex wasn't something she thought she could handle just yet.

The whole evening was going to be a test in her ability to participate in activities that were considered normal for women her age. Activities that she hadn't partaken in for over three years. Not since before. Not since Damien took over. Prior to meeting Damien, she had a very healthy dating life. Attractive and confident, she had friends, she had a job, she had a life. She also had her mom.

She thought the loss of her mother was the lowest point in her life. Looking back now, she knew that wasn't true. The memories of her short marriage to *him* crowded into all the very low points, and that is where they stayed. Damien had been a predator, and she the prey. Weakened by the crippling pain of loss, he hunted her until he had consumed every part of her. She took one more deep, cleansing breath as she looked at her reflection in the mirror, and thought to herself, *or so he thought*.

She was empowered by the fact that she outsmarted Damien. So when she felt down about something, she reminded herself that it had been worse before. Instantly, she felt better. Even after he went to jail, and thought he had left her alone and lacking everything she would need to survive—money, shelter, food—she had outsmarted him. They were small victories that fueled the fire of her survival.

Her internal pep talk was interrupted when she heard a car pull into the driveway. Tessa must have heard it, too, because she took that opportunity to tell Lexi, "Hot hunks like this guy are usually hung like a horse and strive on giving orgasms. In most cases, multiples. Can you say *or-gaz-em*?"

"Tessa! Stop that!" Tori scolded. Tessa was at least smart enough to look a little embarrassed and gave her a sheepish smile.

"Not like she can talk anyway. Besides, this is all very useful information that I wished someone would have told me. She doesn't have a big sister, and I'm her aunt, so it's my job to make sure she is informed."

"How 'bout we wait a few more—or a lot more—years before discussing orgasms with her, okay?" Tori whispered urgently, wanting to end the conversation before Jason could hear it. How awkward it would be to start a first date being caught talking about orgasms.

Moving toward the door, she slipped on a lightweight, blue cardigan over her simple black dress. It was fun and flirty as it flared from her hips, ended above her knees, and was finished off with a pair of wedge sandals that wrapped around her ankles. She was pleased as she took in her appearance, skimming her hands down her front before pulling her hair out of her sweater and smoothing it over her shoulder. She was wearing it loose, per Tessa's instructions, which included the reason: men liked long, loose hair and it made kissing even hotter. Tori preferred to wear it down, because she could without the fear of consequences now.

Tessa picked up Lexi and walked over to Tori. "Give Mommy a kiss, and wish her luck for at least two orgasms." She had stretched out the word to emphasize it. Tori knew she was gonna need to find another sitter soon before Auntie Tessa also told Lexi about erections.

Tori pulled her daughter into her arms for a hug and kiss. When she handed her back to Tessa, she said, "Call me if there's a problem, and please, for the love of God, stop trying to get my daughter to say orgasm."

Tessa shrugged, totally disregarding her request. Tori just shook her head as she turned and opened the door to find the aforementioned "hot hunk," with his hand mid-air, attempting to knock. A slow smile spread across his face as he took her in, and she sent up a quick prayer that he had not heard her say orgasm.

JASON let a slow smile spread across his face. She was beautiful. He let his hand fall from the mid-air position. "Hello."

There was a pink tinge to her cheeks, and she had a hesitant smile as she answered. "Hi. I guess you found the place okay. You could've honked, and I would've come out to the car."

Seriously, what kind of man did that? "I think I'll pretend that you didn't just say that. Even stupid men know that's not how to pick up a beautiful lady."

He extended his hand as she stepped over the threshold when he heard her friend say, "Well shit, they do exist." Looking up, he noticed the woman from the reception holding a squirming Lexi.

Smiling, he offered his hand to shake. "Hi, I'm Jason."

She took his hand and said with a flirty smile, "Hi. Tessa. But you can refer to me as Plan B."

Jason smirked and held back a laugh as Tori scolded her. He ignored the "offer" instead asking, "May I?" as he put his hands out for the baby. Before either woman could answer him, Lexi had already extended her arms in response and was quickly in his reach.

He smiled down at her and said, "Hi there, pretty girl. Make any more phone calls today?" Lexi just smiled at him as she rubbed her fingers on his cheek, clearly amazed with the texture of his beard. His niece, Ella, had the same fascination, so he was used to it. "I sure hope you didn't. I think I would be a little jealous."

He gave her a quick kiss on the forehead and handed her back to Tessa, who mumbled, "I know I'm jealous."

Jason smiled as he turned his attention back to Tori, who was glaring at her friend. "Shall we?"

She turned her stunning green eyes on him and smiled. He suddenly felt like it was a struggle to take in oxygen. In the light of the setting sun, the green of her eyes actually sparkled. The different accents of red in her hair were almost glowing where the light hit them, and he fought the urge to put his hands on her—to glide them down the length of her long hair. She was breathtaking, and all he could do was stare.

"I think that would be a good idea. I'm a little worried about what might come out of Tessa's mouth next," Tori said with feigned irritation and a pointed look at her friend. Jason broke his stare away from Tori, turning it toward Tessa and the baby. "Oh, I'm sure you have nothing to worry about." Unable to help himself, he reached out to Lexi, gave a teasing tickle on her belly, and said with humor, "Can you say orgasm?"

Lexi giggled. Tori groaned and, from the corner of his eye, saw her face drop into her hands. He looked up at Tessa and winked. She fanned her face and said, "Oh hell, it was like a command."

Jason couldn't control his laughter any longer, as Tori grabbed his arm, pulling him toward his car. "Just remember, Tess, payback's a bitch!"

Getting himself under control, he moved her hand to rest in the crook of his elbow as they walked to his car. Looking down at her next to him, he couldn't erase the smile on his face if his life depended on it. Her cheeks were a brighter shade of pink, and she was lightly shaking her head. Her embarrassment was adorable and sexy all at the same time. He silently cursed the sweater she was wearing for blocking his view of her chest, wanting to know if she blushed in other places.

When they got to his car, he opened the door and she stopped to look up at him. "So apparently you have the ability to hear just about everything."

He smiled and shrugged. "I wouldn't say *everything*."

She raised one eyebrow at him. "Then what would you say?"

In a low voice that showed his confidence, complete with a slight smirk, he said, "I would say that two is a minimum requirement of mine."

He heard her gasp before closing the door on the beautiful blushing face with wide green eyes.

TORI was going to kill Tessa. There was no doubt about it. Sure, she'd need to make some solid plans, like where to hide the body and set up a really good alibi, but it was *going* to happen. Jason had heard the whole conversation, and now Tori had to go on a first date with this hot hunk, and the promise of at least two orgasms had already been laid on the table. *'Can you say orgasm'* will be the words she whispers in Tessa's ear as the final breath leaves her body. She could see it all play out so perfectly in her mind.

Jason interrupted her evil planning when he opened his door and got in. The gloating smile on his face made it apparent he achieved some level of satisfaction over her discomfort. She could only imagine the look on her face.

Her cheeks were hot with embarrassment, and goosebumps spread across her skin as she thought of his comment—more like promise. She took in a shaky breath, willing her heart rate to drop. Between the embarrassment, the anticipation of the first date, and now the sudden rampant flow of hormones, she was in danger of combusting.

As Jason put the car in drive he asked, "Anywhere in particular you'd like to go tonight? I know you're not a vegetarian, so I have some thoughts, but I'd like to take you somewhere you'd like."

Where would she like to go? How about his bed, or couch, or recliner, or even a clean carpeted floor? Actually, she'd settle for his lap in any location. Realizing that stupid breath didn't relax her in the least, and her thoughts continued to escalate, she rolled her shoulders in an attempt to gain some control. After a few moments, and hoping her voice didn't betray her, she summoned a witty comeback. "I'm sure I'll find whatever 'thoughts' you've had satisfactory. Unless you don't think you can get us there."

A second later, the double meaning in her words must've registered. He groaned, and all she could do was grin. When he looked over at her, he smiled in admiration. "That was a great comeback. I do believe I've met my match."

She offered him her own smug look as she settled in for the ride. A few seconds of silence passed before he added, "Oh, and Tori, just so you know. I may have met my match in sarcasm, but I meant what I said."

Looking at him in confusion, she waited for him to continue. They stopped at a light, and he reached over to her, taking her hand in his. Gently, he lifted it to his lips for a kiss. She sucked in a silent breath at the warmth of his lips on her skin. Another beat later, it was gone, and her hand was resting in his against the center console. When she looked at their hands, then back up to him, he said confidently, "Two is my *minimum* requirement. Everything past that is just icing on the cupcake."

And just like that, the inferno blazed on.

CHAPTER ELEVEN

JASON was hopeful he hadn't crossed a major line by saying what he said, but he couldn't help himself. He had inadvertently overheard what she and Tessa had been talking about when he stepped up to the door, and it took everything in him not to laugh out loud. But when the opportunity presented itself, he had to take it. He was a pretty straightforward guy, so he let all his colors out for Tori to see.

Fortunately, she seemed very capable of handling him. The surge of satisfaction that passed through him was a rush. The electric current that had been simmering all day spread across his skin, intoxicating him. Oh yeah, it was definitely a rush. One he had never felt before. It was more than lust. It was just ... more.

He knew she was something more than he had experienced before, and he was dying to know what *more* with her would be like. The thoughts and visions that swamped him were almost too much, especially when trying to control himself around Tori. The minute she opened her door to him, his body hardened. And when she blushed at his words right before he closed the car door, his blood pressure dropped as a large volume of blood rushed south.

The combination of her hair color and the blue sweater she was wearing made her eyes even more vivid than he remembered. Add the blush in her cheeks, and he was a goner. It was going to be a long night. One full of uncomfortable shifting and awkward positioning if he didn't get things under control. He made a promise to himself to try and steer their sarcastic remarks away from the sexual undertones they were already dangerously skirting around.

The night was unseasonably warm so he hoped, as he made his way toward downtown, the night air by the water would be comfortable for her with what she was wearing. The silence in the car wasn't unwelcome, it was necessary. They each needed their moment to just ease in to being around each other. When they got closer to downtown he asked, "So, I know you eat meat." He smiled at her before continuing, "But do you eat seafood?"

"I could eat either. I assume it's one or the other?" she asked.

"Well, the steakhouse has both. But there's a great seafood place right across the street," he offered. When he glanced over at her, he saw that her head was leaning against the headrest as she looked at him. Her face showed she was totally relaxed around him. Another surge of ... something ... washed over him. He gave her hand that he still held a small squeeze as he turned his gaze back to the road.

"I can't decide which I want. So we should go to the steakhouse since I'm certain they have a meal that would allow me to have both," Tori stated, her tone indicating she was pleased with her decision. He agreed.

"Sounds like a smart plan to me."

It didn't take long to find parking, and there wasn't really a wait to be seated since it was a Wednesday. Within minutes, drink orders were placed—Jason following Tori's lead with an iced tea. Once the waiter left them, she perused the menu for a moment before setting it down with a satisfied grin. "Definitely a good choice. Steak and shrimp is the way I'm going. How about you?"

He smiled, "Sounds perfect, I'll do the same." The waiter dropped of their drinks, promptly took their orders, then left in silence. *Time for some conversation*, he thought.

As if she had read his mind, she sat back in her seat and rested her hands in her lap as she spoke, "So, Jason, tell me. Why is a guy like you single?"

He huffed a laugh. By the twinkle in her eye, he knew she'd figured out he wasn't a guy who beat around the bush. He would have no problem answering her direct questions.

"So we're going straight to that then. Okay. Let's get it out of the way." He took a sip of his drink and then leaned on his elbows—relaxed, but front and center for her inquisition. He wanted her to know she had his full attention. "Well, the truth of the matter is that I'm single because I'd yet to meet a woman who brought out the need in me to settle down. Now when I say that, it doesn't mean I'm some kind of man-whore. It just means there hasn't been that special person. As it is, I've been pretty content with my life. I have a large group of friends and family all nearby, and we spend lots of time together. I've not been a victim of loneliness."

He paused when the waiter brought their salads, and he watched Tori as she thanked the waiter with a smile. It was a great smile. He wanted more of it. A second later, and there it was, directed at him, a look of excitement shone from her eyes. "I missed lunch today, and I'm so hungry that I think this salad looks better than it really is."

She dug into her salad with gusto, and he felt himself just wanting to watch, forgetting all about what he was saying. Before it could get creepy, she looked up and smiled again, chewing her salad. He could see the movement of her slender neck as she swallowed, his body copying it. A moment later she said with a smirk, "Please, continue. My curiosity peaked after you said man-whore."

TORI watched Jason, just as he watched her. His eyes twinkled with amusement as he kept his gaze firm on hers. He was wearing a charcoal sweater with a high collar and zipper on the neck. It was unzipped, showing off his thick, tan neck, which met up with crisp white V-neck shirt. The obvious color contrast brought out the definition of his jawline and beard.

Oh, dear God, that beard, she thought as she remembered how soft it felt against her face the other day. She quickly shoved another mouthful of salad in her mouth, forcing down her distraction. He once again leaned on the table as he had done before their salads were delivered, and she continued to eat, giving him the opportunity to talk more.

"I guess the only answer I have for 'why I am still single' is it's what I've chosen. I'm not someone who settles for something out of fear of being alone. I've been patiently waiting for *the one*," he said before placing the napkin in his lap and eating some of his salad.

That answer was perfect. It might have been practiced, a move in an arsenal he was waiting to unleash on her. But something told her that this guy, this man in front of her, didn't need moves to get a woman. He used his ability to be frank to his advantage, and she was panting like a puppy. Albeit a very-hungry-starved-for-affection-possibly-too-horny-puppy. Giving herself a mental shake, she looked down to her food and willed her body into submission. When she chanced a glance at him, she lost the hope that he couldn't see her body's response to him. She'd never felt like such an amateur around a guy, acting like a girl on her first date *ever*. But then again, it was the first time she'd ever received such apt attention from a man who overwhelmed her senses. Jason's eyebrows rose, and a smirk appeared. Yeah, she was certain her body was broadcasting its reactions.

"So, did I answer your question well enough?" he asked as he lifted his napkin to his mouth.

She did the same before placing it back in her lap. "I'd say so. No information missing there," she said with a bit of humor.

"Good," he said with satisfaction. "So, how about you, Tori? Why are you *currently* single? I mean, it's obvious that you weren't all that long ago."

She sighed. Did she want to be honest with him right from the start? Of course she did, but not at the risk of him tucking tail and running the other direction. Were the details too much for a first date? Since it was all uncharted territory for her, she really didn't know, but she wished she would've taken the time to ask Tessa. Although Tessa would've told her to let it all hang out, literally.

Then she realized it was good advice. Why should she waste time avoiding details of her life in hopes that someone could accept it later? It was best to be frank, just like Jason.

She took a sip of her iced tea then sat back in her chair, dropping her hands to her lap, clasped in an attempt to quell the emotions of disappointment she felt in herself whenever she shared her fallacy of a marriage. It was something she regretted with all of her heart, but would never change for anything. It gave her Lexi, and she knew she would walk through the fires of hell for her daughter. In some ways, she already had.

Tori was certain Jason would want the information and not tolerate being disrespected with bullshit excuses or half-truths. Taking a deep breath, she straightened her shoulders as she prepared to expose her shame. "Do you want the condensed version? Or would you prefer to have the whole story now, so you can decide if it's ... if I'm worth it?"

Jason once again sat forward, leaning comfortably on the table, his salad completely forgotten. It was as if he was assessing if she was for real. "I'll take whichever version you want to give me, Tori. You can start with the condensed one and progress to the full version at another time. Because understand this, there *will be* another time.

I don't need a piece of your history to figure out if *you* are worth it."

Warmth exploded in her chest, and she could feel the lump forming in her throat. She tilted her head and, with a slight shake to express her astonishment at his response, she said, "You really mean that, don't you? I barely know you, but I feel it in every bone of my body that you wouldn't judge me by my story." A sense of relief stole over her as she absorbed her own words. She felt her guard shift and lower, just a little.

With his eyebrows raised—a look she was quickly identifying as his you-better-hear-my-words-and-hear-them-good expression—he said, "Everyone has a story. Everyone has a past. It doesn't define us; it's what makes us who we are. What kind of man would I be if I passed judgment like that? I wouldn't be someone I'd like very much, that's for sure. Like you said, we barely know each other, but from what I've seen ... whatever you hold in your past didn't destroy you. Which can only mean it made you stronger."

Was he for real? Where the hell had this man been hiding, and how had she been fortunate enough to warrant his attention?

He shrugged but didn't have a chance to continue since the waiter picked that moment to show up with their food. Once he had made sure they had everything they needed and excused himself, Jason's hand reached across the table in search of hers, catching her attention a second before he made contact. Looking in his eyes, she was taken aback by the warmth radiating from them. He gently gripped her hand, allowing his thumb to stroke the skin across her knuckles.

"Based on your apprehension, I can only assume that your story is one that deserves my undivided attention and some privacy. So, how about we enjoy our dinner without any heavy conversation. Then afterward, we can find somewhere else to go and if you want to tell me then, you can?" he offered.

The shame she felt minutes ago was doused by his words. Smiling at him in appreciation, she nodded as she turned her hand over under his. Giving it a squeeze, she repeated his words from earlier, "That sounds like a smart plan to me."

CHAPTER TWELVE

JASON was happy Tori didn't attempt to pay for her dinner. After her insistence at lunch the other day, he was prepared for it. Once he settled the bill, he stood and offered his hand to her. It was a great excuse to touch her, even if it was masked as gentlemanly. She smiled as she accepted it and stood. He ushered her toward the front of the restaurant, his hand now on the small of her back. When they reached the front, he said, "I was thinking we could take a walk down toward Seaport Village."

"That sounds nice. I'm going to head to the ladies room before we leave then," she said shyly.

"I'll wait for you right here," he said as he reluctantly dropped his hand from her back. He was watching her walk away when she looked back over her shoulder at him. Giving him a shy smile, he was grateful he hadn't been caught checking out her ass.

It didn't take long before she returned, and they made their way from the restaurant. A few moments later, they had crossed the busy street and were walking parallel with the San Diego Bay. When he noticed her clutching her small purse, he asked, "Did you want to put your purse in the car?"

Shaking her head, she looked over at him. "No thanks, it has my phone in it. I need that in case Tessa has to get a hold of me."

He understood, but he really wanted one of her hands wrapped firmly inside one of his. “Would you like me to carry it for you?”

She scrunched her eyebrows and looked at him like he was crazy. He laughed. “What’s that look for?”

“You just offered to carry my purse. That’s not normal.”

He smiled bigger at the shock in her voice as he reached over and removed the “purse” from her grip. It couldn’t be much bigger than her phone so it really shouldn't be classified as a purse in his book. Slipping it into his pocket, he reached over and took her hand in his. “It wouldn’t be normal for a guy to swing it by the strap over his shoulder and prance around with it proudly. This,” he said, patting his pocket, “is nothing my masculinity can’t handle.”

“Besides, my offer to carry your stuff was completely selfish.” He punctuated his statement with a squeeze to her hand. After walking a few steps, she removed her hand from his grip. The disappointment was instant, and he looked down at her, about to apologize for overstepping his bounds. His gaze met a smile as he felt her reposition her hand within his.

“This is more comfortable. The angle before felt awkward,” she said as they continued walking. Occasionally moving to the side to allow the pedi-cabs to move past them, they walked along silently. There was a family with a toddler who scrambled into their path to get a better view of the water. A young couple walked with their arms around each other. And then there was an older couple, who looked like they’d been together for decades, walking hand in hand. The older man looked at Tori, then his eyes found Jason's as he gave him a small nod of acknowledgment.

Tori broke the comfortable silence first. "So have you lived in San Diego all your life?"

"Born and raised. All my family is still here, so I've never had the desire to leave." He paused before asking, "How about you, been here long?"

She didn't look at him as she spoke, "Not too long. I've been here for more than a year. Sixteen months, I think."

"And before that?" he asked, trying to keep the conversation going, but hoping to get to the story she was reluctant to tell him earlier.

"Idaho. I was born and raised in Boise, Idaho." She smiled for a moment, apparently caught up in some memory before it disappeared. "I'd never had the desire to leave either. But things changed, and it became a necessity."

He could tell she was trying to work up the courage to tell him more, and he wanted to comfort her—maybe encourage her. Pulling their entwined hands up, he softly kissed the back of hers. When she smiled again, he let their hands drop as they continued walking.

"My ex-husband's name is Damien, and marrying him was the biggest mistake I've made in my life." Her voice was strong, determined. "He is a bastard in every sense of the word, and I hope I never have to see again."

He wanted to say something. The strength he heard in her voice told him that she had plenty more to say. So he waited, content with just holding her hand. Sighing deeply, she said, "I should start by telling you that I was very close to my mother. I feel I need to offer that bit of information up front so you won't think badly of me."

Jason stopped walking, pulling her up short. When she gave him a questioning look, he said, "Tori, I know we just met, but like I said earlier, I'm not the type of man to pass judgment like that."

"I'm sorry. I'm just not used to telling this story," she confessed.

His thumb rubbed the back of her hand, offering reassurance. "And you don't have to tell the story now if you're uncomfortable."

"No, I want to." She gave his hand a tug, and they began walking again. The amount of people walking along the path around them had dwindled, providing them with a sense of privacy. He hoped it made telling her story easier.

"I was very close to my mom. Growing up, it was mostly just she and I. My father died when I was only two, and my mom never remarried. She always said he was the love of her life and once you've experienced that, you can't just go out and find someone else because it would never be good enough." She smiled as she paused.

"I could see that," he agreed.

She looked up at him with a smirk. "She really would've liked you."

It was obvious by what she said that she had lost her mother. "Sounds like she was a great judge of character."

Her smile turned to a scowl. “Yeah, she was … until Damien.” Shaking her head, she paused. He waited. “I met Damien within days of my mom finding out she had cancer. It was pretty advanced when they discovered it, and they suggested she get her affairs in order because her prognosis wasn’t good. They gave her six months, and she lived for seven.”

Unable to remain silent, “I’m sorry.” She nodded and continued.

“It’s been two years, but it’s still hard. When I lost her, I felt like I lost a part of myself. It was my grief that Damien used to his advantage. My mom was desperate to know that I would be taken care of after she was gone. When she met him, he was everything a mother would want for their daughter. He was good-looking, very charming, financially secure—the total package. Mom believed it, and so did I. He proposed quickly, and we got married shortly after. He convinced me to do it quickly so I could have my mom there. Of course I was on board with his suggestion, because I was devastated with what was going to happen. Long story short, we got married, and my mom left this world believing that I would be taken care of in her absence … it was only about a month later when I learned all about the *real* Damien.”

TORI felt Jason stiffen next to her. She avoided looking at him, afraid to see the expression on his face. It didn’t take a genius to understand the meaning of her words. Sure, he said he wouldn’t judge her, and she believed him. It was the pity she didn’t want to see. He didn’t say anything, and she was grateful for that.

She wanted to continue, to get it all out there, so she did. "A month later, Damien was fed up with waiting for me to 'get over it' and decided to teach me a lesson." Reaching up, she ran her fingers along the scar on her cheek. "It was the first of many."

Jason led her to a bench, and they sat. He was still silent, so she chanced a look at him. His expression was one of ... anger? There was no pity, only anger. When she saw the lines of his jaw flexing in tension, she offered him a tentative smile. Not wanting to ruin their evening, she considered not continuing. She needed to lighten the dark that had swirled in around them. Just telling Jason, though, was starting to take some of the burden off her shoulders.

Sighing again, she said, "Fortunately, I'm a smart girl and learned my lesson. It only took me a little while to get out."

"Did he give you that scar on your face, Tori?" Jason asked. His expression was neutral, but his voice was thick with anger. She nodded.

"Where is he now? Can he still hurt you?" he asked in the same tone.

Tori shook her head. "He's in prison ... for now."

Even though he was grimacing, he nodded at her words. "He's back in Idaho, I assume?"

"Yes."

Jason pulled her hand into his lap and wrapped his other one around them. She wasn't sure if he was trying to sooth her or himself as he stroked her skin softly. “And what is he serving time for? It’s not common for a man to serve a sentence for assault on his wife for an extended period of time like that. So there was something more significant to get the attention of a district attorney.”

He wasn’t looking at her, but she watched him. His posture was straight, and his shoulders were tight as he stared down at their hands. The tension radiating from his arms and into her hands wasn’t missed. She was afraid to answer his question—not afraid of him—but concerned about upsetting him. It was her burden to carry, not his, but he acted as if he was a part of it. Not wanting to lie, she answered him, “He was originally charged with attempted murder ... but was downgraded to aggravated assault after he negotiated a deal.”

JASON’S head snapped up, furious at what he heard. “He was charged with attempted murder and was able to strike some kind of deal? What the hell kind of DA do you have up in Idaho?”

His words were laced with anger and fear. The thought of someone harming another human was unthinkable. The thought of someone harming Tori made him see red. It may have been an inappropriate reaction, but it was there nonetheless. He could question it more later, because he needed to tone down his emotions right now. It wasn’t fair to Tori. Here she was telling her story, and he was snarling at her like an asshole.

As he was focusing on diffusing the turmoil in his head, he was surprised to hear her light laugh. Just like that, he softened. “I’d have to agree that the DA wasn’t phenomenal, but he had no choice. I injured Damien in order to get away, so he decided to press assault charges on me. He agreed to drop them if they downgraded the charges against him. If we had tried to push the attempted murder, I would've had to testify, and then I would have had to face him. Avoiding him was important, not just for me, but for Lexi. I didn't want him knowing about her."

The thought of her ex-husband getting off on a lesser charge was infuriating, but Jason understood if it was necessary to protect her daughter. "I can understand that. So he doesn't have any part of her life?"

"No. I hope he still doesn't know she exists," she said in a soft, considering voice. Among normal circumstances, he would probably have a problem with that. As a man, he would want to know he had a child. But clearly her ex-husband wasn't a man of the honorable type.

Jason felt his tension lessen a little with the knowledge that the ex wasn't an immediate threat. He would get more information later. For now, he wanted to file away what he did know and focus on her. He had told her that he wouldn't judge her by her story, and he didn't. He told her that he thought what happened in her past had made her stronger, and it obviously did. The fact that she was able to tell him, and even laugh a little about it, was a testament to that.

Reaching over, he cautiously swept the hair away from her right cheek, exposing the length of her scar to his gaze. Not wanting to make her self-conscience, but conveying his feelings perfectly, he leaned forward and pressed a soft kiss along the scar starting closest to her ear. When she sucked in a breath but didn't pull away, he pressed on, moving down the length of it. She was trembling beneath his lips, and he smiled to himself as he felt her shiver, hoping it wasn't from the chill in the air.

Taking a chance, he moved his attention from her scar to her lips. They were parted as she took in a shaky breath before running her tongue along the bottom one. Leaning closer, he gently kissed them. Nothing demanding, just letting her feel the warmth of his lips against hers. He let himself enjoy a few decadent moments before pulling back. Unconsciously, his hand moved to her cheek, and his thumb rubbed over the rosiness there.

Capturing her gaze, he let a small smile spread across his face. Their breaths mingling in the small space between them, he continued to stroke her cheek. "I'm sorry you had to leave Idaho ... but I'm really glad you picked San Diego."

She answered with a smile of her own and whispered, "Me too."

CHAPTER THIRTEEN

JASON was reluctant to end the evening, but knew it was inevitable. After that kiss, he was struggling to keep himself in check. Or maybe it was because of her story. Probably a combination of both. What he did know, without a doubt, was that if he ever came face to face with Tori's ex, it would take a significant force of nature to prevent him from crushing the man's windpipe with his bare hands.

Standing, he pulled her up with him. They turned and silently made their way back toward his car. He lifted their linked hands and crossed his over her head, resting his arm across her shoulders, bringing her body flush against his. When she looked up and gave him a shy, unguarded smile, he kissed her forehead.

Even though every cell of his body was laced with testosterone, he was content with this simple gesture. For now. A kiss on the forehead was something he'd done countless times, but never to a woman who wasn't part of his family. Jason knew Tori was someone special—worth something more. Sighing his contentment, he turned his attention toward the path in front of them, shortening his long stride to allow her to keep up.

When their destination came into view, she let go of his hand. He sadly went to remove his arm when her other hand reached up and held on to it. A second later her arm snaked around his waist until her hand rested firmly on his hip. He knew he probably looked like a grinning fool, but he couldn't help it. He liked having her pressed up against him. A lot.

When they arrived at his car, Tori stopped and turned to him, blocking the door. Their hands were still locked together, and her other one was now resting on the front of his hip. Her gaze was locked on his chest, and she looked as if she wanted to say something, so he remained silent. Waiting for her.

"Um, I just wanted to say thank you. I mean, I appreciate you listening to me tonight …" her words trailed off, sounding uncertain.

Dropping her hand, he gently tipped her chin up, as he wrapped his other arm around her waist. Pulling her softly against him, he waited until her eyes met his. When they did, he tried to convey as much sincerity with his gaze as he said, "No, Tori. It's me who should be thanking you. I can't imagine telling that story was an easy thing for you to do, but I'm happy you trust me enough to share your painful past with me."

Pausing, he smiled. His hand moved in circles on the small of her back. With each passing moment, he wanted to touch her more, but he was focused on easing the uncertainty he heard in her voice. Continuing, he said, "I'm also certain there is more to that story than what you offered, and you should know that at some point, when you share that part with me, I will listen to as much as you want to tell me. But know this Tori, you *will* tell me all of it. Not because I insist, but because you will *want* to share it all with me. It's my intention to make sure you are comfortable and have no reservations about being near me."

She shook her head slightly before whispering, "I don't have any reservations about being near you, Jason." She paused, and her eyes dropped back down to his chest, even though he still held her chin in his hand. When she found his eyes again, she smiled. "I don't know what it is about you, but I'm comfortable with you, more so than I think I should be. And honestly, that scares me a little bit."

"*It* scares you, but I don't?" he asked in clarification. Without all the details of her past, he could only assume the worst. The scar on her face painted a very vivid picture in his head of what she might have gone through. He could only hope his imagination was overreacting.

Her eyes went wide, and she shook her head with determination, "Oh, no. I'm not scared of you. I'm scared of how easy it is to share things with you. I've only ever told my story to Tessa, and that was because I needed someone to know. Just in case ..."

"Don't even finish that sentence, Tori," Jason insisted as his arm instinctively tightened around her waist. He didn't even want to fathom what 'just in case' could mean. Jason didn't want their evening to wrap up on thoughts of her past—he wanted to lighten the mood.

"That's something we can talk about another time. 'Cause there will be another time, right Tori? Or do I need to hold your spare tire hostage a little longer?"

She smiled at his teasing, and a moment later, with a glint in her eye, she said, "Just be prepared, if one of my tires suddenly has a cluster of nails sticking out of it … I will have no idea how that happened."

"And you know who you'll be calling to take care of that for you, don't you?" he said, as his hand moved from her chin, sliding slowly across the soft skin of her jaw. She nodded slightly, and then there were no words, only need. His hand continued its venture toward her hair and buried itself within the thick, silky strands. Tilting her head, he heard her quick intake of breath as his lips descended to capture hers. Making sure to be soft and gentle, he moved his lips hesitantly. When he felt her lips soften and her body press into him, his reluctance dissolved.

TORI was overwhelmed with the hunger that swamped her senses the moment Jason's lips touched hers. It was a need so strong, she feared its dominance over her … for about a second. She knew the moment his resistance registered in her mind, that this gentle man wouldn't harm her. Physically at least. She was comfortable with him; he was safe. Her body already identified this and was trying to convince her mind. Pulsating with the desire to feel him, she let go. Falling into an abyss of want that was foreign to her, her mind and body went to a place she had never been—a place she never wanted to leave.

She pressed her body harder against his, wanting to feel the strength in his frame—seeking the comfort of his embrace. He answered her body's call, and his hold tightened as he moved them back, against his car. When his tongue slid along the seam of her lips, her hunger intensified. A groan vibrated up her throat and escaped as she parted her lips, wanting to taste him as he had tasted her.

When their tongues met, tentatively sliding against each other, she relished in his tenderness. But her body wanted more. It needed more. It was like it had been starved for years and was finally getting a taste of what it had been searching for, what it needed to survive. Even if she thought she was going to drown in the sensations he evoked, she knew that survival was no longer possible without what she was feeling.

Digging her fingers into his back, she held herself to him with one hand, while she flattened the other against his abdomen and began sliding upward—feeling him, learning him, wanting more of him. As she passed over the muscles of his chest, they tightened and bulged beneath her hand, and she felt him suck in a breath against her lips. Pausing her perusal, she let her hand hover over his chest; she could feel the tension rippling through his muscles. Testing the firmness, she dug her fingers in, kneading his muscle with her fingertips.

Jason groaned as he pulled his lips away from hers. She could feel their breaths mingling in the small space between them. Opening her eyes, she found his eyes locked intently on hers. Hunger and desire shining back at her from their depths. With a shaky breath, he pleaded, "Please ... do that again."

So she did. Her fingers digging in, she watched the hunger in his eyes intensify. She felt his body tighten against hers. His breath, choppy against the skin of her face as his body enjoyed her touch. It was empowering to have a strong man react so profoundly to her touch. It fueled her desire to provoke it more. Moving her hand higher, she met his neck, letting the tips of her fingers flirt with the bare skin above the collar of his sweater, the warmth invading her and radiating up her fingers into her hand.

Their gazes remained locked as she watched him react to her touch, getting drunk off the power of it. Jason then took in a deep breath, and let it out slowly, saying, "I love the feel of your hands on me. When they touch my skin, I feel like I'm on fire."

His words set *her* on fire. Sliding her hand up and around his neck, she pulled his lips back down on hers. He groaned into her mouth as she opened to him, wanting another taste. When his tongue slid against hers, she wondered if he was still going to be gentle. But just as soon as she thought it, his grip on her hair tightened, and his lips pressed firmly against hers. He was in control of the kiss and was going to take what he wanted. She was thankful they wanted the same thing, so it was freely offered.

Responding to his grip, she thrust her tongue more forcefully against his and demanded him to take. And he did. Together their tongues dueled as they fought to taste each other, to seek out more of what was fueling the fire raging between them. Adding another level of stimulation to her already sensitive skin, his lips melded with hers as the softness of his beard tickled her skin. Wanting to feel more, she brought her hand from his neck and cautiously rubbed her fingertips over his cheek. For a moment, Jason's movements got more demanding, before he slowed the kiss down, gently sucking on her tongue as he retreated. With one last taste of her bottom lip, his lips pulled away from hers completely, leaving them swollen and tingling with cold.

Together, they stood there, foreheads pressed together, hands on each other, just trying to catch their breaths. She didn't want to move—afraid to open her eyes—thinking it was a dream she would wake up from and be robbed of the intoxicating sensations pulsing through her. His voice invaded her ears, commanding her to open them and hope the vision of masculine beauty in front of her was still there.

"Damn, Tori ..." he said on a sigh. "Oh, what you do to me."

She let out a shaky laugh as she finally opened her eyes to take him in. His eyes still radiated hunger, but there was also satisfaction there—the look of a man who had just taken what he wanted. A shiver stole through her body at the thought of being captured by Jason. And here he was talking about what she did to him?

"I could say the same thing to you. You're gonna have to scoop me up and deposit me in the car after that. I fear my legs are inoperable now," she admitted. Her hand was still on his cheek, and as she marveled in the physical attraction she felt for him, she couldn't help but run it up and through his hair.

When he groaned, his eyes rolling closed as he leaned into her hand, he said, "I think I'm gonna have to scoop you up now. Because if you keep doing that, I'm liable to do something less than honorable to you, right here in a public parking lot."

He punctuated his statement by securing her body against all the hard points of his. And she felt *all* of them, perfectly. It might not have turned her on in the past, but that wasn't the case now. She had a feeling that when it came to Jason, he wasn't going to be the rule … he was going to be the exception.

Tori was certain she smiled the whole way home. She had never been as grateful for automatic transmissions as she was then since it allowed Jason to hold her hand without interruption. Even though her nervousness about the rest of the evening were beginning to surface, she just sat and continued to absorb the warmth infusing her.

When they got home, Tori was quick to dismiss Tessa under the guise that Jason was staying. It wasn't true, but she would use that to buy her some time. She was certain her phone would be flooded with messages before she even woke tomorrow.

Once Tessa was gone she excused herself to peek in at Lexi, asleep in her crib. When she came back out, Jason still stood by the door, hands in his pockets, making her tiny space look even smaller. There was silence for a moment, and Tori realized that she wasn't sure what to do next. She had told herself that the night wasn't going to end with sex, but her resolve seemed to be wavering, even though she didn't think she was ready for that yet.

Thankfully, Jason took that decision away from her, reaching out his hand, beckoning her to him. Silently she wondered if he remained in the doorway since she hadn't invited him to sit. Moving to him, she placed her hand in his, "I'm sorry for being so rude, would you like to have a seat?"

There was a moment of hesitation where she wondered if he'd see that as more than an invitation to sit, before she quickly dashed it away. He smiled as he gently pulled her against him, resting his hands on her hips. Her hands found his chest as she looked up at him, admiring his strong features, becoming almost entranced by them. "I had a really nice time with you tonight, Tori."

Answering with a smile, she felt herself lean into him more. "I did, too. Thank you ... for everything."

His hands moved around her waist, holding her against him. Being that close brought her a comfort she had longed for, but never knew she could have. "You're very welcome. Thank *you* for sharing with me."

She wasn't sure what to say to that, still a little embarrassed by sharing her story with him. He must have noticed the blush she felt because he let out a small chuckle as one of his hands reached up to cradle her face. His thumb stroked the warmth over her cheekbones while the rest of his fingers caressed the skin of her neck. It was yet another sensation she had missed out on, because she'd never longed for a man after he merely touched the skin of her neck.

Standing in silence, they each took in the other. She wanted to kiss him, but was content just absorbing his touch on her face. After a few moments, he said, "I hope it's not too forward of me to ask if I can see you on Friday. You said you were off then, too, yes?"

With a soft nod and a shaky voice, she said, "Yes, I'm off Friday."

"Can I see you then? Go out again?" he asked, continuing to stroke his thumb over her cheek.

Without hesitation, Tori answered, "I'd like that very much."

He let out a breath and smiled big. Did he think she'd say no to him? After that kiss? She realized that he also seemed to be treading in new territory because for the confident man he was, he was reserved when it came to asking her questions. It was humbling to know he felt that way.

Jason leaned forward a little, appearing cautious as he waited for her to respond, but silently asking for another kiss. Meeting him halfway, she answered his request. It only took him a second before his hand found her hair, cradling her head. At the touch of his lips to hers, she sighed. Their tongues reached for the other, and she was quickly swept up in their heat.

Too quickly, his firm touch retreated as he slowly pulled away from her. Dazed, she opened her eyes to find him staring at her. His face was a few inches from hers, and his breath, slightly labored, whispered across her skin. "I could get lost in your lips for hours."

She licked her lips, tasting him before saying, "I know exactly what you mean."

He smiled and pressed another chaste kiss against her lips. "Until Friday, Tori."

"Friday."

The loss of his touch was felt immediately, desire left in its place. She watched him turn and open the door. With a smile and wink, he left her standing there full of anticipation for Friday.

CHAPTER FOURTEEN

JASON had just finished loading his equipment in the back of the truck when his phone rang. He smirked when he saw it was his brother calling, from his honeymoon. Again.

"Why do you even have your phone with you on your honeymoon?" he asked, completely forgoing a greeting.

Jake laughed on the other end before answering, "Because we have kids, idiot. Do you honestly think I could get Gillian to leave California without the security of being called if one of the kids needed her?"

"Good point, but I don't have any of your kids, so why are you calling me?" He jumped in his truck and started it. The Bluetooth kicked in, so he only picked up the tail end of Jake's response. "Hey, say that again, I started the truck and lost part of it."

Making the turn onto the freeway, he was relieved to see he'd beat the Friday afternoon traffic. The area they were working in was notorious for it, but he'd finished early today.

"I said, Gilly and I fly home tomorrow, and she was hoping everyone could come over on Sunday for a barbeque—to say thank you for helping with the kids while we were gone."

Jason laughed. "Yeah, I know you come back tomorrow. I'm picking you two up, remember? And like Gillian needs a reason to have everyone over. Or that everyone needs a reason to come by."

"Don't I know it. That was the oddest part of being here this week. There weren't people constantly around. It was refreshing, yet slightly unsettling after a few days."

"I can only imagine. Tell Gillian I'll be there." Jason was about to say goodbye so he could focus on his evening ahead when he thought to ask, "Hey, Jake, can I bring someone?"

A moment of silence passed before Jake asked, "And by *someone*, I assume you mean the caterer from my wedding?"

Jason shook his head as he changed lanes and headed for his exit. "You know what they say about people who assume ..."

"Wait, so that's not who you want to bring?" Jake asked, a hint of regret in his voice.

"Yes, Tori is who I want to bring. I just couldn't resist the opportunity to imply you were an ass."

"Okay, good. I can handle you calling me an ass, but I didn't want to tell Gillian it wasn't going to be Tori."

"Totally whipped, the whole lot of you men."

"Seriously, dude, we both know that my beautiful wife could have you eating dirt out of the palm of her hand if she wanted," Jake said with confidence. And it was true, Jason would do anything for Gillian. And Allie or Morgan for that matter. But it was different for him since he wasn't scared they'd take away the goods. He laughed and said, "True, but I don't sound like a pussy when I do it."

“Whatever, your day will come,” Jake said with certainty. Truth of the matter was, Jason was looking forward to it. As much as he gave Jake and Mike crap over it, he would welcome the day he acted like them. Tori’s face, smiling up at him as he held her close to him came to mind. He smiled at the thought of her. Maybe that day was coming sooner than he realized.

“Anyway, just let me know the time on Sunday, and I’ll be there. But I won’t be answering my phone tonight, so just text me.”

“Oh, I see how it is. Call me whipped then ignore everyone while out with a lady,” Jake teased.

“That’s right. Now get off the phone and enjoy the last of the quiet time with your wife before coming home. Text me when you land; I’ll be there.”

“Thanks Jay, good luck on your date.” Jason could hear Jake laughing as he disconnected the call. The guy was in love with a woman for more than seventeen years before making his move, and he had the nerve to tease him? Shaking his head, Jason double-checked the time. Relaxing when he saw he was on schedule, he made the first stop he needed to before heading home to shower.

TORI turned off the blow dryer in time to hear her cell phone ring. Grabbing it, she saw a missed call from Tessa. Calling her back, she put the speakerphone on and continued to work on her hair.

“Hey girl, you’re going to be mad at me, but I got called in to work,” Tessa said immediately upon answering.

“Seriously?” Tori questioned, surprised that work actually called Tessa.

“Yeah, some idiot called in sick. I was next on the rotation, and since I declined covering the last two times … I was *told* to come in, not asked.” The remorse in Tessa’s voice was unusual for her. She really did feel bad, so it wasn’t like Tori could be mad at her or tease her about it, because it seemed so out of character for her.

“Don’t worry, Tessa. I can cancel, it’s not a problem. We can make plans for another day.” She tried to hide the disappointment she was feeling, but it was still there.

“I’m so pissed, I really wanted you to get better aquatinted with Captain Orgasm. When I find out who called in, I am *totally* kicking their ass,” Tessa said with determination.

Tori just laughed. “Calm down, tiger; it’s not that big a deal. I’ll call Jason and reschedule.”

“But I had a motivational speech prepared for you and everything,” Tessa whined.

“I can only imagine what you were going to say. Now get to work before you get written up.”

“Okay,” she relented. “I’ll go, but I won’t like it. I was looking forward to hanging with Lexi, too. Call me tomorrow.”

“I’ll call you tomorrow,” Tori confirmed before hanging up.

Her eyes found her reflection in the mirror. Her hair was tamed, but she hadn’t put any make up on yet, so at least she wouldn’t be sitting at home totally done up with nowhere to go. She sighed with resolve as she picked up her phone and dialed Jason. She hoped that he didn't think she was blowing him off. In reality, she'd been looking forward to seeing him since watching him leave two nights ago.

When his sexy voice came across the line, she fought the need to stomp her foot in frustration. And not all of the frustration was sexual.

"Well, hello there," he said.

"Hi," she said back in a voice that even she thought sounded pathetic.

"Hey, what's wrong?" Good, she obviously did sound pathetic.

"Well, I have to cancel our date tonight. I'm sorry." Unsure of the best way to cancel a date with a man who could have any chick he wanted and wouldn't bother with the likes of her after cancelling on him, she sighed again.

"Why? Are you okay?" His voice came across as anxious, instilling her need to reassure him.

"I'm fine, it's nothing to worry about. Tessa got called into work so I don't have a babysitter now."

She heard him exhale ... in relief? Well, that might not be a good thing, she thought, frowning.

"That's the only reason you're cancelling then?" he asked.

"Yeah. Tess just called me so I'm sorry it's last minute. I hope I didn't ruin your evening completely."

He laughed lightly into the phone this time, and she once again sulked. Why was he laughing?

"Sweet Tori, the only thing that could ruin my evening is not seeing you. Would you be willing to go out still if we brought Lexi with us?" he asked.

"You want to take me on a date with my daughter?" she asked incredulously.

He laughed again. "I love how surprised you sound. Why not? I mean, she's portable, right? And babies are notorious for sleeping in strange places like car seats, so it shouldn't be a problem. I'll just change things up a bit. Does six-thirty still work for you?"

Surprised at his response and alternate suggestions, she found herself nodding. A moment later he said, "Tori, you there?"

"Oh, yes, I'm here. Yes ... six-thirty is fine."

She could hear the smile in his voice when he said, "Great! See you soon."

Caught in a daze of disbelief, she stared at the phone as the call was disconnected. Excitement began to bubble up inside as she realized she was still going out with Jason. And that Lexi would get to come, too. She had to tell Tessa.

> *Tori: Jason still wants to take me out ... with Lexi ... how cool is that!*
>
> *Tessa: OMG, make sure to tell him you're open for business and accepting donations! If you know what I mean.*

Tori: Subtle, Tess. I think everyone would know what you mean by that. Was that the motivational speech?

Tessa: Yep! It's good advice. You should totally take it.

Tori: I'll keep that in mind ... now get to work. Talk to you tomorrow. ;-)

Tessa: I expect details, girl!

Setting down the phone, she glanced at the clock and set about getting both herself and Lexi ready for their date.

JASON pulled in Tori's driveway with minutes to spare. The last minute addition of Lexi to the date had him changing things up. He knew she was a great baby so it wasn't hard to come up with an alternate plan—just required a vehicle change and visit to his brother's house, and he was ready to go. Hopping out of his truck, fresh from the carwash, he made his way to Tori's door.

As he passed the front house, he noticed an older man, he assumed was Tori's landlord, sitting on the back porch. The man appeared to be sizing him up. It was almost funny considering Jason had at least a foot and four decades of youth on the man. But he knew Tori was close to him so Jason understood. Raising his hand, he offered him a hello. Receiving only a nod in response, he smiled and finished the path to Tori's door.

After knocking, it was only a moment later when she answered with a big smile on her face. "Hi there, come on in." Stepping away from the door, she moved about the small room grabbing a few things here and there and stuffing them into the diaper bag he remembered from the weekend before. When she bent forward to pick the baby up from the playpen, Jason was treated to an unhindered view of her ass—shaped perfectly—in the snug black pants she was wearing.

His gaze traveled down the length of her legs, taking in the curve of her muscles shown off by the tight fabric. His sudden appreciation for those exact pants was evident in his own. Clearing his throat as he tried to mentally distract himself, he adjusted his pants. "Is there anything I can help with?"

Standing back up, she swung her long hair around and over her shoulder. It was an erotic vision and didn't help his current problem. Even when she turned around and smiled, wrestling some of her hair out of Lexi's grip. He imagined running his hands through it—almost jealous of Lexi being so close to Tori. When she looked over at him, he made sure to smile back, praying she wouldn't notice his current state of arousal.

"No, I think we're ready. Are you sure you don't mind if Lexi comes along? We could always do it another night. Or maybe we could stay in? I know that sounds lame, but I feel bad."

Walking toward her, he put his hands out for Lexi, and she willingly went to him. He smiled at the baby before turning to Tori. "Did you know you ramble when you're nervous?"

She smirked as she put her hands on her hips. "Picked up on that, did you? How nice of you to point it out."

He wasn't sure if she was trying to scold him or be sarcastic, but he went with the latter and couldn't help but laugh. "I couldn't resist seeing if I could make you blush again, but I guess I missed my mark. I'll have to up my game tonight."

She shook her head and let out a giggle as she picked up the diaper bag. "Great, a man with a mission."

Together they walked to the door, and with Lexi in one arm, he reached for her car seat with the other. He paused for her to lock the door before walking to his car. The old man was still sitting on the porch, just as Jason expected he would be. Tori smiled and walked up to the railing near where he was sitting. The man's face lit up, further confirming the reason for the "sizing up" he got a few minutes before.

Tori introduced Jason to her landlord, Hal. Jason took note of the condition of Hal's hands and understood why Tori helped him around the house. "Nice to meet you sir. Jason Michaels."

Jason received a small glare, which might have worked back in the man's day, but Jason still respected it. "You taking the girls out tonight? Make sure you take good care of them. I made sure to write down your truck information in case you don't."

Tori giggled, and Jason only smiled, not wanting to be rude. He admired the protectiveness. It was similar to something Jason would've said and done. "Absolutely, sir. I'll take care of them as if they were my own."

He got another nod from Hal as Tori leaned in and whispered something in his ear. The old man softened and smiled at her before she kissed his cheek and they were walking to his truck again. Opening the back door to lock the car seat in, he said, "His face lit up when you whispered in his ear. What did you say to him?"

She smiled and gave her a head a small shake. "A girl can't reveal all of her secrets. How else would she remain mysterious?"

He helped her into the front seat, and when she looked down at him, he said, "I look forward to you revealing any secrets you hold, Tori." And with a wink, he shut the door.

CHAPTER FIFTEEN

TORI couldn't remember the last time she'd been to the drive-in. As a child, she remember going quite a bit with her mother. But when the drive-in near home had been torn down for new buildings to go up, there hadn't been any left in the area. The thought of being back at one, with her daughter, caused a couple happy tears. Quickly dashing them away, she waited for Jason to pay before leaning over the center console and placing a quick kiss to his cheek. When he looked at her in surprise, she smiled. "Thank you for bringing us here. This is beyond perfect."

He chuckled as he turned his attention back to maneuvering his truck into a spot. "Feel free to kiss me repeatedly throughout the evening to show your appreciation. I accept all forms and in any location."

With another kiss on his cheek, she settled back into her seat with a bounce. "I bet you do."

"Is this one of those secrets?" he asked with a smirk.

She rolled her eyes, shaking her head. "No, not a secret. More like a really great memory. I used to go with my mom when I was little."

"Then I'm really glad I thought of it. Now, the important question is, do you want to watch it from inside the truck or from the back?" he asked. She looked to the back of the truck and grinned.

"Do you have anything for us to sit on back there? Or would we just sit on the tailgate or something?"

Jason snorted his disbelief. "What kind of slacker do you take me for? I've got whatever we'll need either way, so you just have to pick."

"Then definitely in the back. I've never done it in the back of a truck," she said a little too excitedly. When Jason raised his eyebrows and looked to be hiding a smile, she replayed what she said in head. Closing her eyes, she dropped her face to her hands as she groaned, "Oh my God ..."

"Well then, we'll definitely have to rectify that for you," Jason said with obvious enthusiasm. She didn't have to look at him to know he was smiling. It could be heard clearly in his tone.

Still shaking her head, she lifted it from her hands when he turned off the engine. Certain her face was a bright shade of pink, she glared at him. He put his hands up in mock surrender. "What? You've never watched a movie at the drive-in from the back of a truck, and I aim to please."

Reaching across the distance of the front seat, she playfully smacked his arm. "You're doing that on purpose! You should really be careful because two can play that game."

JASON couldn't help but laugh as he conceded. "Okay, okay, point taken. I see the error of my ways. I'll behave so long as you don't forget to give me those kisses of appreciation."

She didn't confirm or deny, so he'd take that as a good sign. He definitely didn't want to miss out on more kisses. It was like a tiny hit of lust stimulating his nerve endings to pay attention and beg for more. "I'll get the stuff in back ready, and why don't you get Lexi out of her seat."

"Okay," she agreed in a soft voice before he got out. Moving to the back, he unlatched the straps holding stuff down and went about setting up. He'd picked up the small travel playpen they used with Ella and a few things for when the whole gang went camping or had bonfires—cushions, blankets, puffy beanbag-like chairs, and he even grabbed the portable space heater they used for late night sporting events. He had the playpen set up and was sliding it into position before Tori and Lexi came around.

"Wow, did you have all of this stuff just laying around? Or do you come to the drive-in often?" she asked as he jumped out of the back to meet her on the ground. He was certain there was a hidden question in there, so he made sure to answer it.

"No, I haven't been here in a while, and never on a date. Not since high school at least. My friends and I go camping and have bonfires at the beach. We seem to have equipment for anything," he said, reaching out and taking Lexi from her arms. "Climb up, and I'll hand her to you."

Once again, he was blessed with a view of her tight backside. Putting down her bag, she turned to him and bent forward, letting her hair fall all around her. It was a test of his restraint as he fought the need to touch it while he handed her the baby. Once she had Lexi, he closed the tailgate and then climbed up.

"Is this your niece's?" she asked while placing Lexi in the playpen and grabbing stuff for her to play with. Opening the cooler, he pulled out their iced tea and sandwiches, hoping that, of the four he brought, she'd like at least one.

"Yeah, it's Ella's. I ran over to my brother's and borrowed it. Is it okay?" he asked, wondering if maybe it was wrong to assume she wanted to use another baby's equipment. He suddenly second-guessed his plans.

"Oh yeah, it's fine. Thank you for doing this," she said, soothing his concerns. His shoulders relaxed again, and he gave her a smile. Motioning for her to take a seat, he reached out and adjusted the speaker for the movie before settling in. Once seated, he handed her a drink.

"I wasn't sure what kind of sandwich you'd want, so I got a few. I figured there had to be one you'd like. I assumed you'd bring food for Lexi, but now I'm wondering if I should've brought her some milk or something," he said, disappointed he hadn't thought of that sooner.

She smiled and patted him on the arm. "You didn't need to bring anything for Lexi. She already had her dinner, and I brought her bottles just in case."

"Okay, good."

"And I'll eat whichever sandwich you don't want; I'm not picky," she said as she glanced at her options.

He motioned to the food he laid out for them. "No, I insist, ladies first."

Shrugging, she went about picking her meal. When they both had their choices, they settled back just as the movie started. For the next hour, they snacked and watched the movie, but Jason couldn't tell you what it was about. He paid more attention to Tori and Lexi than anything else, just enjoying how comfortable it was to be with them. They chatted quietly about things that really didn't matter, but it gave him more insight to her.

When Lexi started getting fussy, Tori pulled her bottle out, and Jason offered to hold her while she had it. With Lexi settled in his arms, Tori scooted her seat closer to his and tucked a blanket over him and the baby. He was smiling down at Lexi as she stared up at him when he felt Tori press her lips against his cheek again. They lingered longer than the last time, and Jason felt his eyes close as he absorbed her touch. Her lips on his skin had to be one of the most invigorating sensations he'd ever experienced. Intoxicating.

Opening his eyes when she pulled back, he looked over at her. She was still close—her breasts were pushed up against his arm, and her hair was hanging on his chest. Her eyes darted from his, to his lips, and he knew what she was thinking. He was thinking it, too. But he wanted her to come to him. When she ran her tongue along her bottom lip, the sweet anticipation grew. And then she leaned in.

TORI was having trouble fighting the intense need she felt just from being next to Jason. Maybe it was his delicious scent; it made her want to stick her nose in the crook of his neck and inhale deeply. Maybe it was his sexy beard; it made her want to slide her cheek against its soft bristles. Maybe it was his beautiful hazel eyes; the way he looked at her broadcasted the hunger he was holding back. Maybe it was his lips; since they made her want to run her tongue along the seam before slipping inside to taste him.

With thoughts of tasting him, she leaned forward. She had never felt such powerful arousal in her life, and she wasn't sure how long she could hold it back. The only thing preventing her from losing control was the fact that Lexi was nestled in his arms. A momentary feeling of jealousy almost made her laugh. But the sexy sight of Jason doused that feeling and added to the desire burning up inside her.

She brought her gaze back to his. They didn't need to talk because his eyes told her everything she wanted to know. He was fighting the same losing battle she was. Leaning in, to put them out of their misery, she slid her hand up his shoulder to the back of his neck as the other one rested across his body near Lexi. His eyes went half-lidded as her hands stroked the back of his neck.

"Jason," she whispered, "I feel the need the show you a little appreciation right now."

"Thank God," he groaned before her lips made contact with his. He let her lead the kiss for a few moments as she slowly slid her tongue along the seam of his lips. Just like she wanted to. But when his hand reached up and cupped the back of her head, he took over. He groaned deeper as his tongue swept into her mouth, dominating hers. Together, they tasted one another as their tongues dueled. The arousal she had trouble fighting moments before now washed over her in waves, pulsating through her body, as her need for him demanded more.

Tori didn't know how much time passed as they continued giving and taking from one another, but she whimpered her disappointment when Jason pulled away. Using his grip in her hair, he held her still as he peppered small kisses against her lips, all the while they struggled to catch their breaths. When he rested his forehead to hers, he sighed, making her smile. Opening her eyes, she met his and felt another surge of arousal flood her system from just the sight of him. A shiver stole through her body as her nerve endings tingled with awareness.

He smiled and rubbed his nose against hers. The sweetness of the gesture made her feel precious, leaving her a little choked up. It was contradictory to what she was already feeling, but it didn't negate it in the least. Jason broke the silence with his husky voice. "I can't even begin to describe how much I love your lips."

She smiled, moving back a little farther to take in more of his face. Her hand absentmindedly ran over his beard. Clearly she had a thing for his beard. Leaning in for another peck to his lips, she whispered, "That's good to hear because I love having my lips on yours."

Kissing her again, he said, "Best ... news ... ever." He punctuated each word with another kiss. When he smiled big at her, she giggled. Then he reached his arm behind her and made sure her chair was snug up against his before pulling her firmly into his side. Her head rested on his shoulder, and her hand reached up to hold his, which was on her shoulder. In comfortable silence, they finished watching the movie as Lexi slept in one arm and Tori filled the other.

CHAPTER SIXTEEN

JASON found himself once again smiling like an idiot as he looked at his phone. Throughout the day, whenever she'd find time, Tori had texted back and forth with him. Since she was working and he couldn't see her, he'd take whatever he could get. He stood in the baggage claim area waiting for Jake and Gillian, not paying attention to what was going on around him. Even though she wasn't there, Tori had his full attention.

Their date the night before couldn't have gone better, and he was still relishing in the memory of it. Every time he recalled their kissing, his body responded—it was very similar to his teenage years. He chuckled to himself as he wrote back to her. While waiting for her response, his brother's amused voice interrupted him. "With that smile on your face, I can only imagine what you're looking at."

Putting his phone in his pocket, he looked up to find both Jake and Gillian staring at him. He rolled his eyes at Jake then moved to Gillian for a hug. "Hey there sis, good to see you."

Gillian laughed. "Hey handsome, how are you?" She kissed his cheek before stepping aside so he could greet Jake, too. After a handshake-one-armed-hug, he stepped back and smiled.

"I'm great. Did you guys have a good time? You look a little tanner to me."

Together, the three of them moved toward a baggage carousel. When they paused to watch and wait, Gillian asked, “So the boys didn’t give you any trouble when you had them?”

“Of course not,” Jason assured her. “But then again, I had them before Allie did, so who knows what trouble they’ve caused since then.”

Jake chimed in, “Just so you know … I made sure you were top of the batting order for babysitting. You can thank me anytime.”

They laughed, knowing how much trouble they could get into with Allie. Jake managed to grab their bags pretty quickly and before he knew it, Jason was leading them to his car. Gillian had her hand on his arm and gave it squeeze. “So, Jake says you’re bringing Tori with you tomorrow. Does she have anything to do with that smile on your face?”

He shook his head. “I should’ve known we wouldn’t even be on the road before you asked.” Popping the trunk, he and Jake loaded the suitcases before he answered, “And yes, she has everything to do with it.”

“Yay!” Gillian jumped and gave an excited clap. “I’m so excited for you. She was so sweet when we were arranging things for the wedding. How was your date?”

Jason moved to the driver’s side as Gillian jumped in the backseat, with Jake in the front. When their doors all closed Jason said, “You do realize that guys don’t talk about this stuff like you women do, right?”

Gillian just waved her hand at him, dismissing his words. "I'll never understand why you don't. Sometimes the stuff we talk about can be very informative."

Jason looked questioningly at her in the rearview mirror before looking to his brother. Jake just shrugged. "I don't even try to understand, man. Even though I'm worried about what is said that pertains to me, I will say there have been a few things from which I've benefited."

Shocked, Jason looked in his rearview again to find a smirking Gillian. "We talk about *anything* and *everything*. It's why we're so smart and our men are so happy."

"Unbelievable," Jason muttered as he exited the lot and headed toward home.

When he pulled into the driveway at Jake and Gillian's, a small crowd met them as all their kids came out to greet them, with Mike and Allie trailing behind. Jake and Jason grabbed the suitcases, giving Jason the opportunity to ask, "Seriously, they talk about *everything*?"

Jake laughed, "Yeah ... *everything*." He slowly emphasized the word to get his point across. Jason was having some serious doubts about bringing Tori to the barbeque. He had never brought anyone before because he just never had the desire. Suddenly he was a little relieved about that.

"And you're okay with that?" he asked. Jake was nodding when Mike came around the back of the car.

"You guys need help with anything?" Mike asked.

Jake spoke up first, shaking Mike's hand. "We're good. Hey, thanks for helping with the kids this week."

"No problem. It was kinda nice having a baby around again," Mike said with a smile. Jason had to wonder if his smile meant he and Allie were planning on having one. He knew she wanted to be a mom, and it would be great when it finally happened for her.

"Yeah, Ella's a good baby, but I'm sure you'll be happy to have Allie all to yourself again," Jake said with humor.

Jason closed the trunk and helped carry stuff inside. Gillian, Allie, and the kids had already made their way in, so the men were able to speak freely. Mike smiled. "I'm not gonna lie. We'll be out of here just as soon as I can pry her away from Gillian."

Setting down the suitcases, Jake asked, "What about you, Jay? You got time for a beer, or do you have plans?"

"No plans, I'm good," Jason offered. "She's working tonight, if that's what you're asking?"

Jake laughed as the three of them made their way toward the other end of the house. Mike asked, "Is the *she* you're referring to the beautiful redhead from the wedding?"

"Seriously, you sound like a chick when you say that. Call her a hot chick or something like that," Jason threw over his shoulder.

Mike just shrugged. "That's how Allie has been referring to her so it just came out that way."

They made it into the kitchen when Allie interrupted, handing Mike a beer and saying, "We are officially off duty." She took a swig of her own beer before asking, "Okay, so how have I been referring to whom?"

Mike lowered his beer and answered, "The beautiful redhead from the wedding."

Allie smiled big at Jason. "Yes, who I will now call Jason's woman."

He dropped into a seat as Jake handed him a beer. "Not that I mind her being called *my woman* ... but her name is Tori."

Allie shrugged. "I know that, but I prefer to be less traditional and pick my own names, *gigantor*."

"When has anyone ever accused you of being traditional?" Jason asked, pulling on her purple hair.

"Exactly," Allie said smugly as she moved to where Mike stood, leaning against a counter. Jake pulled up a seat at the bar where Jason sat with Ella perched on his lap. His thoughts immediately went to Lexi and how much he enjoyed holding her last night—probably because he was finally able to hold a baby without having to fight Allie for her. But he had a feeling it was more than that, because just like with Tori, he felt connected ... a little possessive.

Gillian came into the room, yelling orders over her shoulder to Ryan and Dylan, before she smiled and asked, "So, is everyone coming tomorrow so we can feed you and say thanks?"

Everyone said yes, and Gillian seemed satisfied with that. Then she directed her stare to Jason and asked, "So you'll be bringing Tori. What about her daughter?"

Jason nodded, assuming she would bring Lexi since there was no reason not to, and Allie perked up. "She has a daughter? How old?"

He smiled smugly. "Lexi is ten months old, and I get first dibs, *half-pint*."

Allie scowled. "You can't call dibs when the baby isn't even here. Standard shotgun rules apply."

"Well, considering I'll already be holding her when I walk in, I'm not worried about it."

"That sounds a lot like a challenge—" Allie was going to say more when Gillian interrupted.

"Stop it you two. Allie, if Tori sees you two acting like that you might scare her away." Jason smirked at Allie before Gillian continued, "And we don't want her being scared away Al; she's a total cow, and I want to keep her."

Allie nodded, and Jason almost spit out his beer. In disbelief and a little defensively, he asked, "Did you just call her a cow?"

Gillian clearly picked up on the irritation in his voice. "It's a good thing, Jason. Do you think I would be mean like that?"

"No. That's why it bothered me."

Gillian and Allie chuckled, and then Jake said next to him, "It's their language, don't even try to understand it."

Jason downed the rest of his beer and nodded. "I don't think I could if I tried." Standing up, he added, "I'm heading home so I'll see you tomorrow at noon."

Accepting a kiss from Gillian, he asked, “Do you need me to bring anything?”

“Nothing but Tori and Lexi.” She smiled. He returned the smile before heading out to his car. When he got in, he checked his phone but found no messages. He sent Tori one anyway, telling her that he was on his way home and would love to talk to her when she had the chance.

About two hours later his phone finally rang. Seeing it was her, he smiled as he answered.

“Hi there.”

“Hey, how are you? It’s not too late to call, is it?” she rushed to ask.

“Of course not; I wanted to talk to you. Are you just getting home?” He hoped she was. He didn’t like the thought of her being out alone at night with Lexi—another thing to add to his list of stuff he’d never really felt before.

“Yeah, we got home a little while ago. Lexi is asleep and I squeezed in a quick shower because I couldn’t wait. I had frosting in my hair,” she whined in a voice that implied he’d understand the horror. If only she knew how turned on he now was—thoughts of her wet and wearing only a towel battled against those of her covered in frosting he could lick off.

He stifled his groan. “Dare I ask how you got frosting in your hair?”

“Tessa,” she said grumpily. He made a mental note to thank Tessa for the erotic image.

“And by Tessa, you mean what exactly?” he asked, trying to form the correct visual in his head.

“I mean that she really has no idea when to behave. We were talking in the kitchen about …” She paused and Jason recalled how Gillian said women talked about everything. He realized that Tessa was her Allie. He perked up more, wondering if maybe he was the subject of their conversation. Her reluctance to continue gave him hope, since he really liked the idea of his name on her lips, but he wanted to know.

“You were talking and somehow got frosting in your hair? That must’ve been *some* conversation,” he said with a smirk he knew she’d hear.

“All right, smart ass. I realize now that I’ve opened the door to a conversation that I had no intention of sharing with you. But I’ll give you the abbreviated version so you can wipe the smug look, I bet you’re wearing, off your face.” She knew what she was talking about, and he loved that she seemed to figure him out so quickly.

A laugh escaped. “One of those secrets to keep you mysterious?”

She sighed. “Yes, one of those secrets. Now listen up because I’m only saying this once. I was telling her about our date last night, and she then proceeded to give me pointers on how she thought I should handle things. One thing led to another and somehow she felt that frosting on my neck would make things interesting between you and me so she demonstrated. So not only did I ice over a hundred cupcakes tonight, but I had the smell of cream cheese frosting overwhelming me for three hours."

He couldn't contain the groan this time as he asked, "Damn, she smeared it on your neck?" Imagining her with the sweet frosting on her neck had him instantly hard and ready for action.

"Yes," she said in a shy voice that added to his already alert status.

Unable to help himself, especially since they always seemed to come back to the sexual innuendos, he said, "I'm really sorry I missed that. I would have loved to help you with that."

"You like cream cheese frosting?" This time her voice had taken on a husky vibration, and he knew he was in trouble.

"Yes I do ... very much," he answered in a voice to match hers, hoping to arouse her the same way she'd done to him.

There was a few moments pause before she said, "I'll have to remember that."

"I can give you reminders if you like," he teased.

She giggled, the sound going straight to his groin. "Oh, I won't forget ... see you tomorrow? At eleven-thirty?"

Knowing he was going to have to take matters into his own hands, even though he didn't want the call to end, he answered, "Yeah, I'll be there to get both of you at eleven-thirty."

"Good night, Jason," she said in a seductive whisper.

"Good night, Tori."

Alone in his bed, he groaned and closed his eyes, giving attention to the erection that had tortured him all week. Caught in the grips of a vision where Tori was holding her long hair up on top of her head, exposing her long neck to him, a thick swipe of cream cheese frosting from her shoulder to ear. He could almost taste her, but with the added element of frosting. Shuddering in release, he thought about how he wanted to devour Tori—just like a cupcake.

CHAPTER SEVENTEEN

TORI licked the little bit of frosting off her finger. Admiring her work, she closed the lid on the container of red velvet cupcakes she whipped up that morning. After Jason's admission to liking cream cheese frosting, and the way it apparently turned him on, she couldn't help herself. And the fact that they were going to a barbeque with his family was the perfect cover.

Hearing his car in the driveway, she pulled off her apron and washed her hands before rushing to the door. He knocked just as she opened it, a grin plastered on her face. "Hey you!"

"Well, that's one hell of a smile to be greeted by," Jason said as he moved toward her. He pulled her against him with a smile and kissed her softly. "Good morning, sunshine. You ready?"

The tingling sensations from his touch made her shudder in excitement. "Yeah, let me just grab my stuff."

He laughed. "And by *stuff* do you mean baby?"

"No, smartass. I made something to bring to the barbeque." She gave his shoulder a playful shove as she moved back to her kitchen area. Picking up the single cupcake she had left out for him, she turned around. Jason paused when his eyes landed on the treat. She smirked at his expression because it was a mixture of more than one kind of hunger. When he grinned and brought his gaze up to hers, she realized she wouldn't mind being that cupcake.

Stepping closer, he asked, "Is that cream cheese frosting?" His voice confirmed what his expression already told her—he was imagining from where he could lick the frosting.

Unable to speak, she nodded and boldly swept her finger through it to offer him a taste. His eyelids drooped and his nostrils flared. It was hard to believe he could have that kind of reaction over her and a cupcake. With a hand wrapped around her wrist, he leaned in to capture her finger in his mouth. Her eyes went wide as her finger touched his tongue and his lips closed around her knuckle. He hummed his satisfaction, and all she could do was watch as it slowly lid from his lips. The suction was felt in more areas than just her finger, and she clenched her thighs together.

When he let go of her finger, he gave her a sexy grin. "Delicious." Then he took the cupcake from her and asked, "Is this mine?"

Again, fearing what her voice would sound like, she nodded. When he swiped his finger across the top, loading the tip with a hefty dose of frosting, she thought she would just watch him eat it. Instead, she was treated to something much better when he set the cupcake down and moved her hair behind her shoulder. Slipping his empty hand into her hair, he tilted her head, exposing her neck. "I'm positive it will taste even better here."

Before she realized what was happening, his finger ran a trail down the side of her neck, leaving frosting in its wake.

She sucked in a breath when the warm heat of his tongue laved the skin at and began lapping the sweetness from her skin. He groaned as he licked and sucked his way up her neck, stopping at the sweet spot just below her ear. She shivered and instinctively reached for him. One hand found his waist and the other found his head. Digging her fingers into his hair, she ran her nails along his scalp. Making him moan deeper and his attentions grew firmer.

When he wrapped his arm around her, she gasped as he lifted her, settling her butt on the counter. Jason settled between her legs as he pulled his face from her neck. She could hear her heart racing, and a whimper escaped as she absorbed the arousal mounting inside her. With a wicked and satisfied smile, he gazed at her and said, "I was right. It did taste better there. But I need to check one more spot."

After another swipe of frosting, his finger was moving across her bottom lip, followed seconds later by his tongue. She sighed at the heady sensation, and he slipped his tongue inside. His taste combined with the sweetness of the frosting was blissful. Her hand tightened in his hair, his body pressed firmly between her legs, and she swallowed his groan as she took the kiss deeper, wanting to remove any and all flavor of the frosting. She could have devoured him—leaving only his taste on her tongue.

Tori was seconds away from wrapping her legs around his waist and demanding he do something about the throbbing sensation she was experiencing when a sound penetrated their lusty haze. Jason must have heard it, too, because he slowly pulled his lips from hers. Lexi squealed a second time, effectively lifting the fog. He smiled and ran his thumb along the side of her mouth before slipping it into his own. "Sorry, I couldn't help myself. After you told me about the frosting last night … and then there you were with a cupcake. It was a sign."

She giggled. "A sign, huh?"

He shrugged, his smile smug. "Oh yeah. And I never ignore the signs." Kissing her one more time, he helped her down. With his hands on her waist, he steadied her before letting go and turning to Lexi. In an attempt to calm herself, she took a deep breath and fanned her face, watching as Jason scooped Lexi up from her playpen. As he held Lexi high above his head, talking to her, it was hard to miss the distinct bulge in his pants. Tori turned to grab the cupcakes and her bag; she needed a distraction not more of an invitation.

Gathering what she needed, she said, "Ready to go." And then they were on their way.

JASON pulled up to the light at the bottom of the exit ramp. Looking down at their joined hands, he smiled before lifting them to his lips. Kissing the back of hers, he set them back down and found Tori's gaze. She had a dreamy smile and seemed completely relaxed. He put that smile on her face, and a sense of satisfaction stole over him at the knowledge.

"Thank you for my cupcake," he said with a smile.

Tori huffed a laugh and squeezed his hand. "You should know from now on, whenever I make you cupcakes, it's for totally selfish reasons."

He barked out a laugh as he started the car forward again. "Oh really? Well, you should know that I would be fine with just the frosting ... and your warm skin, of course."

Tori closed her eyes on a sigh before rolling her head to look out the front window. "Okay, big guy, time to change the subject. We're going to your brother's place?"

"Probably a good idea," he agreed, knowing that it would be highly inappropriate to walk in and greet his family with a hard on. "Yeah, we're going to Jake and Gillian's place. But everyone will be there. Did you want another run-down on the family tree?"

She let out a laugh. "No, I think I can handle the basics. I know Jake and Gillian from dealing with them for their wedding. I remember Ryan and Dylan, but there are other siblings I haven't met, some half and some whole," she added with humor. "Then there's Allie, who I'm not sure her relation to you?"

"Allie is technically not related to me. She's Logan's sister and has been best friends with Gillian and Jake since high school," Jason offered, trying not to overwhelm her.

"I don't remember meeting Logan. Who's he?"

"Logan is my business partner, best friend, and Gillian's ex-husband," he said then looked to see if she was following him. "So he wasn't at the wedding."

"No, I bet he wasn't."

"I'm sure he'll be there today; though; he lives next door, and he still can't tell Gillian no. So if she wants him to come hang out with everyone, he will."

"Seriously?" Tori asked, surprised.

"We're all a pretty tight-knit group, even after Gillian and Logan split. I'm sure it seems a little odd, but it works." He shrugged as he turned down the street toward the house. "After everything that happened, Logan is paying some heavy dues right now. But that's a long story I can tell you another time 'cause we're here."

She looked a little nervous all of a sudden as she glanced out the window. "Did they know we were coming with you? Are you sure they won't mind? I can always call Tessa to pick us up if I need to."

"Hey." He turned in his seat, taking her hand in both of his. "You're doing that rambling thing again. There is nothing for you to be nervous about. I promise." He kissed the back of her hand again and waited for her to relax. Wanting to reassure her more, he added, "Besides, last night, Gillian told Allie not to scare you off because you were a cow and she wanted to keep you."

Jason nodded with a smile, believing he had just given her what she needed to be more comfortable. But it seemed to have the opposite effect. Her eyes widened and her nostrils flared. "Excuse me?" She took a deep, slow breath, before asking, "Did you just say she called me a *cow*?"

Shit! "Um, yeah, but Gillian said it was a good thing. She says she really likes you." Trying to think of what more to say to convince her, he added, "When she found out you and I were going on a date she scolded me and said that I better treat you right. She defended your honor by accusing me of giving you a wrong phone number, and that was why you had to call Jake for it. Please, give them a chance. I promise they are really good people."

She gave him a reluctant look as she considered it. A scowl was lodged on her face and when she took another deep breath, he held his own, waiting for her answer. A few moments later, she asked, "Did you know you ramble, too ... when you're worried you did something wrong?"

He let out his breath and smiled. "I'm figuring that out, but it only seems to be when I'm worried about upsetting *you*."

When she sighed and her shoulders dropped, he knew he'd won. "Fine. I'll give them a chance, but now I'm apprehensive. If I'm not comfortable, Lexi, me, and the cupcakes are outta there."

Relief swam through him. He would have Gillian make it right because he wanted her there with him—and he wanted her comfortable. Getting out of the car, he leaned into the back to get Lexi. She was still smiling and happy, just like when he'd put her in the car. He realized he hadn't heard her cry yet and couldn't help but smile back at her. Holding her against him, he met Tori at the front of the car, and they walked to the door. Wanting to calm her more, he kissed her forehead. "It'll be fine, I promise."

TORI followed Jason through the open door and was immediately met with the sounds and smells one would acquaint with *home*. It pacified some of the tension still gripping her shoulders. Women could be catty and scornful creatures, and just knowing they referred to her in such a manner had her on guard. When Jason placed his hand on the small of her back, she realized she had stopped walking. She was taking in the homey feel, and her heart ached just a little with it. *Mom …*

He directed her toward the back of the house, where all the noise seemed to be coming from. When they walked into the kitchen, the conversation stopped and everyone turned to them. *Nothing like having all eyes on you*, she thought as she fought the urge to cower under the attention. Then everyone seemed to burst out at the same time. Gillian moved toward her, hugging her around the cupcakes, like they were the best of friends. "I'm so glad you could come today, Tori. Welcome."

At least she sounded genuine. Tori smiled in response. "Thank you for having us. I made some cupcakes for everyone." Holding the tray forward, Gillian's response was cut off when Allie jumped forward and swiftly took possession of it.

"I have a new best friend, and her name is Tori because she brought us cupcakes," Allie said in a sing-song voice. Tori couldn't help but laugh and look up at Jason as he did the same.

"See, I told you they liked you."

Gillian overheard him and moved in closer to them. "And why would she think we didn't, Jason?"

Tori wanted to laugh at how Jason seemed a little worried to explain. When he told Gillian what he'd said, she understood. Because a second after, his body jerked to the side as he yelled out in pain. Tori looked over and saw him rubbing his side, as Allie promptly removed Lexi from his arms. Tori was thinking she should intervene but stopped when Allie scolded him, "No baby for you! You can't go speaking our language to others when you don't even know it yourself."

"Seriously, Jason, it's a wonder she even came in here today. Now go away so we can explain it to her before she jumps ship and runs the other direction," Gillian chided. Tori watched him smile indulgently before kissing Gillian's cheek and whispering something in her ear. Then Gillian smiled back at him and said, "I got this, now go."

Jason leaned down, pressed his lips against Tori's for a moment before saying, "You're in good hands, but come find me if you need me."

She watched as he strode out of the room with a few other men, and she wanted to follow. Not because she was worried about being with the women, but because she preferred to be in his good hands. Smiling to herself, she turned her attention to Gillian and Allie who both wore huge grins. When she was about to ask them why they were looking at her like that, Allie nudged Gillian's hip and said, "Oh yeah, *Jason's woman* for sure."

CHAPTER EIGHTEEN

TORI failed at disregarding Allie's comment. A sense of longing set up camp in her chest at the idea of being considered Jason's woman. Oh yeah, she wanted that ... a lot. Allie's voice caught her attention. Looking over, she saw Lexi's little hand was weaved tightly into Allie's hair. Letting out a little laugh, she moved to help her disengage it. "Sorry about that. She seems to have a thing for long hair."

Allie smiled at Lexi. "Girl after my own heart. You can play with my hair anytime." She said the last part in baby talk, producing a giggle from Lexi.

As she was watching Allie talk to her daughter, Gillian said, "Okay, so I feel the need to explain myself to you." Giving Gillian her full attention, she raised her eyebrow in question and waited.

"So, when Allie or I referred to you as a 'cow,' it was in no way an insult. In fact it was a compliment," Gillian said, pausing to examine the cupcakes. "Oh my God, Allie. They're red velvet cupcakes."

Allie leaned in to see. "Nice. Good thing I already claimed her as my new best friend; those look orgasmic." The three of them let out a laugh before Gillian continued.

"Anyway, when we were younger we would call the all the pretty girls cows because we were jealous and wanted to be them. As we got older, it turned into our little way of acknowledging that we liked a person, that they were the whole package, someone we envied. So ... when talking with Jason last night, we referred to you as a cow. I thought you were so sweet and wonderful helping with the food for the wedding, I felt we could definitely be friends. And when I found out that Jason had asked you out, I was so excited for both of you."

Tori smiled. She felt a little bad that Gillian had to explain herself. In truth, Jason probably shouldn't have said anything, but she was glad he did. She, too, thought these were people she wouldn't mind being friends with. "Well, I guess that's good to know. I had come up with my own choice words for you when I heard you called me that."

"I bet you did," Gillian said with humor as she turned to pull something out of the fridge. Placing a tray of veggies and dip on the table in front of Tori, she gestured for her to help herself.

Allie snorted. "I bet it started with a capital B and ended with an itch." She smiled down at Lexi before she added, "And just so you know, I totally am one, but when calling me that you must put the *super* in front of it."

As she relaxed and enjoyed the conversation, she realized she was pretty hungry. Grabbing a napkin, she picked up a few things and proceeded to nibble on them. Gillian groaned and gave Allie an exasperated look. "Please don't start with the superhero names again."

Tori giggled as she quickly finished chewing what was in her mouth. Grabbing a bottle of water from the table, she looked to Gillian. "Your son actually had a debate with me over superheroes. It was quite amusing."

When Allie literally laughed out loud, Gillian sighed, her shoulders dropping in defeat. She wiped her hands on the dishtowel before throwing it in a laughing Allie's face. She looked back over to her and asked, "Please tell me they didn't call you Super Bitch. Because I will have to kick a certain someone's ass for that."

Tori had just taken a sip of her water, so coughing to clear her throat, she asked, "What? No!"

"Okay, good," Gillian said. "Stop laughing Allie. You guys really need to pay attention when you bring up the superhero names in front of Dylan. Ryan doesn't repeat things, but you know damn well Dylan does. I am not looking forward to the call from school about how he called some boy his "Little Bitch."

Allie only laughed louder, and Tori couldn't help but join in even though she wasn't sure why. Gillian smiled but continued to shake her head at Allie. "Allie has taken a liking to designating superhero and sidekick names to herself and others. Her two favorite to use are for her, Super Bitch, and for Jake, Little Bitch. It's all fun and laughable until the nine year old repeats it."

Tori covered mouth, trying to stifle the laugh threatening to bubble over. She didn't want to offend Gillian, but it was funny. Gillian rolled her eyes. "Go ahead, you can laugh, too." So she did. She thought it was funny as hell and wanted even more to be a part of this group. Tessa was really her only friend, but right then she felt she was part of something more.

Allie's laugh was interrupted when Jason stepped in the room and swept Lexi out of her arms. "Hey, no fair."

Jason just held Lexi up high so Allie couldn't reach her, and declared, "You didn't call dibs, so I am. Standard shotgun rules apply, your words half-pint. She's mine." As the outsider again, she wasn't sure what was going on, but it was fun to watch. When Jason brought Lexi down to his chest, he hugged her to him and kissed the top of her head. He turned his attention to Tori, completely ignoring Allie who continued to complain. When a cocky, one-sided smile spread across his face, she couldn't help but answer with one of her own. He winked and then left the room with a firm grip on Lexi, Allie trailing behind him.

"Well, if I didn't think you were *Jason's woman* before, I sure as hell do now," Gillian said with a smirk. Tori felt her cheeks redden in acknowledgment, even though she really wouldn't mind being Jason's woman.

~*~*~*~

JASON went in search of Tori. He was happy she was comfortable around his friends and all, but he wanted to spend time with her, too. Feeling like he was one step away from pouting about it, he was ready to track her down and get out of there.

He found the women relaxing on the couch, giggling about something. But when they realized he had entered the room, they all stopped and seemed to be holding something in. Shaking his head as he recalled Gillian's admission of talking about everything, he feared what they might have been discussing. Slightly comforted by the fact that nobody in that room could say anything of a sexual nature about him, he decided not to worry about anything else.

When Tori's eyes met his, he smiled and crossed the room. Squatting in front of her, he placed his hand on her knee. "Hey you, I was thinking about us getting out of here. Would that be okay with you?"

"Yeah sure," she answered with a smile. "Let me just get Lexi from Ella's room."

"I'll get her for you." He stood and made his way to Ella's room. Lexi and Ella were both asleep in the large crib. Jason smiled at the sight. Carefully, he picked up Lexi and rested her against his chest. Kissing his finger, he placed it against Ella's forehead before leaving the room.

Tori had gathered all her things and was waiting in the front room. The women quietly said their goodbyes so not to disturb Lexi. It was probably the quickest goodbye ever where Allie and Gillian were concerned, and he kissed Lexi quietly in thanks. They were loaded in the car and pulling out before Jason asked, "Did you have a good time?"

Smiling big, Tori said, "I did. They were all so great. You're so lucky to have such great friends. I felt like I already knew them. Thank you for bringing me."

He reached across the console and rested his hand over hers. "Thank you for coming with me."

With the smile still on her face, she relaxed back in the seat for the drive. When they made it back to her place, Jason knew he wasn't ready to leave. He realized now that he should've asked if there was somewhere else she wanted to go, but with the baby, he just assumed she'd want to bring her home. Getting out of the car, he lifted the baby carrier out, and they walked to the door in silence. They both turned and began talking at the same time.

Both of them laughed before Jason said, "Go ahead, you first."

With a shy smile, she said, "Well, it's still early, and I wasn't sure what your plans were for the rest of the evening. But I thought that you'd probably need to eat dinner at some point, and I would too, so maybe, if you want, you could hang out here. I'm a great cook, so it wouldn't be like I was going to give you crappy mac-n-cheese or anything. You can say no ..."

Placing his finger to her lip to stop her nervous rambling, Jason said, "Tori ... I would love to spend more time with you today. You don't even have to bribe me with the offer of a meal. I was sold when you smiled."

Sighing, her shoulders visibly relaxed. "Okay ... great."

Unlocking the door, she let them in and quickly went about the task of putting a still sleeping Lexi in her crib. When Tori came back out, he asked, "Does she usually take long naps?"

Tori nodded. "She takes two naps, but her morning one wasn't very long because I woke her up to make sure we were ready when you came. So this one might last a little while longer."

"I'm sorry for interrupting her schedule," he said in a mischievous voice as he crept closer to her. "But I'm a little happy she'll sleep a while longer."

Her gaze followed his as he moved right up against her. Looking up at him, she asked, "You are?" Her voice had dropped to an almost whisper. It was low and husky sounding. It was sexy.

He nodded. "I am."

Placing his hands on her hips, he walked her backward toward her couch. Moving to sit down, he pulled her down onto his lap. She squealed an adorable sound, which had him smiling. Her bottom rested over his legs, while her arm had found its way across his shoulders. In the position he had her, he could access any part of her body—her plump lips, her long neck, her thick, silky hair, her curved hips, her toned legs ... any and all of it.

Caressing her cheek, he slowly moved her hair over her shoulder before leaning in to kiss her neck. "I was kinda hoping that we could make out like teenagers here on the couch." He heard the hitch in her throat when his lips touched her warm skin again. He continued, "You know, get lost in each other, not knowing when it will end ... wondering who'll catch us wrapped around one another."

His tongue snuck out and ran up her neck. When he got to her ear, he wrapped his lips around the lobe and gave it a small nibble. She shivered in his arms, and he knew she was right there with him—aroused and needy. Pulling his face from her neck, he found her eyes closed and leaned in to kiss each lid.

“Tori?” Jason said.

When she opened her eyes and met his, he smiled, “What do you say, *Cupcake*?... wanna get lost in me?” She answered by pressing her lips to his and taking everything he was offering.

CHAPTER NINETEEN

TORI pulled the tray from the oven, the smell of enchilada sauce wafting to her face. Her mouth watered, and she wanted to laugh at how hungry she was. Apparently making out like a teenager burned some calories and her body needed more—especially if they were going to pick up where they left off. Tori could only recall not smiling when hearing Lexi wake up a handful of times. Sleep had been the only thing Lexi had ever interrupted until now.

Even with the interruption, it had been one of the most sensual experiences of her life. Just recalling the feel of his lips and beard brushing against her skin caused her to shiver. She'd thought it was distinctly possible it might go further, but it hadn't. She could safely say they moved slowly between first and second base, which was strangely disappointing.

Pulling down plates, she quickly dished out food for both of them. After carrying them into the living room, she set them down on the coffee table. Jason smiled. "Mmm, that smells delicious. Thank you."

Tori retrieved Lexi from his lap and moved her back to the playpen before grabbing them some napkins. When she returned to the couch, she found Jason had waited for her before he started to eat, proving once again his thoughtfulness. Together, they ate in silence. The only noises were the sounds of utensils against plates, with the occasional noise from Lexi. At first she wondered if his silence was because he didn't like the food, but she soon realized how quickly he had eaten. As he finished the last bite, he said, "Oh, please tell me there's more in the kitchen?"

She laughed. "Of course there is. Do you want one or two more?"

He stood with his plate. "You don't have to get up; I can get it. Would you like more, too?"

Such the gentleman, she thought as she answered him with a shake of her head. Damien had always expected her to serve him. Immediately, she felt bad for even comparing the two men when it was obvious there was no comparison. It didn't escape her that with Jason, she *wanted* to do things for him.

The evening progressed with casual conversation while they simply got to know each other better. Even though he offered to help, he played with Lexi on the floor while she cleaned up after dinner. Shocked as she was by him offering to even change Lexi's diaper, she told him not to bother since it was almost bath time. She was a little disappointed thinking he might take that as the opportunity to leave, but he didn't. It seemed Jason was the "total package."

After bathing Lexi and putting her to sleep, Tori returned to find Jason relaxed and watching TV. When he saw her, he set the remote down and put his hand out for her. Moving to him, she took his hand and let him guide her down to his lap again. He pulled her tightly against him, securing his hands around her. Once nestled up against him, he asked, "Comfortable?"

Nodding, she said, "Yes, very."

"Good. Is it okay that I'm still here? I keep telling myself I'm being a jerk and inviting myself to stay. The truth is, I can't find the will to leave, and I don't want to," he said in a soft, sincere voice. "But if you want me to, just say so, and I'll be gone."

Tori was quiet for a moment, reflecting on the insecurity in his voice. Her hand lifted and began teasing the hair at the base of his head. Holding his gaze, she said, "I don't think you're being a jerk. I like having you here."

He smiled, and leaning in, he whispered, "How about here? Do you like me here?" His lips met hers and with a quick swipe of his tongue, he was gone again—teasing her and restarting the fire that had been simmering low in her belly all evening. All day really. She whispered her agreement as her lips followed his retreat, going in for her own taste. Marveling at how quickly her body flooded with need, she fed the desire. Her tongue slid against his lips and then back before his took over, dominating her, telling her what she wanted, and giving her what she didn't realize she needed.

JASON felt like a caged animal. Hunger like no other gripped him, and he was having trouble holding it back. With each stroke of her tongue against his, it escalated. He wanted Tori on a level he didn't think he'd recover from. With her draped across his lap, he let one hand travel down her back and over the curve of her hip before finding the back of her knees. Then, tightening the hold on her back, he slipped his arm around her bent knees and pulled her firmly against his body. He used his hold on her to stand up and reverse their positions.

Letting her knees go, he moved between them. Now cradled between her thighs, her heat pressed firmly against him, he pulled his lips away and looked at her. Really looked. He needed to make sure she was right there with him, that he wasn't getting carried away. His concern for scaring her away was clawing at his conscience, and he needed to settle it.

"Tori, I need you to look at me." His voice came out strained and foreign to him. When she opened her eyes, he focused on the hunger he saw reflected in her emerald pools. He let the haze clear from her eyes before saying, "I don't want to push too far and mess this up ..." His hands moved to cradle her face, "Please tell me you're with me, that you want me like I want you."

Time seemed to slow down as he waited for her response. Lying there beneath him, her hair spread out to tease him with its allure, her eyes sparkled with lust, and her soft skin beckoned him to caress it; he took it all in. When she licked her bottom lip, he fought the need to chase her tongue with his own. Instinct to claim was riding him hard. Then she whispered his name, and every part of his body hardened in anticipation.

"Jason ... it's beyond that." She licked her lips again. "It's not just want, it's *need*. I physically *crave* you." And that was all he needed to hear. His lips slammed down on hers, and they both let go. The dam had broken, and the lust they'd restrained swirled in the air around them as hands and lips sought out their targets. Hips ground against one another reflexively. Tori's hand found the bare skin of his back, and he couldn't help but rip at the fabric to expose more of it for her. Suddenly, the cramped space of the couch wasn't enough. He wanted room to move, to spread her out, and feast on every part of her.

Standing quickly, he pulled his shirt all the way off, tossing it aside. Taking her hand, he pulled her up and divested her of her own shirt, exposing more of her creamy skin. The temptation won as he dropped his lips to her shoulder and tasted. Her breath hitched, and the sound went straight to his cock. Dropping his hands to her ass, he hoisted her up his body. She wrapped her legs around his waist, and he shuddered when her moist lips found his neck. Tori nipped and sucked, prompting his feet into motion.

Finding her bed quickly, he lowered them on the soft surface and began to explore. He let his hands roam up and down her sides, enjoying the way the curve of her hip fit his hands. His tongue traveled down her neck, teasing the soft mounds of her breasts. The hushed moans escaping her fueled his endeavor. Sliding her bra strap off her shoulder, he slowly exposed her breast. Groaning, he let his tongue tease the tip before swirling it around the nipple.

"Perfection," he whispered. Repeating his movements on the other side, she gripped his hair tightly, holding him against her as she squirmed beneath him, seeking more. Rising to his knees, he slid his hands under her to remove her bra, uncovering her completely. Then his hands went to the hem of her pants and made quick work of them.

Now, lying before him in only a pair of pink panties, he stared down at the beauty. Mesmerized, he slid a fingertip from the top of her chest down her midline. His eyes followed the path as it circled her navel before reaching the little pink waistband. His cock throbbed in his pants, demanding to be set free. He ignored it, and found her gaze, "God, Tori ... you're even sexier than I imagined."

Tori blushed, smiling shyly. "My body isn't as sexy as it used to be."

Jason shook his head. "I really don't see how that's possible, Cupcake. You've got my body at war; I *want* to slide my tongue all over you and taste you everywhere." He ran his finger deeper below the waistband, and slid it back and forth, teasing both of them. "But I *need* to feel the heat of your body as I slide inside you."

With eyes half-lidded, she squirmed below him, hunger radiating from her body. He had to have her. Moving off the bed, he ditched his jeans and underwear quickly before sliding on the condom he was thankful to have. Reaching out for her, his hands found her ankles and brought them together. Stroking the soft skin, he slowly slid them upward until he reached the last piece of clothing in his way. When he paused, she voiced her impatience, "Jason ... please ..."

Capturing her gaze, he smiled and then slid them off. Tossing them aside, he almost lost it at the sight of her legs falling open for him, exposing her wet, swollen center to him. Unable to help himself, he said, "I have to taste you." And he did.

One swipe of his tongue wasn't enough. Tori gasped as he sucked her sensitive flesh into his mouth. Releasing it, he moved quickly up her body, making sure to tease her breasts along the way. Jason rested his body against hers and sighed at the sensation of his hardness nestled in her softness. Taking himself in hand, he got in position for the slow slide to ecstasy. When her wet heat fisted him, he prayed for control. Fully engulfed, he buried his face in her neck and groaned. He could feel her pulse pounding, her breathing erratic, and almost worried if she was okay.

Pulling back, he looked at her to find her eyes closed and legs squeezed tightly at his hips. "Are you okay, baby? Look at me."

When she opened her eyes, a single tear leaked out the side, and he almost came undone. "Oh, Jason, it feels so good ... please, I need you."

Instinct took over as his hips began to move. Keeping his eyes on hers, he slowly and thoroughly made love to her. Sliding in and out over her most sensitive spots, he listened to her responses. He absorbed her expressions, her sounds, as they alternated from need and desire to pure satisfaction. Every whimper, every moan were a plea for more. Answering her request, his thrusting increased, as his need to finish became almost unbearable. Her body began to tighten and tremble beneath him as her breathing became loud and insistent in his ears. *More, she needs more.*

Reaching down, his hand found the curve of her knee, and he hooked his arm under it. Tori gasped, and her muscles contracted around him. Pulling her knee up and changing his angle, he thrust harder and she cried out. "Oh God! Jason!"

They were both teetering on the edge of release. Keeping the pace, he spread her leg a little more to the side, further exposing her sensitive nerves to his body's assault. Her whimpers matched every thrust as he drove to find her pleasure. With his lips latched on to the spot on her neck he discovered she liked, she exploded. Crying out, she buried her face in his neck and bit down, muffling the sound as her body convulsed around him. The sharp bite of her teeth on his neck sent him over the cliff, and his body pulsated deep within her.

Holding her to him, he slowed his movements until they were lying in silence. Only the sounds of their breathing filled the air. Tori's hands slowly stroked up and down his back. Lifting his head, he found her gaze, praying to God there weren't any tears. When she smiled at him, he relaxed, and his sated body became heavy.

Smiling back at her, he cautiously asked, "Are you okay? You had me worried ..."

Tori shushed him with a finger to his lips. "I'm perfect, Jason. *You* were perfect."

CHAPTER TWENTY

TORI blinked the sleep from her eyes as she tried to assess what had woken her. A small snore escaped from Jason, and she smiled, figuring it must have been that. Closing her eyes again, she snuggled in closer to his sleeping form. With one arm and one leg crossed over his body, she couldn't help but sigh in contentment, especially since it was still early. She heard a small sound come from Lexi's room, so she turned her face into Jason's chest and gently kissed it before getting up.

Grabbing a pair of underwear and a tank top, she first slipped into the bathroom. After quickly dressing and simultaneously brushing her teeth, she pulled her hair up the best she could. It was a mess, but she wanted to take care of Lexi before she woke up Jason. Opening the door, she was met with the sight of one sexy backside covered in boxer briefs, standing in the doorway to Lexi's room.

Jason turned, Lexi already in his arms. Smiling, Tori said, "So much for not letting her wake you up. I'm sorry."

He smiled down at Lexi, who was currently digging her fingers into his beard. "I can think of far worse ways to wake up in the morning." Placing a kiss to her forehead before turning back to Tori, he added with a wink, "I can think of far better ways, too."

Moving to them, Tori said, "I agree, on both counts."

When she went to take Lexi, he tightened his hold and then wrapped his arm around her, too, pulling her against him. Kissing her forehead, he said, "Good morning, sunshine."

"Good morning to you, too. Did you want to go back to sleep? I know it's Monday, but I don't know what time you go to work," she said while grabbing a reluctant Lexi from his arms.

Jason laughed at Lexi's disgruntled expression. "No, I'm an early riser. In fact, I would usually be on my way to work already if it were any other day."

Feeling instantly bad, she rushed to say, "Oh, I'm sorry. I didn't think to set an alarm for you."

"You have nothing to apologize for. I'm a grown man, I know how to set an alarm." He kissed her on the forehead again and added, "Did you think maybe I didn't want to get up any earlier?" His expression was questioning. When she didn't respond, he gave her a smirk before excusing himself.

She watched him walk away until the bathroom door closed, blocking the view of his tight ass. Flashbacks of the night before, and her hands gripping those toned cheeks, made her body instantly hum with awareness. Turning to leave the bedroom, Tori shook her head and whispered to Lexi, "Can you say *Captain Orgasm*?"

A little while later, Tori was perched at the end of the couch, breastfeeding Lexi when Jason came into the room. Her position allowed her to see him before he noticed her. He'd put his jeans on but left off his shirt, and she was more than okay with that. Not only did she get to stare at his bare chest and strong back a few moments longer, but it meant he wasn't leaving yet. Having had a few quiet moments to reflect, she was battling her own insecurities. Would he leave and not call her? Nothing he'd done up to that point indicated he would do something like that, though she felt her fear was justified. Going from a man like Damien to one like Jason—too good to be true was definitely a possibility. And even though he might be, she was hoping to enjoy him for as long as she could.

When he turned his head and found her, his surprised expression made her laugh. He walked to the couch and sat close to her and Lexi, watching as she nursed. "Never seen a woman breastfeed before?"

His hand stroked over the back of Lexi's head, almost reverently, before he brought his eyes up to hers. Shaking his head, Jason answered, "Gillian and Morgan breastfed under a cover, and since they're like sisters, I really didn't pay attention. But this," his gaze fell back to Lexi, "... this is beautiful, Tori."

"Really?" she asked. For *her*, it was a beautiful thing. The beauty for her was the fact that only she could provide for Lexi in this way. For him, a person on the outside witnessing it, she was curious to know why he felt that way.

"Yeah, really. It's amazing to think what women can do with their bodies. I mean—when you think about what men can do in comparison, it's definitely a one-sided contribution." He laughed and she agreed as he continued, "Without sounding all philosophical, a woman can produce and sustain a life. Where all we were given was fertilizer and the overwhelming need to spread it everywhere."

She snorted a laugh, disturbing Lexi. When she got her latched back on she said, "That provides one hell of a disturbing visual."

Jason slipped his arm across the back of the couch and positioned himself against her shoulder. Reflexively, she leaned into him as she continued to nurse Lexi. A few moments later he asked, "Is it okay that I'm sitting with you? I don't want to intrude or make you uncomfortable."

Tori just smiled, because for as confident as he almost always was, every once and a while he'd show a bit of insecurity. She considered his supposed intrusion, especially since she cherished the time with Lexi—it was their mommy-daughter time. But she realized it didn't feel like an intrusion to her. Not with him. "It's okay, I don't mind."

She felt his body relax further. After a few moments of silence, he asked in a soft voice, "What time do you work today?"

"My shift starts at one o'clock. We have an off-site job today," she answered, shifting Lexi to her other breast. The change in position allowed Jason to rub the top of Lexi's head. His touch was so cherishing that Tori couldn't help but watch. Lexi deserved that kind of attention.

Without looking to her, Jason asked, "Do you have plans for breakfast, 'cause I could make us something or go pick up something. Or if you have the time, we could go somewhere and grab a bite."

She really didn't care what they did; she was just happy that each option involved a 'we.' Shrugging her shoulders, she looked to him. "I'm fine with anything, really. You can decide."

Jason kissed her quickly on the lips before he smiled and said, "Then I pick making something here, that way you can stay in just those panties and tank top." He waggled his eyebrows suggestively then added, "Hey, there's more cupcakes, right?"

She laughed as she recalled what Jason would do with his cupcakes. "Sadly, the cupcakes are all gone. Sorry." His disappointment was evident, and as endearing as it was, she wanted to replace that look with another one. "But there *is* frosting," she added with a smirk, and he groaned before burying his face in her neck.

~*~*~*~

JASON finally pulled up to the jobsite around one o'clock. Walking into the office, he set his laptop on the desk before placing his lunch in the fridge. It was so nice to be sent to work with a care package. From a woman he was dating. Just another first for him. How he had survived that long without experiencing it, he'd never understand. But it didn't matter, because he had a feeling it wouldn't matter if it was another woman. It was all Tori.

Sitting at his desk, he got himself situated so he could get to work. A few minutes later, Logan walked in. "Well, look who finally made it to work today."

Jason ignored Logan's condescending tone; he'd expected it. In fact, he welcomed it. After the morning he'd had, it was definitely worth it. Jason and Tori had had breakfast together, then went for a walk with Lexi. She'd let him drive her to work and had teased him about needing to return her spare tire. He'd reluctantly agreed but promised he'd find something else to use as collateral, just in case she needed an excuse to see him. It was a simple morning of them continuing to get to know each other, but it was more than satisfying, filled with stolen kisses, gentle caresses, and promises for more to come.

Smiling to himself, he flipped Logan off and continued working. Logan laughed as he dropped into his chair. "Oh, come on. You come in over five hours late, after no more than a text saying, *I'll be late*, followed by the middle finger salute. That's all I'm gonna get?"

"Fine, I promise to give you a more definite timeframe next time, boss man," Jason offered sarcastically.

"Seriously Jay, I'm not your mom or anything, but that's not like you. It's more like the crap I would pull. Is everything all right?" Logan asked. Jason agreed, as once upon a time, Logan did do stuff like that.

Jason sighed and turned his attention to Logan. "I know, but I didn't know how late I was going to be. I was keeping my options open." He finished with a smile. "And yeah, everything's good. Really good."

The two of them went about doing their own things as Logan continued the conversation. "So, I assume you were with Tori this morning, *and* you said everything's good. Congrats man, she seemed great yesterday."

"She *is* great," Jason clarified for Logan.

"You really like her?" Logan asked, though it seemed more like a statement, his voice a cross between humor and surprise. "I mean you *like her* like her, don't you?"

Looking his friend straight in the eyes, he nodded. "Yeah, I really do. Damn." He sat back in his chair and ran a hand through his hair as he evaluated his words. "It's kind of crazy, man. I was barely able to leave her this morning. If she didn't have to work today, I probably wouldn't have come in."

The pull he felt to be with Tori was shocking, to say the least. His days usually consisted of a steady routine of work, home, friends, and whatever else came up. With Tori, it was like he was just doing stuff to keep busy until he could see her again. There had been a shift in his balance. Looking at the time, he was counting down how long until he got to pick her up from work. He was comforted knowing he was definitely going to see her; there was no question as to *if*.

Logan nodded and smiled. "Sounds like the real deal for you. I've never known you to talk like that. It's kinda fun watching you fall for a woman."

He considered that, not really thinking about *what* was happening, just knowing that it was different—more. Was he falling? He wasn't sure, but he knew he wasn't going to worry about it. If he was going to fall for someone, he had no problem with it being Tori.

"Glad I could entertain you," he tossed at Logan. "Now can I get some work done?"

Hours later, he shut down the site office and headed out to pick up Tori. It didn't take too long to get to her work, so as he sat waiting for her, he assessed the possibilities for dinner. She'd fed him leftover enchiladas for lunch, so it was only right for him to take care of dinner. *Not presumptuous at all*, he told himself. Besides, if she didn't want him to stay, he still needed to feed her. Examining the route between Lexi's daycare and Tori's place, he came up with a few options.

Engrossed in his phone, he hadn't known she'd come out until there was a knock on the window. Though saddened he missed the opportunity to watch her walk to him, he hopped out and made his way to her side. "Hey you," Tori said when he rounded the car.

"Hey yourself," he said as he stole a quick kiss, not wanting to be inappropriate at her work. "How was your day?"

"Great. How was yours?" she asked as she got in. He closed the door and quickly walked around to his side before answering.

"It was good. Had a fantastic morning with this amazing woman, then she packed me a lunch that had Logan jealous, which is always fun. And now I'm going to buy her some dinner to say thank you. So my day couldn't have been better." He winked, and she gave him a smile so genuine, he wanted to lock the car doors and never let her out of his sight.

"Is that so? Well, I'm afraid that isn't going to work for me."

Instantly, his ego deflated, and he couldn't contain the disappointment. But then she smiled and said, "You're gonna have to cancel with that other chick because *I* was hoping to have dinner with you."

His smile was instantaneous. "Oh, that was good. I totally set that up for you."

"Total amateur move, big guy." Her voice was laced with laughter. "I couldn't resist."

"Ah, so you're saying you can't resist me. That's good to hear, Cupcake." She blushed before he leaned over and stole a kiss. Putting the car in gear, he pulled away from the curb and gave her the choices for dinner. He was anxious to get their evening together started and hoped his day ended much like it started ... with Tori.

CHAPTER TWENTY-ONE

TORI grabbed her make-up bag and stuffed it in her overnight bag. When she left the bathroom, she tried to think of what else she would need for the night. Excitement and nerves warred with each other as she thought of their plans for the evening. Over the past month, she and Jason had developed a routine of sorts—they spoke on the phone every day, sent each other messages, shared meals whenever time allowed it, and basically built their schedules around each other. On days when she worked in the afternoon, he would try to go in late and work late, so he could spend the time in the morning with her. She never asked him to do it, he just did. Of course, he asked if it was okay with her, which was so not what she was used to in a relationship.

It was obvious he was being cautious and trying not to smother her, and it only emphasized exactly how different he was from Damien. Even though she didn't compare the two men any longer, she couldn't help but notice simple things Jason did that had never been done for her in the past. A phone call when he was on the way over to see if she needed anything. Asking her preferences for dinner and if she even wanted to go out. All questions that never existed in her marriage to Damien.

Even before she'd married Damien, he'd simply made decisions based on his needs and expected her compliance. To him, it was her job to meet his needs. Getting lost in thought, she hadn't realized her hand had ventured up to her scar. It was an unconscious move and she didn't do it as often as she used to, but wanted to stop altogether. Refocusing on the night ahead, she prayed she wasn't out of line in assuming Jason wanted her to stay at his place. Over the past month, they had slept together plenty of times, but always at her place, and she had yet to actually sleep in his bed. Sure, they'd had sex at his place, but it was always stolen moments when Lexi was asleep or with a sitter. There was even a time or two on his lunch break. She was ready to get a little more carried away with him—to feel sexier with him.

Throwing a change of clothes into her bag, she zipped it up as Tessa strolled in the bedroom. "Okay, I have to ask, are those clean sheets on your bed?

"Of course I changed the sheets for you," Tori answered, irritated that Tessa would think she was a bad host. But when Tessa muttered a curse of disappointment under her breath, Tori looked to her in question.

Tessa flopped down on the comforter and mumbled, "I was hoping I'd be able to smell Captain Orgasm on his pillow. That way it would be like I was sleeping with a man, too."

Tori laughed and shook her head. "I don't know how you still surprise me with the shit you say, Tess."

"That's because I keep coming up with new and improved shit," Tessa said as she waggled her eyebrows. Sitting on the corner of the bed, Tori pulled on her new boots. They were a lot like a pair she used to own that Damien had thrown away, among other things of hers. Smiling down at them, she hoped Jason liked them.

Standing up, she moved to the mirror and took in her appearance. Her hair was falling in soft curls down her back, contrasting the light color of her dress. It was a strapless, cream-colored dress with a layer of eyelet lace and a thick brown belt resting high on the waist. The dress was shorter than she preferred, with the hem landing just below mid-thigh, making her legs look longer. And the position of the belt seemed to emphasizing her breasts. Overall, she was happy with how she looked, and she hoped for Jason's approval, as well.

Turning to get a view of the back, she made sure the curve of her rear didn't shorten the dress too much. From the bed, Tessa said, "You look hot, all you're missing is a cowboy hat to match your boots."

Tori smiled. "I know, right; it would totally make the outfit. I used to have one ... maybe next time."

She grabbed her bag, and Tessa followed her into the living room. Tori leaned forward and kissed a napping Lexi. It was the first time she would spend the night away from her, and she couldn't help the small dose of anxiety that surged through her system. She wanted to be alone with Jason, but didn't like feeling as though she was abandoning her daughter—no matter how irrational the thought.

"She'll be fine, Tori; don't worry about her. As soon as you leave here, you get to have Jason all to yourself. Parents do this all the time."

Taking a deep breath, Tori let it out slowly, feeling some of the apprehension lessen at Tessa's words. "I know, but I still feel a little guilty."

"Totally normal," Tessa said as she slung her arm around Tori's shoulder. "Now, did you bring something sexy to wear later? Alone time doesn't happen often so you have to make the best of it."

"Honestly, I thought about it, but I think Jason would be just fine with me in nothing but my boots and panties." She smiled at the image of her standing before him like that.

They both turned at the sound of Jason pulling in the drive. Tori slung her bag over her shoulder and went to the door, wanting to escape without waking Lexi. If she woke up before they left, it would be too hard to leave. Waving to Tessa, she grabbed her cropped denim jacket to wear after the sun went down. As she gently closed the door, she heard Jason before she saw him. "Holy shit ..."

She looked over her shoulder to find Jason staring at her from a few yards away. Flipping her hair back, she turned and smiled before walking to him. By the time she stopped in front of him, he hadn't said anything else, but his expression screamed loud and clear—he was a fan of her outfit. The ability to render him speechless was empowering.

With her best flirty voice, she said, "Hey handsome, you wanna be my date for the night?"

His hand met her waist, and she found herself anchored against a hard, very aroused man. He let out a long, shaky breath and with a low, husky voice, he answered, "Your date? Hell, Tori, I want to be your *everything* tonight."

Holy shit is right. She didn't know what to say to that, so she just smiled. With his eyes locked on hers, the hunger and passion he showed her so well was there, lingering in the icy depths. After finally pressing his lips against hers, she could feel him trembling, holding back. She knew if she said the word, he'd unleash all that hunger. It made her feel like she was *his* everything.

Pulling his lips from hers, he bent down and wrapped his arms around her legs, before standing back up. Tori squealed as her body was lifted straight up in the air—against his. Now looking down at him, she giggled, resting her hands on his shoulders as he turned and carried her to the truck.

"I so badly want to throw you over my shoulder and carry you back inside, but I'll settle for carrying you like this. Because at least you're against my body."

"Sounds good to me," she said, kissing him again. He groaned and placed her on the ground by the passenger door. Opening it, he took her bag and helped her in.

"What's in the bag? Cupcakes by chance?"

She laughed and rolled her eyes. "No. Have you thought about having your cupcake addiction to checked out? It's borderline obsessive."

Jason started the truck and said, "Oh, I'm addicted for sure, but it's not the baked goods kind." He winked and turned his attention to the road. *Damn, he really said the best things.*

"Got the charm on full force tonight I see. You hoping to get lucky or something?" she teased.

"Hell, I've already gotten lucky, anything else is just a bonus, *Cupcake*."

~*~*~*~

JASON was ready to call it a night. He was ready to blow off the rest of the concert and find a place where he could devote all his attention to Tori. Friends be damned. The only thing keeping him from storming off with her—caveman style—was the smile on her face. She was enjoying herself, and he wasn't about to ruin that. Scanning the crowd, he tried to find her again. The three women had ventured to the bathroom, leaving the men to stand in line for drinks. Personally, he thought one of the men should have gone with them.

The ratio of men to women at the concert was definitely tipped on the testosterone side. Everywhere he looked there were cowboys prowling around everything in a skirt. And Tori was wearing a skirt—a very short skirt in fact. He perused the crowd again, anxious to lay eyes on her. Focused on finding her, he was startled a moment later when he felt a hand on his arm. Looking down, he found a young woman smiling up at him. The line moved so he excused himself and stepped forward, tapping Jake on the shoulder.

When Jake turned around, Jason moved in to tell him he was going to look for the girls, but a hand on his arm held him up. Thinking it was Tori, he was disappointed to find it was the same woman from a minute ago, and she was now leaning into him, wearing an expression that could only be described as an invitation. While it wasn't an invitation he would've accepted ever, it especially irritated him right now. He wanted Tori's hands on him.

"Excuse me," he said more curtly and moved his arm. Ignoring her, he looked back to Jake. "I'm going to find the girls. It's too much of a meat market around here, and I don't like it."

Jason laughed and gestured behind him. "Relax Jay, they're right there."

He spun to look for Tori, relaxing when he finally laid eyes on her. Taking the water Jake handed him, he moved quickly. Once she was close enough, he wrapped his arm around her waist and pulled her against him. Giggling, she asked, "Whoa, did someone miss me?"

"I don't think you should go anywhere without me the rest of the night," he grumbled, giving her the water.

She took a sip. "Hmm, well, if you insist. I bet you'll have loads of fun in the ladies room." With a wink, she continued, "There would be plenty of admirers ... like that one in line with you."

Jason huffed a laugh and wrapped both arms around her, "Well, if you want to bring up admirers, you should know there are at least ten sets of eyes on those sexy legs of yours right now. And every one of them is trying to figure out a way to get them wrapped around their waist."

Her finger trailed a path up and down his chest, teasing him. She smiled coyly and asked, "What about you? Is there a set of legs around here that you're wishing were wrapped around your waist? 'Cause I can totally be your wingman. You just show me who, and I will definitely talk you up."

She wanted to play, huh? Jason loved her sarcastic side, but also knew he didn't want to joke about some things. He wanted to make sure she understood her legs were the only ones he was thinking about. *Only hers*. "Baby, the only legs that have my attention are yours."

She smirked, and he felt her slip one of her legs between his, rubbing up and down like a cat. He wanted to purr at her sexiness.

"So, you're not the least bit interested in any other legs?"

"Not in the least," he assured her, giving her leg a squeeze between his.

"Positive? Because we might be able to find someone who would be open to joining us." The sultry tone of her voice coupled with her words were almost his undoing.

Jason's eyes widened, and he sucked in a breath. "Did you really just say that? Holy shit ... are you trying to kill me?" His beautiful little smartass was playing hardball.

Again, she giggled. "What?" she asked with feigned innocence. "Are you saying that's not something you'd like? Tessa has offered plenty of times. I could just call her ..."

His nostrils flared, and he pressed firmly into her, his erection obvious through his jeans. A man could only handle so much. "You feel that?" he growled in a low tone.

Tori nodded, unfettered desire sparkling in her eyes. "That's all you. I've been dealing with *that* since you walked out of the house wearing that dress and those boots." His body ached as he pressed into her again to emphasize his point. "*You* are the one who got me like this, and only *you* can satisfy my cravings." Jason hoped his expression conveyed just as much as his words did.

The world around them had already disappeared, but when the lights in the venue fell, shrouding them in semi-darkness, he could feel the hum of their combined arousal cloaking them. The music for the main act began to fill the air, followed by excitement of the crowd, but all he could see was her. Shielded in the darkness, he wrapped his arms around her waist and lifted her up.

Unable to wait any longer, his lips descended on hers, and he took. When he felt her legs wrap around his waist, his hips pushed forward on reflex, seeking more contact. He moved his hands to her ass, securing her tightly against him. She whimpered as she ground herself against the bulge of his jeans, torturing them both. His hold was firm as held her immobile, trying to prevent instincts from taking over. They were in public, and her pleasure was for him alone. When she tried to move again, he growled and dropped his lips to her ear. "You are playing with fire my little Cupcake."

CHAPTER TWENTY-TWO

TORI wanted to crawl out of her skin from the anticipation. She and Jason had been torturing each other all evening. As the concert progressed, it became harder not to just grab his hand and drag him out of there, all while making demands like *'Take me to your place and make me scream your name over and over.'* Every time she came in contact with Jason's body, she realized he was suffering all the same. Between the straining bulge in his jeans and the rumbling growl she felt coming from his chest, she knew he was right there with her. Thankfully the concert was over.

Their whole group walked out together. At the beginning of the evening, she'd thought it silly that they all had their own vehicles. Now, though, she was grateful. She didn't want to deal with dropping people off. It might have been a bit callous of her, but she was dying to be close to Jason. After saying quick goodbyes and making promises to drive safely, Jason was finally helping her into his truck.

Before he closed the door, she felt a breeze as her skirt lifted, followed by the undeniable presence of his teeth pressing into her butt cheek. She let out a squeal and turned to look down at him. He was grinning like a Cheshire cat, obviously happy with her reaction. Keeping his gaze on hers, he lowered his lips and kissed the area he'd just bitten. Then the grin was back as he said, "Couldn't help myself. I've been dying for a piece of that ass all night."

Shaking her head, she laughed at his not-so-subtle innuendo, saying, "Well, is that all you want, just a piece?"

He hopped onto the side step and crowded into her space. His voice was low and firm as he gripped her chin between his thumb and forefinger. "Oh, I want a lot more than just a *piece,* Tori. I want it all."

A shiver moved down her spine, leaving goose bumps in its wake. Her hands found the back of his neck, and her fingers teased the short hair there as she said, "Then I think you better take me back to your place so you *can* have it all ... all night long."

One side of his mouth lifted in a half-smile, and his eyes brightened. "Really, I get to keep you tonight? All to myself, at my house, in my bed, for the entire night?"

Excitement laced his words as he finished his sentence. She wanted to laugh at how something so simple as being at his house, alone, could make him that happy. She nodded. "You sure do."

As if he needed to make sure he understood, he asked again, "Tessa is staying with Lexi overnight, and I get to keep you?"

Tilting her head to the side, she asked, "Is that okay with you?"

Leaning in, Jason captured her lips for a chaste kiss. "It's more than okay, baby. I'm just so excited I had to make sure I wasn't hearing you wrong. Are *you* okay with it? It's your first night away from Lexi."

Tori was pretty damn certain she loved Jason. She knew it, but she just hadn't told him yet. And when he put his own desires aside to acknowledge his concerns for her, she wondered why she hadn't. Tori was in love with Jason, and it was something she needed to make sure he knew. Even if she was a bit chicken-shit for not saying it. She would. Soon.

Until the right moment came, she would do her best to show him her feelings. Stroking his cheek, he leaned into her hand, seeking more of her. "Could you be any sweeter?" she asked in awe. "Yes, I'm okay with it. You deserve a night of my undivided attention. I want all of you, too."

His lips were on hers a heartbeat later, consuming her. The passion they had been battling all evening, which had temporarily dimmed there in the cab of his truck, ignited again. Needing to rein it in, she broke the heated connection. With her hands on his face, she leaned her forehead against his, their breaths coming deep and hard. "Take me home, Jason," she whispered.

After one more quick kiss of his lips on hers, he hopped down from his perch and closed the door without another word. Tori smiled to herself. Yes, she loved Jason Michaels, and tonight seemed like the perfect time to tell him.

JASON once again found himself trying to control his inappropriate thoughts. His desire to drive his truck through every vehicle slowing his exit from the dirt lot. His need to slide Tori across the front seat and into his lap. His longing to pull over to the side of the road and slam his over-hardened body into hers over and over again.

These extreme emotions had plagued him since he first caught sight of his emerald-eyed beauty. And as he thought on those emotions, he recalled all the times he gave his friends crap over being whipped. It didn't take a genius to figure out he'd fallen hard on his ass for Tori. He wasn't lying when he said he wanted all of her, and he intended to *take* all of her.

It didn't take them too long to get out of the packed parking lot, but it was still longer than Jason liked. These strangers sitting in traffic with him were wasting his time—his alone time with Tori. Reaching over, he took her hand in his, needing to touch her. They smiled at each other, not speaking and not needing to. He could see the excitement in her expression and loved that it mirrored his own.

Not long after, he was pulling into his driveway. Instructing Tori to wait there, he exited the truck and grabbed her bag from the back. When he opened her door, she gave him a questioning look. Taking her hand, he pulled it as he dropped his shoulder to her waist. With a surprised yell, followed by her laughter, he was striding toward his front door, Tori resting firmly over his shoulder.

Her hands were hovering on the waist of his jeans, playing with his bare skin before slipping below the waistband. One of his hands caressed the softness of her legs and the other brushed over the mound of her ass. Giving it a playful smack, he said, "Behave yourself back there, Cupcake."

Tori giggled again, "So says the caveman carrying me to his lair. I can only imagine what your neighbors would think."

The image of her draped over his shoulder, her long hair reaching for the ground, firm ass high in the air, popped in his head. He groaned at the erotic vision that tugged at every testosterone-laced cell in his body. Given the lack of blood in his brain, he was impressed by his ability to still function with menial tasks such as opening the door. And closing it for that matter. After securing the locks and tossing his keys on the table, he headed straight for the stairs.

Tori's arms, now wrapped around the front of his body, were making their way toward his straining erection. *A man could really only handle so much*, he thought as his hand captured both of hers, halting their assault. "I said, behave."

"How do expect me to behave myself when your ass is in my face. I need to touch!" she said in a voice mixed with arousal and sarcasm.

Jason strode into his bedroom, dropping Tori's bag on his way toward the bed. Stopping in front of it, he let her body slowly slide down his front, his hands gliding up the back of her thighs until her ass filled them. She wrapped her legs around his waist, and their eyes met. Silent as they stared, his hands cradled her against his body while hers rested on his shoulders. Her hair was tousled from her upside-down journey, making her even sexier than before—easily the most beautiful thing he'd ever seen.

They were tightly wound and their breathing was shallow, as the current between them grew in intensity. Tori's hand moved to his neck, finding his hair. For a moment, she stroked it gently. Then, fisting it tightly, she held his head immobile as she leaned toward his face. In a sexy voice she asked, "Can I misbehave now?"

TORI watched as lust flared in Jason's eyes. She'd never been so brazen as she was with Jason. Something about him and the way he looked at her fueled her desires to the level of combustion. He was a drug her body craved. With her hand still gripping his hair, she held his gaze while she slowly slid her tongue across his plump bottom lip. Teasing the beast. He sucked in a shaky breath, and she felt the band on his restraint snap.

His lips claimed hers, then she was falling. Held tight in his arms, her back met the bed. His hands found her hair and angled her head to the side, exposing her neck to him. Jason knew her body well; he seemed to take note of every noise and every whimper she made. Telling him where to return again, and he always did. Sliding his tongue upward, he found her weak spot and nibbled on it. Each scrape of teeth across her sensitive nerve endings sent a pulsing sensation down to her core. Never had she imagined there could be a direct current passing between the two areas. When he sucked hard on the sensitive area, she gasped, and her body began rubbing against his, seeking more contact.

Like always, he knew she needed more. Lifting off her, he pulled the top of her dress down, exposing her chest to his hungry gaze. He shifted his weight so he could cup her aching breasts before feasting on her feverish skin. She watched as he nipped, sucked, and licked. Wetness pooled between her legs, and she once again arched her body into his.

She sighed, closing her eyes as she whispered his name. Not knowing what else to say, it was all she could get out, but it was all he needed to hear. His weight left her body and her eyes shot open. She watched as he tore his shirt over his head before getting to work on her belt and dress. Within moments, she was lying before him in only her panties and boots. He slid off the bed, and she continued to watch as he removed his own boots and pants. Standing above her, his eyes traveled the length of her almost naked body before landing on her boots, causing a shiver to overtake her.

Reaching out, his finger found the skin of her inner leg and followed the path his eyes had just made. When he reached her foot, he picked up her leg and kissed her just above the boot before sliding it off. "I really like your boots, baby. But I'm feeling a bit selfish tonight." Placing her leg down, he repeated the action with the other leg as he continued, "I don't want any of your skin hidden from me."

Staring at his boxer briefs, she gave him a sultry smile. "The feeling is mutual. Lose the briefs, handsome."

He grinned back at her before his hands found the waistband, and he lost the briefs. Standing before her, gloriously naked, she watched as he gripped his hard length. He slowly moved his fist as he waited. "If you like those panties, baby, you better get rid of them ... now."

At his command, she moved without hesitation and quickly removed the final barrier. He didn't take his eyes off hers as he retrieved a condom and rolled it on. Her eyes bounced from his to the movements of his hands.

The stark rawness of his actions brought her wanton side further to the surface. Lying back on the bed, she could no longer stand the distance between them. Beckoning him, she held her hand out. "All of me, Jason ... come get what's yours."

With a growl, he moved to her. Prowling up the length of her body, his hands squeezed, his tongue stroked, and his teeth grazed until his body was nestled in the cradle of her legs. His skin was hot against hers, and her body relaxed at the sensation of rightness just from having his weight against her. Jason's hips moved, sliding his erection against her hot center. She gasped, and he caught it with his lips. When he broke away, he stilled above her, capturing her gaze. Then he slowly slid inside.

He watched her as he always did. She knew everything she felt played across her face. The sweet ecstasy of how he filled her never got old, and she could feel him respond to her expressions. It was a loop of actions and reactions that fueled each other. Jason paused, letting her body stretch and accommodate his intrusion. Tori's hands traveled the planes of his back, from neck to ass, loving the strength she could feel residing there.

Jason slowly started to move his hips, pulling away from her, before doing it all over again, pulling a sigh from her. There really were no words to describe the pleasure she felt, just from being with him like this. The love she felt for him began to swell in her chest and threatened to pour out. Biting her lip, she wrapped her leg around him, urging him to move faster.

One of his hands found the back of her neck, and the other found her hip as he moved with more urgency. Bracing her body under his, he rocked his hips, grinding them against her enflamed nerve endings. It was the sweetest torture. In and out, his body pounded into hers as they both reached for the release that hovered in the distance. Feeling his need mount, her body responded and clenched around him, pulling a groan from him. Jason dropped his face to her chest and once again began an all-out assault on her sensitive flesh.

Taking her nipple in his mouth, he sucked on the tip before letting his teeth bite down gently. She gasped, and the sensation shot down to her now throbbing core. The loop of sensations continued as her responses fueled his actions. His hand moved from her hip to ass, lifting her into his body more firmly, sending him deeper. Grabbing his hair, she pulled him from her breast to her mouth. She needed to taste him, too. Together, they fed off each other as Jason's movements quickened, demanding their release.

Moments later, her body coiled like a spring and then let go. Her head fell back as she cried out his name and dug her nails into his shoulders. Jason grumbled a curse before dropping his face to her neck. His teeth found the tendon there as his thrusts became more labored and his body tightened above hers. Riding out the waves of her own pleasure, she felt him swell moments before his body exploded within her.

When their movements slowed to a stop, she relished the weight of his body on top of hers. With a smile, she thought to herself how this was exactly where she was meant to be.

CHAPTER TWENTY-THREE

JASON had taken full advantage of having Tori all to himself. It wasn't that he didn't enjoy having Lexi around; he just hadn't realized the how great it would be to have Tori's attention solely on him. And vice versa. Did that make him greedy? Probably. Did he care? Maybe a little, but he tried to ignore it. Lexi was in good hands, and they'd both see her in the morning. Right now, though, Tori was all his.

Nestled tightly into his side, Tori lay with a soft, naked leg draped across his. Her arm was resting on his chest, and her fingers were currently tracing an unknown pattern on his skin. Her long hair was spread out behind her, and Jason found himself twirling the ends of it around his fingers, loving the silky texture. Loving the feel of her body against his. Loving her. His arm reflexively tightened around her at the thought of love, breaking whatever trance she was in.

Lifting her head, she propped it up on her fist resting on his chest, and gave him a shy smile. Reaching up, he swept her hair out of her face, tucking it behind her ear. Everything felt right, and he knew it was time to lay it all on the table. He wanted her, all of her, just like he said earlier. She may not have realized that when he said *all*, he really meant all. He wanted to own her heart the way she owned his.

Tilting his head to the side a little, he asked, "Do you know how beautiful you are?"

She rolled her eyes and scoffed at his words. "I'll accept pretty as a description, but I think beautiful might be a bit above me."

Giving his head a shake in disbelief, he said, "It really doesn't matter what you think you are, because the facts are clear as day. You. Are. Beautiful." He punctuated each of his words by tapping the tip of her nose. She didn't respond, but he could see the doubt in her eyes. Rolling them over, he positioned her beneath him, wanting her full attention. "Why wouldn't you believe you're beautiful?"

She tried to turn her face to avoid his question, but he caught it. Planting his elbows on either side of her head, he boxed her in so she had no choice but to hear him. He leaned forward and kissed the tip of her nose. "Tell me how you could be considered anything other than beautiful."

When he pulled back, he could see tears welling in her eyes before she blinked them away. In a small voice she whispered, "My scars."

Scars? He made a mental note to revisit the subject later. Not wanting to disregard it, but wanting to keep the conversation on track, he said, "You have more than one scar, baby? I've only noticed the one on your cheek, and the only reason I can see it, is because I see *all* of you." He pressed his lips against her scar. From the corner of her mouth to the end by her ear, he kissed it repeatedly. When he reached the end, he whispered against her ear, "You are beautiful."

A small giggle escaped her, making him smile. Pulling back he caught the blush on her cheeks, which only made her more attractive. A woman who could shy away from direct attention but accept it when given intrigued him. When she caught him looking at her, she said, “You know, when you say it, it’s almost believable.”

He gave her a satisfied smile as he swooped down and stole another kiss. Her body went soft beneath him, and he groaned in response. He wanted her again, but not before he said what he needed to say. In an attempt to gain control, he rolled them to their sides, so they were facing each other with their heads on one pillow. Running the back of his fingers down her cheek, she sighed and closed her eyes.

“You are beautiful, Tori. And if I have to say it over and over each and every day to make you believe it, I will. I can make it my mission in life to prove it to you,” he said with clear sincerity.

Opening her eyes, she stated softly, “That’s a pretty big commitment.” He acknowledged her statement with a small nod. A few silent moments stretched out between them before she rolled to her back and stared at the ceiling.

“Why me?” she asked, doubt evident in her voice.

He threw his leg over hers and pulled her body firmly against his. Propping himself up on one elbow, he gently swept her hair away from her face, exposing her long neck. The softness of her skin enticed him. Finding her gaze, he smiled. “I could ask you the same question.”

She scoffed at his comment and rolled her eyes. "Don't be ridiculous, Jason. There's nothing more obvious than why *any* woman would want you."

His gaze moved to the vibrant colors of her hair as he ran his hand through it, once again marveling in the silky texture. She was an aphrodisiac in the purest form. Her hair, her skin, her voice, her gaze. All of it turned his blood to boiling and set his nerve endings on fire. It had never been like this before. There was no other woman whose smile had the power to bring him to his knees. He needed to make her see—to know the extent of her power over him.

"You want to know why?" he asked as he slipped his hand into the hair behind her neck before bringing his gaze back to hers.

She whispered, "Yes."

"Because from the moment you walked into my life, everyone else disappeared. You're the first thought I have when I wake and the last thought I have when I fall asleep. Because when something happens during my day, you're the first person I want to share it with. Because I know without a doubt, that if you were to walk away from me, I wouldn't survive it. I choose you, Tori." Leaning forward, he rubbed his nose back and forth across the tip of hers. Pulling back, he watched as a tear slipped down her temple, getting lost in her hair. "Why you? Because you're *the one*. I love you."

TORI felt her eyes widen and her heart stall in her chest. He loved her? The shock of his statement didn't drown out the irony of how she was battling her need to tell him how she felt for *him*. Here she was, holding it back, fearing his rejection. No, not his rejection; she feared exposing her heart like that. When you did, it left you vulnerable to pain. But she knew there was far more to love than the pain of loss. She was ashamed she had withheld her feelings from him.

They were silent as she pondered how to reply. *I love you too* could be seen as a reflex answer, and she didn't want him to think she was just saying it, even though it was true. The silence must have triggered his insecurity, and she wanted to curse as she saw him begin to withdraw. His eyes averted from hers and looked to be questioning himself. Dislodging her legs from under his, she pushed him to his back and climbed on top. Straddling him, she distracted his thoughts with a fevered kiss.

It took him a moment to respond, but when she felt his hands on her ass, she relented her assault. Lifting up, she let the veil of her hair fall around them. With her hands on his chest, she could feel his heart beating hard, and she wanted to smile at how it mirrored hers. When she finally felt like her voice was strong enough, she said, "Please don't mistake my silence as anything other than being taken by surprise—"

Jason cut her off. "I know you probably think it's too soon. I understand, but I've seen what happens when people lose someone, and I couldn't handle not telling you how I felt ..."

He looked as if he was going to keep going, and she needed him to stop. Placing a finger to his lips, she said, "Did you know you babble when you're nervous?"

A smile graced his face. "Apparently, but only when it pertains to you."

Dropping her lips down to his, she kissed him thoroughly before pulling back and finishing what she'd been trying to say. "As I was trying to say, please don't mistake my silence as anything other than surprise because I was trying to figure out how to tell you that I feel the exact same way."

His hands tightened on her waist when she spoke, but he didn't say anything. So she pushed on and told him, "I love you, Jason."

That magnetic, full-toothed grin spread across his face. "You love me?"

She nodded, her hair shifting around them. "I do."

"Why?" he asked with a grin. *So he was going to play it like that?* He poured his heart out, and now wanted her to do the same. Okay, she was the girl in the relationship, so she could do it, too.

Sighing, she said, "I love you because you see me. All of me. Because when we're in a crowd of people or friends, I can always look for you and find your eyes on me. I love you because you treat me like I'm a treasure, to be cherished and valued. Because when I call you at any time of the day, you take the time to listen to me like my words are the most important part of your day. And if all of that wasn't enough, I love you because of how you love my daughter. I never thought it was possible to find a man who would treat her as if she were his own."

Tears formed in her eyes and had now run down and dripped on to his chest. But he remained silent. "I love you because I, too, know that if you were to walk away from me, I'd die inside. Because you ... are my everything."

Jason sat up quickly and captured her lips. She wrapped her arms tightly around his neck and kissed him back. All the passion they normally had multiplied with the admission of their love. He held her against him and shifted their bodies so he was again lying on top of her. Sweeping her hair out of their faces, he continued to kiss her as he rubbed his body against hers. He blindly reached for a condom and only left her long enough to put it on.

When he finally slid his body into hers, they both sighed. Capturing her lips again, he set up a fevered pace as he pushed her body to the limits. Demanding she take what he was giving her until she was once again relishing in the ecstasy that only Jason seemed able to provide, she gasped at the force of his thrusts, and cried out his name before burying her face in his neck. He held her there as he continued to push them both to the top, before finally letting them both fall over the edge together.

Lying together in a heap of sweaty limbs, trying to catch their breaths, she tasted the salty skin of his neck. He shivered and pulled back to stare at her. She let him see all of her as she smiled. "I love you, Jason."

"I love you, too."

CHAPTER TWENTY-FOUR

TORI had just laid Lexi down for a nap in the room Jason had set up for her when her phone rang. She didn't recognize the number, but it was the second time that day it had called. No message was left the first time so she was apprehensive to answer. She ignored the call and headed downstairs, hoping the caller would choose to leave a message this time.

Dropping onto the couch, she set the baby monitor down and picked up her book. She wanted to enjoy a few minutes of quiet while Lexi was asleep and Jason was out. Since he was picking up pizza for dinner, and Logan was coming over, she knew it was her only opportunity. A few minutes later, her phone rang again showing the same number. Annoyed, she answered, her tone reflecting her feelings. "Hello."

"Is this Victoria Chambers?" the unidentified voice asked. His use of her full, married name had her immediately on alert. With no idea who this person was or how he got her name and attached it to her number, she denied it. She wasn't that person anymore.

"I'm sorry, but you must have the wrong number." Before she could hang up, she heard him desperately trying to get her attention. "Please, Victoria, it's Mack, don't hang up."

Oh my God. "Mack?" she repeated his name hesitantly. As if that would change the fact he was calling her. Tears immediately began to blur her vision.

"Yeah, sweetheart. How are you doing?" he asked in a soft voice, as if approaching a scared animal, afraid she would flee at any moment. She didn't blame him for that, since it was how he knew her. Until the day he saved her. She'd never forget how her neighbor, who she'd never been allowed to speak to, saved her life. When so many people would've looked the other direction, thought of themselves, he didn't.

A sob escaped as she was overcome with emotion for how much she owed this man. "I'm good Mack ... I'm really good."

"That's so great to hear, sweetheart. I'm sorry if I scared you, but I didn't know what name you went by now," he said apologetically.

A few tears escaped even as she smiled. Dashing them away, she told him, "I go by Tori now."

"It suits you; not that your full name doesn't, but I can see you as a Tori."

"Thank you," she said, not really sure what else to say. She was still Victoria and always would be. But hearing it out loud now reminded her of Damien, it was something else he took from her. A few moments of silence passed before she asked, "How did you get my number, Mack?"

"It took a little work, but back when you needed a reference for your landlord, you called me from it. Do you remember that?" She nodded. Even though he couldn't see it, he continued as if he had. "I went through my old cell phone records and tracked it down."

"Why did you need to track it down?" she whispered, dread creeping in to her chest.

He heaved a sigh and paused a moment, as if he was trying to gather the strength to tell her. His apprehension confirmed what she knew he was going to say before he said it.

"He's being released ... I was given a courtesy call two days ago since I'm listed on a restraining order for him. When I asked the person calling if you were, they said there wasn't one in place with your name on it. So I knew I had to track you down." His tone was full of regret as he explained. A virtual stranger to her up until the day she cried for help, and he was thoughtful enough to seek her out. To protect her. Again.

Closing her eyes, she took a deep breath, trying to clear the lump in her throat. It was threatening to choke her as that day played through her mind. Tears were steadily falling now, unbeknownst to her and completely out of her control. Holding the tears back, she said, "Thank you, Mack ... for everything."

"You don't have to thank me for anything, sweetheart. I just knew I had to find you and make sure you knew. After the way he managed to manipulate the charges against him, I was concerned you weren't protected. That you were alone."

Alone? No, she wasn't alone. Jason would protect her; she knew this in her heart. But guilt crowded in at the danger she could be placing him in, just by being with her. Damien wouldn't accept that another man had what, in his mind, belonged to him. As if conjured by her thoughts, Jason walked in the house. She watched as he entered the kitchen and set down the pizzas he had picked up, not knowing the turmoil she was experiencing only ten feet away from him. When he turned to ask her a question, he could immediately tell something was wrong and rushed across the room to her.

Dropping on his knees in front of her, he asked, "What's wrong, baby? Are you hurt?" His voice was panicked as his eyes roamed over her body, clearly looking for any indication as to why she was crying. When he noticed the phone against her ear, his eyes went to hers in question.

Her free hand lifted to his face and cupped his cheek. His hand covered hers as his other one found its way around her waist. Kneeling in front of her, he pressed his body against hers, comforting her. Even if it wasn't his intention, that's what it did. Taking a shaky breath, she soothed Mack's concerns. "No, Mack ... I'm not alone anymore."

Jason's body tensed up, but he didn't say anything.

"That's great, it makes me feel better to know that," Mack said, relief clear in his voice. She smiled through her tears as she watched a surplus of emotions cross Jason's face. Strain, pain, fear, anger. He would protect her. He would protect Lexi. She wanted to make sure Mack could get a hold of her if needed, so she asked, "Mack, can I give you an alternate number to reach me? It's not just me I need to look after anymore, and if I need to know something immediately, I want to make sure you can reach one of us."

"You got it, sweetheart. Give me the other number." She gave him the number and finished the call, promising to check in with him periodically. He, too, promised to let her know if Damien resurfaced at the house. After his arrest, because he owned the house free and clear and was at no risk of losing it while in jail, he made sure she was promptly locked out. It was assumed the house would remain empty until he returned. Which was apparently sooner than hoped.

Hanging up the call, she closed her eyes and let her head fall back. Jason didn't waste any time getting into her space. He quickly lifted her into his arms and took her seat on the couch. Pulling her tightly against him, he cradled her body, infusing it with warmth and strength, fighting off the paralyzing fear she could easily get lost in. Jason was her rock, her anchor in the storm, and she held onto him knowing the waters were about to get rougher. She knew he needed information, he deserved to hear the whole story. He deserved to know what he was getting into just by being with her, just because he loved her. It was time for Jason to learn about Victoria.

JASON felt like his heart might explode in his chest. The pain he saw etched on Tori's face gutted him. But there was fear, too. Instinct to protect and destroy whatever caused her that pain overwhelmed him and threatened his capacity to breathe. Now that he held her tightly in his embrace, he calmed a little, but not by much. He needed to know what was wrong, so he could fix it and prevent it from putting that look on her face again. So he could destroy it if necessary—all she had to do was tell him.

Tori clung to him, her arms wrapped firmly around his neck. Little sobs escaped periodically, and the shoulder of his shirt was wet against his skin. He knew she had to let it out, so he let her do it silence, content just holding her for now. Noticing Lexi wasn't in the room, he spied the baby monitor and figured she was napping in her room. Well, it wasn't her room, yet. But if he had his way, it would be.

When Tori's sobs relented and her body relaxed under the soothing strokes of his hand down her back, he kissed the top of her head. A few minutes later, she pulled her head from his neck and found his eyes. Red, puffy eyes stared back at him as she sniffled.

He smoothed her hair out of her face and waited for her to talk to him. Fortunately, she didn't make him wait much longer. With a hitch in her voice, she told him that Mack was her old neighbor, that he was the one to save her from Damien. She explained about the scar on her stomach and how she thought it had ended Lexi's life before it even began.

Tori explained how Damien threatened to 'take care of the problem' because her body belonged to him. Tori told him how her full name was Victoria, but she went by Tori now because her full name reminded her too much of Damien. Also hoping it made it harder for him to find her. Then she told him that she'd understand if all of this was too much to take on, and that if he chose to be without her, she would let him. But he had heard enough.

In a stern voice, he silenced her, "I've heard all I need to hear, Tori." He paused and watched as her eyes widened at his words, so he continued, "Out of everything you just said to me, do you want to know what pisses me off the most?"

A tear slipped from the corner of her right eye, crossing over her scar. Unconsciously, his hand sought out her cheek, and his thumb gently ran over its path. She hadn't answered him, and she didn't need to, because he would tell her anyway. "It was the part where you said that if I wanted to go, you would let me. Now I can't say for sure which is worse. The fact that you think I would want to go, or that you would let me go."

"Jason ..." Her voice came out choked and pleading. He hushed her with a finger to her lips.

"Tori, did you believe me last night when I told you I loved you?" he asked, hoping she couldn't tell how scared he was she'd say no. So when she answered with a nod, the tightness in his chest released. Pushing forward, he asked, "Did you mean it when you said you loved me?"

She wrapped her hand around the finger he still had pressed against her lips and pulled it away. She cleared her throat and swept her tongue across her bottom lip before saying, "Yes, I love you very much."

Again, his chest tightened as her words washed over him. Never before had he felt so vulnerable at the hands of another. Yes, she'd said it before, but in the shadow of her fears, it had a more profound meaning to him. Leaning his forehead against hers, he sighed her name.

"I love you, Tori. You and Lexi are mine, and I vow to do whatever is necessary to make you understand that. We can handle whatever the future—or your past—hurls at us. You understand that? You and Lexi are *mine*. Mine to protect. Mine to keep."

Another tear escaped when she nodded, her eyes holding his. "I understand ... we're yours."

CHAPTER TWENTY-FIVE

JASON knew Logan would be arriving shortly. Standing up, he pulled Tori with him. After giving her another hug, he kissed her forehead, and said, "Why don't you take a minute to freshen up before Logan gets here."

Her puffy eyes widened. "Oh, I must look terrible. I should just go home." She wiped at her cheeks, blindly looking for evidence of her makeup.

"Sorry, baby, but you're not going home tonight. Until we know more details, you and Lexi are safer here," Jason said, as sternly as he could. He didn't want to come across as a controlling asshole, but there wasn't going to be any give on this. She and Lexi were staying there, end of story. When she tried to speak up, he silenced her with a finger to her lips. "Don't even try to argue with me about it. We have spent most nights together at your house, so now we'll just spend them here. I'm not budging on this."

"Okay," she whispered.

"Now, I'd like to call that Mack guy back. Can I have your phone?" he asked, putting his hand out for it. She handed it to him without question. He was happy she was letting him take the lead on this. "Thank you. Go ahead and freshen up, take your time, and I'll listen for Lexi."

She nodded and gave him a weak smile before turning and heading for the stairs. Jason closed his eyes and took a deep breath, trying to control the roll of emotions that were beating at his insides. He fell onto the couch, and his head dropped to his hands. Between the new information he got from Tori about her marriage and the actual threat of knowing her ex-husband was being released, he thought he might lose it. His heart hammered in his chest as he recalled her entire story. As if he didn't already have a mountain of respect for Tori, it had increased exponentially with the new details.

Jason also realized what a sadistic bastard Damien really was. He needed to come up with a game plan to make sure she wasn't in any danger. He needed details.

Dialing the last number that called her phone, it rang three times before a man's voice came across the line. "Victoria, are you okay?"

Jason didn't like this guy calling her that. She was Tori. Not only was that the name of the woman he met and fell in love with, but Jason also knew she didn't want to be called Victoria any longer. Without coming across as rude, he said, "Tori is fine. She's a little upset, as I'm sure you can understand, but she'll be all right."

"Who I am speaking with?" Mack asked.

"My name is Jason Michaels. I'm the reason Tori isn't alone anymore," Jason said. He wasn't sure why he said it like that, but just calling himself her 'boyfriend' didn't seem to sound important enough. He felt like more, because she was more than a 'girlfriend' to him.

"Good, I'm glad she isn't alone. I was worried about calling her, but knew I had to find her. She didn't leave any information with the officer that handled her case so I knew she wouldn't have known otherwise," Mack offered.

Jason nodded to himself. This man seemed like a good guy, and Jason appreciated that he took the time to find her. "Thank you for tracking her down. She not only has to worry about herself, but her daughter, so I'm grateful you did."

"I couldn't sleep thinking of her out there somewhere, unprotected. I was there when her ex went to court. I saw how he manipulated a deal out of them, saying she assaulted him in his own kitchen. Though I will say, I was pleased to see she'd permanently injured him."

Jason's curiosity got the best of him. "Oh really. I don't have all the details, and I know she didn't see him after he was taken away. What did she do to him?"

"She flung a pan full of boiling sauce over her shoulder and into his face. Pretty sure she was burned on the back of her shoulder in the process. Last time I saw him, it looked mighty painful. One whole side of his face was scarred," Mack said with satisfaction. It made Jason like the guy even more.

"Well, considering I've never seen the man before, it's good to know he has identifiable marks. Should make it easier to spot him should he show up here." Jason made a mental note to examine her shoulder later in bed.

"It certainly should," Mack agreed. Jason set about asking Mack questions, in order to get the information he needed. What he knew about Damien. What he was told when he got the call informing him about Damien's release. He asked for whatever information he could think of, knowing he would get together with Sean and figure out how best to ensure Tori and Lexi were protected. Before getting off the phone, he asked Mack if he could keep an eye on the house. Jason wanted to know if Damien was there on a daily basis, because if he was in Idaho, there was no way he could be a threat to Tori in San Diego.

He knew it was probably a lot to ask a man who really didn't have any obligation to Tori. But the fact that he tracked her down, gave Jason hope. Before they hung up, Jason made sure they both had all the information they needed to contact each other, then agreed to check in daily via text. It was a bit extreme, but Jason didn't care; he had to do what he could and felt he had an ally with Mack.

Standing from the couch, he was making his way toward the stairs to check on Tori when Logan walked in. Holding up the six-pack he was carrying, he said, "Sorry I'm late, but I come bearing gifts."

Jason's mood must have been obvious because Logan's smile instantly faded. "What's wrong man?"

"A lot. I'll explain in little while, but can you do me a favor and call Sean. It's important that I talk with him. Tori and I need his advice," Jason explained. His mood was somber but determined.

"Sean doesn't like me too much, but I'm sure he'll come over. You need him now?" Logan asked, pulling out his phone to dial.

"Yeah, we need him now," Jason said as he turned to climb the stairs. Tori had been upstairs for too long, and he needed to see she was okay. Taking the stairs two at a time, he was in his room seconds later. When he found it empty, he had a moment of panic before finding her in the room where Lexi was sleeping. He used the room when any of his nieces or nephews stayed with him so there was a playpen, a bed, and a couch. There were toys piled in a basket, sporting equipment standing in a corner and a gaming system set up opposite the bed.

Tori was sitting on the couch, her legs stretched across the length of it, with Lexi asleep on her chest. Her eyes were closed so he approached with caution in case she didn't know he was there. Whether she knew she needed him or not, she had him, and he was going to make sure she realized it. Positioning his hip on the edge of the couch beside her legs, he rested one hand on Lexi and the other stroked Tori's tear-streaked cheek. She opened her eyes, and another tear escaped. He caught it with his thumb and wiped it away. Taking in a shaky breath, she whispered words that gutted him to his core. "He can't know about her. I'll do whatever I have to, but he will never get his hands on my daughter."

TORI watched as anger washed over Jason's face. "You're fucking right he'll never lay his hands on her. I told you, she's mine, and I'd kill for her."

She believed him; there was no way she couldn't. The look on his face said it all. Lexi deserved to have a man like Jason caring for her. Tilting her head and giving him a knowing smile, she agreed, "I know you would, and I'm beyond grateful for that."

Lexi stirred in her arms but didn't wake up. When Tori came upstairs to freshen up, she gravitated to Lexi immediately. Holding her daughter infused her with peace, almost making her feel stronger than she was. She was terrified of the fact Damien was being set out in the world again. Whether his sights would be set on finding her, or on another woman, she didn't know. But she knew she wasn't his victim anymore, and just like the day she got away from him, she had more to fight for than herself.

With a kiss to Lexi's head, she stood before placing her gently back in the playpen. Smiling, she took in how big Lexi was getting and couldn't help but marvel at the fact that her first birthday was only a week away. Standing over her, she felt Jason's arms wrap around her from behind and his chin rest on her shoulder. He, too, gave her strength, and she leaned into him, seeking more of it.

After a few silent moments, Jason said, "I called Sean over to talk. He can help us figure out how best to protect you and Lexi. I'm not taking any chances knowing that bastard is out there."

Turning in the circle of his arms, she wrapped her own around him. Pressing her face into his chest, she inhaled his scent. As it washed over her, she calmed a little before placing a kiss there. Looking up, she captured his lips for soft kiss and said, "Let's go talk then."

~*~*~*~

It was several hours, a couple six-packs, and two pizzas later before Sean and Logan left. Tori was mentally exhausted, and though she knew they were helping, she was ready to stop talking about her drama for the night. Lexi's bedtime was approaching, and a bath was in order. Jason returned from walking the guys out, Lexi in his arms, as Tori was cleaning up the remnants of dinner. When she went to take her from him, he pulled Tori into his embrace.

Kissing her on the forehead, he said, "Why don't you go take a bath and relax. I'll take care of Lex."

A bath did sound like a great idea. With all the tension coursing through her body, she could use a little relaxation. Hugging the two of them, she asked, "You don't mind?"

"Not at all. Do you have another change of clothes for both of you?" he asked. She nodded and he added, "Good. Tomorrow we'll make sure to grab more stuff for you to bring here."

He must've seen the reluctance in her eyes because he pushed on, "It's not up for discussion, Tori. You and Lexi are not safe at your place. This house has an alarm, and not to mention, me. It's better for you to be here, and you know that, so you should just accept it."

She sighed and dropped her gaze to his chest, hesitant to say what she was thinking. "I know, but I just don't want you to get sick of me. I hate the thought that we're being pushed on you out of obligation."

Jason let out an exasperated sigh. "You're gonna have to stop saying stupid shit like that, Tori. It really pisses me off."

Surprised, she met his gaze. "It's not stupid; it's true."

Jason let go of her and walked over to where Lexi's playpen now sat. Setting her down, she voiced her disappointment but was easily distracted by a toy. Tori watched as Jason strode toward her, determination set in his eyes. When he reached her, one arm wrapped around her back and the other gripped the hair at the back of her neck. Pulling her forcibly against him, he angled her head so she had no choice but to meet his eyes. At another time, with another person, his actions might've scared her. But with Jason, it set her emotionally strung-out body on fire as arousal began to spread—awakening her.

"I'm really not sure how else to make you understand this. Maybe you're not used to the idea of being loved by me yet. Maybe you're not used to the idea of having someone strong enough for you to lean on. But you should know something about me. I don't do *anything* out of obligation. Every single thing I do, I do by choice. I chose you to be mine. My heart chose you to fill an empty spot I had no idea existed until I laid eyes on you. It knew you were mine before I did." Jason's voice was strong and steady. It didn't waver as he told her exactly what he wanted her to hear.

"And you are not being *pushed* on me. I'm taking what I want ... *you*. Having you close to me isn't just necessary because I don't think your place is safe. It's necessary because I'm a selfish bastard and prefer to have you here."

She watched him watching her, absorbing his words. When her hands went to his face, he pulled her lips to his. He took what he just claimed was his. And she handed it right over.

CHAPTER TWENTY-SIX

TORI figured she'd soaked in the tub long enough. After letting the water drain, she stood and dried off. Feeling marginally better, she took in her still slightly puffy eyes and sighed. Not much she could do about them at the moment. It was nothing a good night sleep wouldn't fix. Wrapping her hair in a towel, she slipped on Jason's shirt. When she walked out of the bathroom, she was surprised to not find Jason waiting for her in the bedroom. Moving to the hallway, she heard the shower running and felt bad he was using the guest bathroom. She was also a little disappointed he hadn't joined her.

On her way to kiss Lexi goodnight, she walked past the bathroom door, which wasn't all the way closed, and could hear him singing. She smiled at the thought of him singing in the shower. Her smile only grew when she realized *what* he was singing. Quietly, she opened the door and caught sight of his body looming behind the fogged class. Fully entering the bathroom and angling herself so she could see him better, the tears she'd thought were all gone made another appearance. But this time, they were happy tears, because seeing Jason in the shower with Lexi, singing *The Itsy Bitsy Spider,* was one of the sweetest things she'd ever seen. Dropping her gaze, she took in his body and couldn't control the giggle that escaped her.

Jason stopped singing to look over his shoulder at her. Her hand covered her mouth in a failed attempt at holding back more laughter. Jason smiled and shrugged as he said,

"I was going to use the bathtub but then realized how unsafe it is. This was the better option."

Tori dropped her hand and gestured to his body. "Did you forget to take off your clothes before getting in, or do you usually shower in shorts and a t-shirt?" She couldn't help but laugh again, as he seemed to be a little embarrassed by it.

He shrugged again. "I couldn't shower naked; that just wouldn't be right."

Lexi let out a squeal as she splashed her hands against the wet shirt covering Jason's chest. He closed his eyes to block the water, and when she stopped, he looked at Tori. "She does that when I stop singing."

Tori picked up a towel and moved to the shower. When she opened the towel, Jason handed Lexi over. Once Lexi was wrapped up, Tori turned to leave but took one more glance at Jason and said, "Just so you know, you are *so* getting lucky tonight."

His eyebrows lifted and a grin spread across his face. "Yeah I am."

She laughed and shook her head as Jason began removing his wet clothes. Tori left the bathroom, saying, "Not even one yet and I catch you showering with a man." Lexi reached up and started tugging on the towel wrapped around Tori's head. It fell over them, and she laughed. Her daughter's laughter helped relax whatever the bath had not.

Tori got her dried off and dressed for bed before sitting down and reading her a story. A short while later, Lexi was asleep in her playpen and Tori was sneaking out of the room. Closing the door quietly, she came in contact with a warm body and smiled. When Jason moved her hair to the side, he kissed her neck. "Is she asleep already?"

She turned to him and nodded. "She was exhausted—busy day for her. First, the playdate in the morning with Ella, then she flirted with Sean and Logan for a few hours. And then she topped it off by showering with a man."

Jason pulled her to him. He only had a towel wrapped around his waist, but his skin was already dry. "Don't say it like that ... 'a man' makes it sound creepy."

Even though she was only joking, she didn't want to belittle what he did for her. So she gave him a serious face and apologized, "You're right. I'm sorry ... forgive me?"

Standing up on tiptoes, she placed a quick kiss to his lips. He squeezed her to him and lifted. As he carried her toward the bedroom, he said, "I can think of a few ways you could earn my forgiveness."

Dropping her lips to his neck, she bit him gently. "I bet you could."

She felt his body shudder against hers as he walked them to the bed. Setting her down before him, he took her lips in a demanding kiss. His tongue swept in and stroked her own, seeking her attention. Responding to his actions, she gave as good as she got. Their tongues caressed each other as his hands found the hem of her shirt and lifted. They separated for a breathless moment, before his lips were back on hers. Her hands dropped in search of the towel, needing to feel him, searching for his heat.

Jason's hands stopped her pursuit and she voiced her displeasure. He chuckled as he broke the kiss. Finding her gaze, he said, "Hang on, baby, you'll get what you want soon. But there's something I need to do first."

Confused, she waited for some indication as to what he needed to do. His hands rested on her bare hips, and he used his grip to turn her body away from him. She wasn't sure what was going on, but she enjoyed his hands on her skin nonetheless. His right hand slid up her side and moved to her back, a fingertip stopping over her shoulder blade. When it slowly traced a pattern, she realized what he was doing.

Trying to turn toward him, he halted her movements before placing his lips on the scarred skin. Then he moved his lips and began to kiss every spot that she'd damaged when trying to flee from Damien. Each press of his lips released the tension that had formed in her shoulders. She stood quietly, letting him do what he needed to do.

JASON didn't know how he'd never noticed them before. Small, irregular-shaped patches of skin were spread across her shoulder blade. Some were bigger than others and had a bit of a raised texture to them, but they were subtle enough to remain unseen. When looking closely, they reminded him of the spots on a cheetah. He made sure to kiss each and every one of them, cataloged them, and committed them to memory.

Her body had tensed for a few moments before relaxing to his touch. Making her uncomfortable was the last thing he wanted to do, but it was necessary. Tori's history was rough, albeit for a short period of time, and it left physical scars. But those scars did nothing to take away from the beauty he saw in her, both inside and out.

When he finished kissing the last scar, he turned her around. Claiming her lips in a sweet kiss, he whispered, "You are so beautiful."

Dazed, she opened her eyes and stared at him. "You make me feel beautiful."

"Good," he said with a smirk before he dropped to his knees in front of her. She followed his descent and watched him as he slid her panties down her legs. Tapping her ankle, he let her step out of them, then returned his attention to her stomach. His eyes scanned the soft skin, which showed proof of motherhood, until he found it. Mixed in with her stretch marks, he found a long, thin line. It was clean-cut, which explained its near invisibility. Pressing his lips to one end of it, he repeated his actions.

Tori's hands cupped his head as he covered the scar with kisses and tiny strokes of his tongue. When she thought of her scars, he wanted her to think of him on his knees in front of her, and not how she got them. Finishing, he stood quickly and cupped her face in his hands. Pressing his forehead to hers, he whispered again, "You are beautiful, Tori."

She gave him a shaky nod before her hands yanked the towel from his waist. When her small hand wrapped around his hard length, he hissed at the contact. He hadn't realized how aroused he'd become as he tended to her scars. But now, as her hand stroked him, he was ready to explode. Stilling her hand, he took a deep breath, willing his excitement down a notch.

“Please, Jason … I need you.”

With a groan, he dropped them onto the bed. “I need you, too, baby.”

Together, they worked in unison. Her hands gripped at him, pulling him tightly into her. His hard body found her heat before sliding in. They both sighed as his body rested firmly against hers. There was no space between them; they were one. When her body clenched around his, he pressed his face into her neck and swallowed hard. “You’ve gotta stop that, baby. I’m barely holding on here.”

She squirmed beneath him, her breathing labored as she said, “God, Jason, please let go!”

Knowing he could never deny her, he pulled his body back before slamming into her. She cried out, and her fingers dug into his back. Doing it again, he repeated the motion, loving every sigh and whimper she gave him. Feeling his release threatening to end things sooner than he wanted, he shifted his body slightly and thrust into her again. The new angle was a direct hit to her clit, and her body pulsed around him.

Giving her what she demanded, he felt her let go and explode around him. Her loud cries became muffled as she buried her face in his neck and rode out the pleasure he’d given her. Once he’d gotten what he wanted out of her, only then did he take his own pleasure. Sliding into her one more time, his body vibrated in release as his orgasm settled over him.

She sighed, and he pulled his face from her neck to see to her smiling. To see the look of satisfaction on his woman's face was a heady sight. His body, which still hummed from his own release, responded and began to ready itself for her again. He knew she felt it, because her eyes widened in surprise before she asked, breathlessly, "Seriously?"

He kissed her hard as his body continued to demand more. Pulling back, he rolled their still connected bodies over so she was on top. She gasped as she thrust gently upward. He smirked and said, "Get used to it, baby. It's what you do to me."

~*~*~*~

TORI awoke a few hours later, startled by the dream she'd had. Her heart beat loudly in her chest, the sound of it filling her ears. A moment later, Jason was sitting up next to her, "Are you okay? What's wrong?"

His arm came around her, and she immediately turned into him, trying to calm herself down and erase the haunting images from her mind. Jason ran his hands down her back and kissed her forehead.

"Did you have a bad dream?" he asked, his voice thick with sleep. She nodded into his chest.

"Do you want to talk about it?"

She thought she could, and she tried, but all she could get out was Lexi's name before a sob escaped her. Jason pulled them back down on the bed and held her tightly. She knew it was only a dream, but the sight of Damien with his hands on Lexi was enough to make her stomach roll. Fighting it, she took a breath and knew she needed to check on Lexi. She had never had a dream like that before, and it was terrifyingly real. Sitting up straight, she went to get out of bed, but Jason stopped her.

"Hold on, let me get her for you. Just lay back down ... okay?" All she could do was nod. Jason pulled on a pair of shorts as Tori found her shirt from earlier. Just as she pulled it over her head, she watched Jason walked back into the room with a sleeping Lexi. She felt bad about disturbing her, and Jason for that matter, but nothing was going to clear her head better than her daughter being safe in her arms.

Jason whispered, "Lay down, baby." So she did. He stood over her and laid Lexi in the space between where she and Jason were sleeping. Excusing himself, he went into the bathroom for a moment before he climbed back in on his side. Tori looked at him in question. He yawned, then said, "You'll sleep better with her in here."

He pulled the blanket up over the three of them and rested his arm low over her hip. Before long, he was sleeping, and Tori was just watching the two of them. The soothing sounds of their combined breathing lulled Tori back to sleep in no time.

CHAPTER TWENTY-SEVEN

TORI picked up the container of cupcakes she had saved for Hal. She'd invited him to join them to celebrate Lexi's birthday at Jason's house the day before, but he declined. Since Tori had been staying with Jason all week, she felt bad leaving him all alone. Even though she had seen him on Wednesday when she brought him his meals, she missed seeing him daily. Hal was like the grandpa she'd never had.

Jason walked around the corner into the kitchen, Lexi perched on his shoulders. When he spotted the cupcakes, he lifted his eyebrows in question. "Are those my cupcakes?"

Tori giggled as she shoved the container into her purse, hoping they'd make it out of the house with her. "You really need to get that cupcake obsession checked out."

Jason set Lexi on the ground. She was still trying to walk on her own, but managed to get around fine in the kitchen with all the surfaces to hold on to. He crowded into her personal space and stole a kiss. "I've told you, I'm only obsessed with *your* cupcakes, Cupcake." Then he winked and planted a scorching kiss on her lips. Seconds later, Tori broke the kiss at the sound of Lexi laughing and pulling on her pant leg. They both looked down at her and laughed.

Jason picked her up and shook his head. "Little Cockblocker should be the next words Aunt Tessa teaches you. Or Aunt Allie."

Tori smacked him on the arm and scolded him, "Stop it! She is really gonna start saying everything you guys say to her."

Jason chuckled. "Okay, we'll work on Mommy first. Would that be better?"

Taking Lexi from his arms, she said, "Yes, much."

He kissed them both before heading to the fridge. Pulling out his lunch Tori had made him, he finished gathering his stuff to head into work. All week, he had kept close tabs on them, completely disrupting his life and work to make sure they were safe. Jason spoke with Mack on a daily basis and the two of them discussed whether or not Damien had been seen at the house. Between those phone calls, and Sean confirming that Damien had checked in with his parole officer, she felt safe.

According to today's call with Mack, Damien was seen at his mailbox the day before, and he had pulled his car out of the garage early that morning, leaving it in the driveway. With the knowledge that Damien was in Idaho, Tori would be going to the mall with Tessa today.

Putting her bag on her shoulder as Jason came back in the room, she asked, "Have you seen the keys to my car? I thought they were in my purse, but I can't find them."

Jason pulled out the keys to his car and handed them to her. "I told you I'd prefer you driving my car. Yours isn't as safe."

She scowled at him. "My car is perfectly fine and gets me where I need to go."

He pulled her to him, wrapping his arms around both her and Lexi. “I’m sure it does, but my car is safer and more reliable. Besides, Lexi’s new seat is already strapped in, so you might as well.”

Still scowling and unable to move from his hold since her hands were full, she grumbled, “Was that part of your plan? Use my reluctance to move the oversized car seat to my car.”

Jason smiled and kissed the tip of her nose. “I plead the fifth ... a guy has to keep some secrets.”

“Oh, using my own lines on me ... I see how it is. You just wait until tonight. Two can play at game, mister.”

“Promises, promises,” he said with humor as he hugged her tighter and dropped his face to her shoulder, kissing it. The brush of his beard against her skin awakened her body, as always. Her nerve endings were slaves to the sensation, and he knew this. Jason Michaels fought dirty for sure.

Nudging him away from her, she laughed. “Okay, stop that. We both have places to be.”

“But I’m the boss, so I can be late,” he said, moving toward her again. She quickly ducked out of the way and moved around the kitchen island.

“You already had me today so you’ll just have to go to work and wait until tonight for more,” she said while trying to counter each of his moves. He went left, she moved right.

Finally, he gave up and his shoulders slumped in defeat. Giving her a pouty lip, he relented, "Fine. If you can resist me, I can resist you. So long as we're not in the same building, I can totally wait until tonight."

She shook her head and grabbed his keys he'd put on the island. "That pouty face isn't going to work. Now let's go before you're late for work again and Logan starts to hate me for being the cause."

Jason huffed a laugh as he moved to pick up his computer bag, "Logan likes how happy I am right now."

Tori stopped and looked at him. "He does."

Jason took Lexi from her and proceeded to carry her out to the garage. Loading her in the seat, he turned back to Tori and kissed her. "Yep, so you're stuck with me now. Just think of all the people whose happiness would be directly affected if you ever leave me."

Giving him her best *I'm-dead-serious* expression, she said, "I'm not going anywhere."

"You're damn right you're not," he said sternly before taking her lips in another kiss—one meant to drive his point home. After she was good and breathless, he pulled away, smiled, and walked to his truck. "Call me later, please."

Shaking the dazed feeling off, her fingers touched her tingling lips as she nodded. She watched him leave before getting in the car. Looking back at Lexi, she teased, "Looks like someone might be skipping her afternoon nap so she can go to bed early tonight."

Lexi picked the appropriate time to blow a raspberry at her. Tori laughed and backed out. "We'll see, little girl."

JASON had just dropped down into his chair when his phone rang. It wasn't a number already programmed into his phone so he assumed it was business related.

"Jason Michaels."

"Jason? It's Tessa." Her voice was serious and not playful as it usually was, immediately putting him on edge. The tone of her voice, coupled with the fact that she was calling him when she was supposed to be with Tori, had him bluntly asking, "Is everything okay?"

"Yeah, I think ... I don't know. I was just checking to see if you've seen Tori. She said she'd be here over an hour ago, and I can't get ahold of her. That's not like her so I was starting to get worried."

Standing abruptly from his chair, it slammed into the wall behind him, catching Logan's attention. Maybe his reaction was unnecessary, but he had reason for it. Tessa was right; it wasn't like Tori to be late or to not answer her phone. Something could very well be wrong. "I haven't seen her since she and Lexi left the house well over an hour ago. She said she was running by her place to drop off something for Hal, then she was picking you up." He was already making his way out to his truck so that he could get to her place, with Logan close on his heels. "Do you have her landlord's phone number?"

Tessa answered, "Yes, want me to try his number?"

"Yeah. I'm on my way over there, but call him now and see if he's seen her."

"Okay, I'll call you back. Bye."

He ended the call, and Logan grabbed his arm as he was climbing in the truck. Jason looked at his friend and got straight to the point. "Something is wrong. Tori hasn't shown up at Tessa's, and she isn't answering her phone."

Logan's hand dropped from Jason's arm as he cursed. "Fuck, go! I'll call Sean."

Jason nodded as he slammed the door and threw the truck in drive, yelling out the window as he pulled away, "Tell him I heading over to her place."

He found Tori's number at the top of his call list. Pressing send, he waited as it rang. When he got her voicemail, he hung up and dialed again. As he heard her sweet voice telling him to leave a message, he couldn't help the surge of fear that crept up his spine. Something was wrong.

When the recording ended and gave him the beep, in a voice full of concern he said, "Tori, baby, call me back as soon as you get this." Panic had him clinging to the phone, not wanting to move it away from his ear. When the phone ended the call for him, he reluctantly pulled it away and looked at it. Something was definitely wrong.

A honking horn alerted him to the now green light he was sitting at. Driving blindly as he'd called her, he hadn't even realized where he was. All his focus was on getting to Tori's place as quickly as possible, so he floored it. Under normal circumstances, it would take about ten minutes to get there—but not this time.

As Jason was weaving around cars on the freeway, speeding to the exit he needed, his phone rang. Quickly grabbing it, he answered with the hope Tessa had found Tori. "Tessa?"

"Jason, her landlord isn't answering his phone either. Are you at her place yet? I'm worried," Tessa said in a small voice, nowhere near as large as her personality. He wanted to comfort her a little, since she was Tori's best friend after all, but the truth of the matter was he didn't know what to say.

"I'm worried, too." Taking a deep breath when he saw his exit come into view, he added, "I'm getting off the freeway now, so I should be there in three minutes or less. Call me if she shows up, okay?"

"Okay, let me know when you find her," she pleaded.

"Of course." Ending the call, he turned right onto the main road leading to her street. Less than a mile down, and he was making the quick right turn toward her house. Even though he was in a residential neighborhood, he punched the gas. The truck picked up speed as he made his way to the end of the cul-de-sac.

His fears began to conjure all sorts of scenarios as to what horrible things could've happened to Tori. The fact that he couldn't see any emergency vehicles or smoke coming from where her place was only provided a small comfort. When her driveway came into view, and he could see the tail end of his car there, a bit more relief bubbled up inside. Now he could eliminate car accident from the list of fears he mentally made on the reckless drive over.

Pulling in the driveway far too fast, he slammed on the brakes and simultaneously flung his door open. After throwing the truck in park, he was out the door a second later, jogging past the front house, through the gate toward the converted garage where she lived. He called her name as he got closer to her door, but heard no response. Trying the door handle first with no luck, he began to pound loudly on the door, calling her name again.

Nothing looked out of place as he abandoned the front door and went to the small window next it. Everything was quiet, and he didn't like it. The ruckus he was making should've at least warranted a response from Lexi. If they were in there and something was wrong with Tori, he would've heard Lexi. He wasn't sure if he should be comforted or frightened by that fact. Where the hell were his girls?

Deciding to get inside at any cost, he needed tools. As he started to run past his car to get some from his truck, a movement inside the car caught his attention. The front seat was empty, and the dark tinted windows prevented him from seeing much, but he knew he saw something. Throwing open the back door, he almost crumpled with relief when he found Lexi belted into her car seat. Her cheeks were lined with tear tracks, and she was sucking her thumb voraciously.

Leaning into the car, he crooned, "Hi there baby girl." Making quick work of the belts, she made noises between crying and whimpering—but happy to see him. He could totally relate to how she felt. After pulling her out, he stood up and held her tightly to his chest as she snuggled into him. Her little body hiccupped from crying so much, so he knew she had been in the car by herself for an extended period of time. Rubbing her back, he rocked her and tried to calm her, all while the sickening feeling of dread threatened to take him to his knees. Tori would never leave Lexi ... ever. Something was horribly wrong.

CHAPTER TWENTY-EIGHT

JASON turned himself in a circle, taking in everything around them, hoping for a clue as to where she might have gone. When his gaze landed on the back door to Hal's house, he could see that it was open. Moving closer, he noticed damage to the frame and something on the floor, just beyond the doorway. Knowing he needed to investigate, he glanced down at Lexi in his arms and debated whether or not he should take her in there with him.

He didn't have many options, and the thought of putting her back in the car was not appealing in the least. *What if Tori's hurt in there and needs help*, he thought. Deciding she'd be safer with him, he stepped into the yard to get a closer look. His gut was screaming at him that something just wasn't right, so he pulled out his phone and dialed.

"Nine-one-one, what's your emergency?" A firm feminine voice came across the connection.

He wasn't even sure how to answer her question. "I'm not sure what the problem is yet, but I just know that something is wrong. I wanted to call you guys before I entered the house to see what is happening."

"Sir, can I have your name and location please?" she asked.

As he began walking toward the open door, he answered her. He could hear her saying things into the line that were clearly meant as orders to others. Although he was glad that help was on the way, it did little to calm his fears.

"Thank you, sir. I'm dispatching a unit to your location now. Can you tell me what kind of help you need? Is someone hurt?"

"I'm still not sure. All I know is that when I got here, my girlfriend wasn't here, but her one year old daughter was still in the car. She would never leave the baby alone like that. I can see the back door to her landlord's house open so I'm going in to check it out," he said as he continued to hold Lexi tightly against his chest.

"Sir, do *not* go inside the house if you think there's something wrong," she insisted.

"With all due respect, there is no way I'm *not* going into that house. What if she's hurt and needs me?"

"I understand your concern, but I can't allow you to place yourself in danger. The unit is three minutes out, sir, please wait."

"I can't do that," he answered with a lowered voice as he stepped up onto the back stoop. Angling himself so that he was shielded by the doorframe, he assessed the view inside the door. Not seeing anything other than a turned over chair, he cautiously stepped inside. He was thankful that the baby had calmed down and wasn't making much noise, but she still clung to him, so he held her tightly. In his attempt to comfort her, he realized she was providing him a level of calm he didn't think was possible otherwise. Not with the horrible thoughts running through his head.

"Sir, the officer is pulling up out front. Are you inside, and what are you wearing?" the dispatcher asked.

"Yes, I'm inside. I have on jeans and a black t-shirt. I'm holding a baby, and I'm unarmed," Jason answered, knowing the dispatcher needed to relay the information to the officer outside. He knew this was for his safety as much as it was for the officer's. He could hear her communicating what Jason was wearing to the officer at the same time he heard car doors close outside. Ending his call, he moved toward the front of the house, intent on getting the door for the police, when he spotted Hal lying on the floor.

Rushing to him, he knelt down next to him in a position that shielded Lexi from what he might find when he rolled the older man over. Gently placing his hand on Hal's shoulder, he felt the man tense up underneath his touch. "Hal, it's Jason Michaels."

The older man relaxed and turned his head, looking over his shoulder at Jason before breathing a sigh of relief. "I thought that bastard was back. Why the hell didn't you announce yourself when you came in? I've been lying here pretending to be knocked out since I heard you!"

Jason helped him roll to a sitting position as he responded, "Sorry Hal, I had no idea if someone was in here. Where's Tori?"

It wasn't until he was fully seated that Jason could see Hal's legs had been duct taped together. His hands weren't restrained, but the fact that he suffered from severe arthritis must not have escaped whoever did this. There was no way he would've been able to get out of the binding.

"Shit, Hal, are you hurt anywhere?" Jason asked as he went to help release his legs.

Hal's hands shot out quickly. "Don't touch anything!" Confused, Jason looked at him before he continued, "That bastard wasn't wearing any gloves. Don't mess with anything. I can tolerate being in this position until the authorities remove it properly."

Jason slumped back onto his heels; he was right. Feeling a little helpless, he asked, "Hal, where's Tori?"

Hal just shook his head slightly, "She's not here. I saw a man stuff her into a trunk."

Jason felt the blood drain from his face at the image Hal had painted for him. His hold on Lexi tightened as Hal confirmed his fear. "The guy was wearing a hood, but she put up a fight and it fell back. That's when I saw scars on his face." Hal sighed and shook his head in disgust. "I was clumsy and knocked the chair over getting to the phone. He obviously heard me because he broke down the back door, and he must have knocked me out because I woke up to the sound of the car leaving. And my legs like this."

Hal shook his head again before groaning in discomfort as he rested his head against the wall. "I'm sorry I couldn't do more. But she put up a fight, because I heard him howl in pain and that's how I knew something was wrong."

Jason wasn't sure what to say, but just then a police officer came into the room. Gun drawn, he yelled, "Police! Hands where I can see them."

Jason lifted his free arm in the air. “Officer, I’m the one who called.”

The officer demanded again, “I said put your hands where I can see them!”

Taking in the situation, he understood the officer didn’t have a clear view of Jason, so he was unaware he was holding Lexi. “I can’t lift my other arm … I’m holding a child. Can I turn around and show you?”

“No, stay right where you are,” the officer stated authoritatively, but Jason just thought he sounded like an overreacting asshole. He heard him say, ‘Cover me,’ to what he assumed was another officer. Hal sat in front of him, with his crippled hands as high as he could hold them, but Jason knew that his big body shielded Hal from the officer’s view.

Jason knew the exact moment Hal could see the officer since he barked at him, “Put that gun away, rookie! If you point that gun anywhere near that child he’s holding, I’ll make sure to kick your ass myself.”

Jason wanted to laugh. Hal clearly wasn’t capable of inflicting harm on the other man, but Jason appreciated his threat. The officer came into Jason’s view on his right side—the side where Lexi was being held. He knew this was done because if Jason was armed, there would be no way he could turn and shoot the officer quickly enough.

“Slowly turn toward me until I can see both of your hands,” the officer instructed.

Jason complied, turning as slowly and awkwardly as he could while kneeling on the hard ground, holding Lexi.

Once fully facing the officer, whose gun was still drawn, he said, "Officer, my name is Jason Michaels. I'm the one who called 9-1-1. I'm not armed, and Hal here took a blow to the head."

The "rookie," as Hal called him, ordered, "Stand up and move away from the other man."

Jason made sure to roll his eyes as he stood to his full six-foot three-inch height. His broad shoulders and imposing appearance probably didn't put the officer at ease, so Jason cautiously stepped backward. He knew it was important to do what he was told, regardless of the fact that he wanted to wrap both of his hands around the officer's neck and squeeze until he passed out. Being distracted by Hal's situation had lessened his anxiety over Tori being missing ... but only momentarily. Now it was coming back full force, and hostility was crowding in with it. Tori needed him, and he had no idea how to find her.

Lexi had remained huddled against him, obviously sensing the tension around her. Still with his hand in the air, and unable to hug Lexi with both hands, he pressed his lips against her curls. He took in a deep breath filled with her scent. Filled with Tori's scent. It was like a hit of Valium and a dose of a stimulant at the same time.

Once he was backed up against the wall, about five feet away from Hal, both officers holstered their weapons. Jason dropped his raised arm and wrapped it around Lexi, giving her the comfort she needed. The rookie said, "We got a call about an abandoned child, and we arrive to a busted in door and a restrained man. You mind telling us what the hell is going on here? And is this the abandoned child?"

Jason didn't have time for this shit. "My girlfriend lives in the back house. When she didn't show up where she was supposed to, I came looking for her. What I found was her daughter alone in the car, and Hal, here, with tape around his legs."

The officer interrupted him and took a step closer. "So this child has been abandoned by her mother?"

What the hell? Jason was going to throttle him if he said it like that one more time. Tori would never abandon Lexi … ever. "No," he growled. "This child's mother was taken against her will, and the child was left behind."

He took another step closer and asked, "Is this child yours then?"

Jason's hold around Lexi tightened once again. He wasn't sure he liked where the officer was going with his questions, but they were taking them off the subject of Tori. "No, not biologically," Jason said with exasperation.

His need to get back on track had him distracted, and he almost didn't realize what was happening until the officer had his hands on Lexi. "Let go of the child, sir. I have no idea who you are and if you had anything to do with her mother's disappearance."

Jason bared his teeth and, in a menacing voice, said, "Get your fucking hands off her … now!"

The officer stepped back and put his hand on his gun. Jason angled Lexi away from the situation that seemed to be escalating out of control for no reason.

“Sir, I said ...” the officer began, but was interrupted by a voice coming from the back of the house.

“Lt. Sean Cooper entering the premises. Stand down officers.” Jason sagged in relief at the arrival of Gillian’s brother. When Sean walked in, he took in Jason’s defensive posture and the officer’s offensive one and began ordering him around. “Officer Jennings, you better have one hell of a reason for treating my brother-in-law like that.”

The rookie, or officer Jennings as he now knew, didn’t back down. His hand remained on his gun, the other arm outstretched toward Lexi. He looked to Sean and said, “Lieutenant, this man claims the child’s mother is missing, and he is not the father. I have yet to determine if he had anything to do with it so I wasn’t about to let him keep the child.”

This officer clearly was a rookie and had seen one too many *Law & Order* episodes. While there was some drama around the events, it wasn’t with him. Hal picked that moment to say, “You’re a dumbass! I saw the man who took Tori, and if you’d taken a moment to ask me that three minutes ago, you could already be trying to find her.”

Everyone looked down at Hal in surprise. Then Jason looked over to Sean and said, “Damien has Tori.”

CHAPTER TWENTY-NINE

JASON found himself sitting on his bed, his back propped up against his headboard, staring down at Lexi. He didn't even know how he got there, let alone how long he'd been sitting there. She was cradled against his chest, safe in his arms. He knew she'd probably be more comfortable lying on the bed, but he was afraid he wouldn't be able to put her down. Feeling her weight against him reminded him to stay calm and focused. For her. For Tori.

Sighing, he ran a hand through her hair—the fluffy out of control curls that held the same color as her mother's. Tori. His pulse rate picked up, and panic once again flooded his system as he fought the need to run out the door and look for her. The vision of her being stuffed in a trunk by Damien threatened to destroy him. But he was grounded by the fact that Lexi needed him. A lone tear rolled slowly down his cheek, and he let it. He recalled the last time he'd cried, and the thought made his stomach roll. *Marc*. Losing Marc brought out pain he hadn't been familiar with until that day. The fear and pain he felt now, though, was far worse.

What if ... He couldn't even finish the thought and quickly threw the comparison away. Tori had to be okay ... she had to be. For Lexi. For him.

The bed shifted next to him, but he didn't take his eyes off Lexi. The rise and fall of her chest was his focus, the only thing providing him with a sense of calm. It was a front, but he held on to it tightly. When he felt a hand against his shoulder, another tear escaped along with a chink in his façade.

Allie wrapped her arm around his shoulders and pulled his head against her. Still, he kept his eyes locked on Lexi, pulling strength from her. Allie ran her hand over Lexi's hair, too, and he found himself following the motion, watching how the reddish-brown strands would separate before springing back upward. Together, they sat in silence. Allie's presence offered both comfort and threatened to destroy his barriers.

After a while, he felt his eyes getting heavy, the soft, repetitive sounds of their breathing and Lexi's weight on his chest, lulling him. But he fought it. Even when he felt Allie's hand stroking his hair, he resisted. "It's okay to close your eyes, Jay. I know it's a scary thing to do, but you need to," Allie whispered.

He sighed, because he wanted to. "I can't, Al. I feel like if I do, Lexi might disappear, too."

Allie's hold tightened. "Not gonna happen. There is a small army of people downstairs willing to kill for her ... for both of them."

Comforted by her words, he once again fought the fear that had a firm grip around his heart. Swallowing the lump in his throat, he voiced his fear to a person who knew the pain of loss. "I can't lose her, Allie." His eyes welled up. "I've waited so long for her. I just *can't*."

"You won't," she said with a resolve she had no way of supporting. "She's strong, and strength like that doesn't disappear. I refuse to accept any other alternative. And neither should you."

Allie's determined hope fed into his own, bolstering its strength further. Jason settled against her, still clinging to Lexi, and closed his eyes. If only for a few moments.

Startled, he realized he'd fallen asleep. Opening his eyes, Gillian loomed over him, a soft smile on her face. "Let me take her for a little bit, Jay."

Blinking the sleep from his eyes, he processed her words. *Take her*? Panic seized him and he sat straight up.

"No!" he barked in a tone he had no business using with Gillian. It startled Lexi awake, and he regretted it even more. Lowering his voice, he consoled Lexi before looking back at Gillian. "I don't want to let her go."

Allie was still next to him, her hand on his shoulder. She squeezed it, offering her silent support and understanding. Gillian sat opposite him, her stare unwavering as she placed one hand on his cheek. He felt weak right then, surrounded by these strong women. A sense of longing for *his* woman slammed into him, and he closed his eyes to fight the tension and despair. Lexi squirmed in his arms, obviously sensing his turmoil.

"I know you don't want to, but you have to. Let me take her, change her, and put her in her crib for the night," Gillian said in a soothing voice. Jason drew his attention to the window to see that the sun had set. He knew she was right, but it still didn't mean he liked it. Seeing the resolve in his eyes, Gillian leaned in and gently took Lexi from his arms. “She will only be in her room, safe and sound. I promise.”

Unable to speak, he nodded, before pressing his lips to Lexi’s head. He watched as Gillian walked out of his bedroom and had never felt so alone. Sitting in the middle of his bed, he dropped his face in his hands and let the tears fall. Allie was there immediately, wrapping her arms around him. She didn’t say anything ... she just let him get it all out.

~*~*~*~

JASON wasn’t sure what time it was when he finally lifted his aching body from bed. The sun was rising, and soon, so would Lexi. After being awake until the early hours of the morning, he needed to make sure he was cleaned up and ready to face the day for her. At some point in the night, Allie had traded places with Logan, and he was now sleeping in the corner chair. Jason knew he had great friends, but he’d just never been the one they had to look after before. Shaking his head, he took off his shirt, grabbed a clean pair of jeans, and headed toward the bathroom.

After a quick shower, he was making his way out when he heard Lexi come over the monitor. Grabbing a shirt, he was in the hall before he had it on; he needed to see her. Lexi was standing at her crib bars, waiting for him. She began to bounce up and down, her obvious excitement at seeing him warranted a smile. “Good morning, sweetheart. How’s my baby girl today?”

He felt like a hypocrite asking the question. Of course, she was blissfully unaware that her mother had been kidnapped, so she was perfect. Pushing back his fears, he focused on Lexi. After lifting her from the crib, he hugged her to him, absorbing her, before he went about changing her. Since Tori no longer breastfed, there would be no impact of her absence in that sense. And there had been that night where Jason and Tori had been able to get away, so he hoped Lexi was none the wiser today. He liked to think that because *he* was there, it wouldn't be as obvious that Tori was not.

Going about their usual routine, he made his way to the kitchen with Lexi. On the couch in the family room, he could see there were at least two sleeping bodies covered with a blanket. He wasn't sure who they were, but as soon as Lexi hits the floor, they were gonna get a surprise. Setting her down, she took off for the bumps on the couch as he got her breakfast ready.

A moment later he heard a squeal from Lexi followed by Allie's laughter. Coffee was most definitely required so he started a full pot, still having no clue as to how many people were in his house. Once the coffee was brewing, he made Lexi's oatmeal and set it out to cool while grabbing her milk from the fridge. Allie came into the kitchen carrying Lexi. Up on tiptoes, she kissed him on the cheek and said, "Today will be a good day, Jay. I can feel it."

Jason gave her a nod, knowing he needed to stay positive. The problem was that every time he did, his mind went immediately to the alternative. And that was not something he wanted to focus on.

“Thanks, Al. You guys didn’t need to stay, you know.”

“Shut the hell up.” Allie dismissed him as she put Lexi in her highchair. When she turned back to him, she added, “Next time you say something stupid like that, you will be pinched.”

Jason’s sides tightened in response; she dealt some painful pinches. The other bump on the couch, now known to be Mike, called out, “We both know you don’t want that.”

He smiled, regardless of what was going on. His friends being there was what he needed. They knew this and he expected nothing less from them. Allie walked over to the couch and kissed Mike, before excusing herself to clean up. A few moments later, he heard Logan yell from upstairs, followed by Allie laughing. Jason shook his head, and Mike said, “Sounds like Logan’s up now. I can only imagine what she did to him.”

Logan came lumbering down the stairs with a scowl on his face. As he slipped his shirt over his head, he said, “Mike, could you at least try to control your woman. She just ripped hair out of my leg.”

Mike snorted as he stood and stretched. “She’s been your sister longer than *my woman*. Why on Earth would you think *I* could tame her?”

Jason offered, “He’s got a point, Logan. Besides, in previous times she would’ve laid a wax strip on you or something.”

Logan grabbed himself a cup of coffee. “You mean, again. A strip of wax *again*.”

He let out a small laugh when Mike's eyebrows shot up in question. Jason just said, "True story."

Mike stifled a laugh as he went upstairs in search of Allie. The front door opened, and Jason could hear Gillian and Jake talking as they came in. When they rounded the corner, Gillian smiled and set a box of pastries on the counter. "Good, you're up. I talked to Sean already, and he said they have a make and model on the car Damien was driving. So they've put out an APB for it. They've got eyes on his house in Idaho, and he promised to stay on top of things and call as soon as he has more information."

He accepted a kiss on the cheek before she moved around him and helped herself to some coffee. Jake was holding Ella, and gave Jason a pat on the shoulder. "You doing okay today?"

Jason's throat clogged up, and he tried to swallow, unsuccessfully, so he nodded in answer. Logan dug into the pastry box. Jake accepted coffee from Gillian. Mike and Allie came downstairs laughing about something. Lexi was playing with her oatmeal, and somehow Ella had ended up in his arms. This was his family, and they were doing the only thing they could do for him right then ... distracting him. *Thank God for them*, he thought. Because the alternative was for him to go crazier with each passing minute, wondering where his Cupcake was.

~*~*~*~

TORI groaned. Her body felt like she'd gone three rounds with a prized fighter, after drinking a bottle of tequila, but not before being thrown down a flight of stairs and then locked in a sauna for days. Not recalling going on a bender, she tried opening her eyes, only meeting more darkness. There was a throbbing in her head that began to pulsate harder, and she moved her hand to rub at the offending area. It was then she felt that both of her hands were restrained and awareness crowded in. Damien!

Her body jolted in shock just remembering the threat of her ex-husband. The movement brought another wave of pain down her arms and back. Feeling as if she'd been in the same position for days, she tried to roll a little to ease the discomfort, but her lack of mobility was astounding. Her limbs felt heavy, and her mouth was dry. Tape covered her lips, which she only realized as she went to lick them. Her eyes burned like she was crying, but nothing escaped as she took in the magnitude of her predicament. She was locked in a trunk, with her hands and mouth taped, in what felt like sweltering heat. Just thinking of the heat made her voracious thirst roar to the front of her mind.

She had no idea where she was, or how long she'd been there, but just that she needed to get the hell out. There was no way she was going down without a fight. Gathering all the strength she could, and taking in all the oxygen her nose would allow, she screamed through the tape, hoping to God someone was nearby. Someone other than Damien.

CHAPTER THIRTY

JASON stood at the door leading to his yard, staring at the landscape, making mental notes of things he wanted or needed to do back there. Anything to keep his mind off things. Things that could be happening to Tori. Things that could've already happened. Things he couldn't prevent from happening. Closing his eyes, he took a deep breath, willing the calm to stay. It wasn't working, though. With each passing hour, his anxiety mounted. It crowded in with the fear, the pain ... and the disappointment. Never before had he felt like such a failure. He'd failed Tori in every possible way, and if given the chance, he'd never do it again.

He sighed and told himself, "I failed. I'm so sorry I failed."

A second later, a sharp pain stabbed at his flank, and he spun to see the source. His eyes met a scowling Allie, hands on hips for a brief moment before one of her fists socked him in the chest. "I dare you to say that again!"

Jason rubbed his side, momentarily thankful for the physical pain to distract him from his emotional pain. Glaring at Allie, he said, "Knock it off, Al. I'm not in the mood."

"I'll knock it off when you do," Allie insisted, challenge in her voice. Turning back to the window, he sighed again, ignoring Allie's words. It didn't matter what she thought, because he knew he'd failed Tori. When staring at the yard no longer worked, he found his way to the couch and sat amongst his friends, hoping whatever they were watching on daytime television would distract him. Lexi would be asleep for at least another thirty minutes. He mentally ran through what he would have to do next for Lexi to make sure her day wasn't altered too much in Tori's absence. It had been twenty-four hours since she was taken. *A lot could happen in twenty-four hours*.

Turning back to the television, he focused on that. A loud knock at the front door had his attention immediately. Everyone in the room looked in the direction of the door. Logan was up and moving to answer it as the rest of them also stood. Whoever was at the door clearly had something important to say—the knock sounding determined.

When Sean barged in the room wearing his uniform, Jason wasn't sure if he wanted to hear what he had to say. The thought that it could go negatively had Jason's knees ready to buckle. He stepped forward, and Jake's hand landed on his shoulder. He didn't know if it was in support or restraint. Sean finally nodded his head and said the three words Jason needed to hear. "They found her."

Jason was in motion immediately. He had no idea where he was going, just that he needed to move, to get to her. Shrugging off Jake's hold, he rushed past Sean, his sole thought was that Tori needed him. He'd almost made it to the door, only to be held back again. "Jason, wait. You can't leave ..."

All Jason heard was *you can't leave*, and he lost it. Before he knew what he was doing, his fist landed across Sean's jaw, knocking him backward. Turning back to the door, he pushed forward with one intent—getting to Tori. He didn't know where she was, but he knew she wasn't there. Strong arms banded around him from behind and pulled him back. His chest heaved, and he tried disengaging from the hold. "Calm down, Jay. She's okay, and she needs you … so you have to control yourself, man." Jake's voice filtered through the buzzing in his ears.

He tried again to free himself from his brother's hold, but Logan got in his face instead. "Cool it! Where you gonna go, huh?" Jason's heart began to hurt from the speed of his pulse. He *was* losing it. It felt like he was wound as tightly as he could possible get, and he was beginning to snap. Blinking rapidly, he tried to focus as he looked at Logan, Jake's hold like steel bands around his arms. "You need to hold it together. Listen to what Sean has to say, and then we can figure out what to do. We'll get you to her, I swear."

Jason's jaw clenched and unclenched, "I need to be moving. I have to get to her."

"I know that, and you will," Logan said firmly. Then he looked over Jason's shoulder and said, "Sean, what do we have to do, and where do we need to go."

Sean came into Jason's view, rubbing his jaw. Jason hadn't meant to punch his friend; it just happened. Sean stretched his jaw from side to side. "Shit man, that hurt!"

Jason glared at him, wanting to do it again. Sean put his hands up. "Okay, she's not in San Diego. The bastard was actually trying to take her back to Idaho. She was found in the trunk of the car, at a store just north of Vegas. Someone heard sounds coming from the trunk and called it in. Luckily, there was a unit nearby, and they ran the plates. Minutes later, they were forcing their way into the car. Damien was nowhere to be found, but they have Tori. She's safe."

Jason was trying to process the information Sean had just spilled. His brain was trying to determine what question he needed to ask next, but he couldn't figure it out. She was far from there … too far. Fortunately, his friends were there to speak for him because Gillian asked, "Where is she now, Sean? Is she okay?"

Why didn't he think to ask that? Because she had to be, that's why. If she weren't, Sean would've told him otherwise. He needed to get to her. How long would it take to drive to Vegas? He was mentally calculating just that when Sean answered, "She's been taken to one of the hospitals in Vegas. She was dehydrated and has some bruising, but overall, she appears to be good. They're expecting you, Jason. I listed you as next of kin on the reports so you shouldn't have trouble getting in."

That was all he needed to know. Trying to shake Jake off, he was again met with Logan in his face. "Calm the fuck down! I know what you're thinking. That you can just get in the car and drive to her, but that's not happening." Jason scowled at his closest friend, wishing his hands were free to inflict some kind of pain on him. "You get in that car and try driving like this, you won't even make it. Plus, you'll take out a few people with you. Gillian?"

"Yeah?" Gillian answered from somewhere nearby.

Logan said, "Can you use the company cards and book me and Jason on the next flight to Vegas and get us set up with a car there?"

"On it," Gillian said quickly.

Jake declared from behind him, "I'm going, too."

Logan leveled a look at him, "I know he's your brother, but he needs you here. Sean said they didn't find Damien, and that means he could be coming back. And since we can't take Lexi on a plane with us, you need to keep an eye on her here."

Jason stiffened at the thought. *Damien could not get his hands on Lexi.* Jake's hold on Jason lessened as he said, "Not gonna happen. I'll take care of her for you." Jason nodded, still able to speak.

Logan then said, "Allie, can you throw a change of clothes in a bag for Jason?"

Allie responded as she ran toward the stairs, "I'll throw in a change for Tori, too."

Logan nodded, and Jason watched him, thankful his friend knew what he needed. Whether it was to yell in his face, or get him a change of clothes. Jason took a deep breath and calmed a little more. Gillian walked back in, papers in hand. "Got you both on a flight that leaves in two hours. That should give you enough time to run by your place for a bag, Logan." He nodded then she turned to Jason. "You have a plane ticket and a car reserved. I will get you both a hotel room and text you the information as soon as I have it. I don't know which hospital she's at yet, and I want to pick one close by. Okay?"

Jason gave her a nod before whispering, "Thank you."

She hugged him. Allie came down the stairs and pulled Gillian off him before pushing him to the door. Shoving a bag in his hand, she said, "Go get your girl."

Logan walked quickly to the driveway and jumped his truck, Jason following. Before they left, Sean leaned on the open window. "I'll send you any information I get as it comes in. Keep me posted."

Logan agreed, and then they were moving. He felt almost numb, not knowing what he was supposed to feel. The pain was there, but duller. The anxiety still simmered, and the fear remained hovering in the distance. There was a new kind of fear, too. He had to wonder and worry—what if she blamed him? Shaking that feeling off, he focused on remaining calm. Tori was okay, and he was on his way to get her.

Together, he and Logan went through the motions of airport security, and they were soon waiting at the gate. None too patiently either. Jason paced in front of the window, waiting for the call to board the plane. Looking to his watch, he willed the time to pass quicker. He thought about how long the flight was, then how long it would take to get from the airport to the hospital, mentally calculating how long until he would be with her again. How long before he could touch her.

Logan interrupted his thoughts, "Jay, you need to sit the fuck down. TSA is probably watching you and getting ready to pounce on your ass any second. Then how will you get to Tori?"

"I can't help it. My skin is crawling," Jason admitted with defeat as he dropped to the seat next to Logan.

"Just try and channel it. We'll be on our way soon."

Jason nodded and let his head fall back on his shoulders. Closing his eyes, he tried to relax, but failed miserably. When his phone vibrated in his pocket, he jumped up and fought with himself as he pulled it out. It was a number he didn't recognize, but he answered it quickly.

"Hello?"

"Jason ..." Tori's voice came through the line, scratchy and weak, but hers nonetheless, choking the breath right out of him.

Dropping his heavy body to his seat again, he whispered, "Tori? Baby, is that you?"

"It's me. Where's Lexi? Is she safe?" she asked, almost desperately.

He nodded as he answered, "Lexi is safe, I promise." Tori's sob hit his ear like a punch, and tears filled his eyes. Between the overwhelming relief at hearing her voice, then the sounds of her sobs and being powerless to console her, he thought he might lose it. Thinking the only thing he thought would help either of them, he said, "I'm coming, baby. I'll be there in about two hours, okay? Just hang in there until I get there."

TORI hiccupped as she tried to hold back the tears. Lexi was safe, and Jason was coming. That was all she needed to know. "Okay ... I'll hang in there."

“I’ll be there before you know it.” He paused, and she could hear the noises of the airport around him before he said, “They’re boarding us now. That’s the only reason I’m hanging this phone up. You hear me? The only reason.”

Another sob escaped her as she smiled. “Okay. See you soon.”

“I love you, Tori.”

“I love you, too.”

CHAPTER THIRTY-ONE

TORI felt a warm hand stroke across her cheekbone, before she felt lips press against her forehead. Taking a breath, she filled her lungs with Jason. He was there. Smiling, she opened her eyes and met his. Sadness lurked in their depths, and the guilt washed over her knowing she was the reason for it. Not sure what to say, she gave him a smile. He answered with one of his own as he let his eyes roam her face.

When they landed back on hers, he smirked and whispered, "Hey you."

"Hey yourself." Tears were once again falling, and she had to fight the sob clawing its way up from her chest. Wanting nothing more than to throw herself in his arms, she resisted.

Jason swept the hair off her forehead and asked, "Are you in pain? Where are you hurt?"

Shaking her head, she lifted her wrists and showed him the bruising. "It was really hot in that trunk so I was pretty dehydrated. And my wrists were torn up from the tape, but other than that, I'm not hurt. He didn't have time."

His body tensed over her, and his jaw flexed when she spoke those words. Taking a slow breath, he asked, "So it won't hurt if I hold you? 'Cause if I don't get my fucking arms wrapped around you in the next thirty seconds, I don't know what I'll do."

Relief coursed through her. She needed his touch, too. "I feel the exact same way." Swiftly, Jason's large arms engulfed her, making her feel small, vulnerable ... yet she felt cherished and loved. She soaked him into her pores, wanting to climb inside him and never leave. She felt his lips press against her hair and just stay there. With her one arm attached to her IV, she held him as tightly as she could with the other arm. They stayed like that for minutes before the sound of a throat clearing interrupted them.

Jason didn't let go, but shifted so they could both see who had come in. Logan stood just inside the doorway with her doctor. He smiled and said, "Sorry to interrupt, but the doc here says she needs to examine Tori. I told her so long as she doesn't try to make the oversized caveman in there leave, she shouldn't have a problem."

Tori snorted a laugh. "Hi Logan. Thanks for making sure my oversized caveman got here safely."

Logan winked. "Sure thing. Now, would you please tell the doctor he can stay so they don't have to call security?"

Tori looked up at Jason and smiled. "It sounds like you've been a handful."

He shrugged. "I was having Cupcake withdrawals."

She laughed out loud and looked at the doctor. "Yeah, he's not going anywhere. Can you do what you need to do with him here?"

The small, Asian woman just nodded. "I will need him to let go of you for a few minutes, though."

Jason grumbled his discontent with that, and Tori patted him on the chest. "Let the doctor do her job."

"Fine," he mumbled under his breath and obediently moved out of the way. Logan took the cue and left. One set of vitals and visual inspection of her bruises later, and the doctor told her she wanted one more bag of fluids in her IV before discharging her. Since her dehydration wasn't for an extended period of time, she was rebounding quickly. Tori was relieved she didn't have to stay there for too long.

Before the doctor excused herself, Jason asked, "Is she allowed out of bed while you give her those fluids?"

The doctor nodded. "So long as she has assistance at first, and she isn't experiencing any dizziness, its fine."

"Thank you," Jason offered as she left the room. As soon as the door closed, Jason had her hand in his and was pulling the sheet back for her. Helping her shift her legs, he helped her to a standing position, not saying a word. When she was upright, he asked, "Dizzy?"

"No, I feel good. Maybe a little tired, but good."

Jason nodded and then moved to sit in the chair beside her bed. Once seated, he moved her in front of him and gently guided her to his lap. Cradling her against him, he pulled the sheet from the bed and wrapped it over the lower half of her body, shielding her from anyone who might walk in. With the right side of her body snuggled up against him, it left the IV exposed on the other side. So when the nurse came in and hooked up the bag, she didn't say anything about it. The two of them just sat there, holding one another, soothing the other merely from their proximity.

JASON knew the moment Tori had fallen asleep. Her body relaxed further into his, and her breathing leveled out. He loved that she could fall asleep on his lap so easily, regardless of what she'd been through. Trying not to let his mind wander down that dark path again, he reached for his phone to text Logan. A few minutes later, he quietly entered the room as Jason had requested. Logan planted himself at the end of the bed and smiled—his features full of compassion as he took in Tori asleep on his lap. "Glad she's okay, man."

Jason held her tighter, confirming to himself that she was, in fact, okay. Nodding, he agreed, "Me too."

"Okay, so, Gillian texted me the hotel information. I had her get us two rooms since the doc said she could go today. That gets us through until tomorrow. We can't fly home with Tori because, as my oh-so-smart-ex-wife pointed out ... we don't have Tori's ID since her purse is back in San Diego. According to Sean, she could use the police report, but you'd have to wait until it's ready."

Jason hadn't even thought about that. "Shit, I don't want to have to wait for a report."

Logan nodded, his voice full of sarcasm. "Yep, that about sums it up. So you thinking we should drive?"

The drive home wasn't a big deal for him. They'd done that drive countless times over the years. But when he thought about bringing Tori back to San Diego, he realized he didn't want to. She was in more danger now than before, so he couldn't take her home. They needed to come up with a plan. When he asked Logan if he'd be willing to carry to the load back at work, he expected nothing less than full support.

"Of course. And if anyone has a problem with any delays, given the circumstances, we don't need them as clients."

Jason agreed. As he continued to think on a plan, his stomach growled against Tori's side, and Jason was surprised it hadn't woken her up. Lunch the day before had been his last meal. Now that the nerves and fears had dissipated, his body was quickly returning to normal—meaning, he was famished. Jason asked, "You think you can get us some food while her IV finishes?"

Logan stood. "Sure thing, but since I'm buying and flying, I get to pick."

"Thanks, man," Jason said with sincerity. It was for more than just the offer of food and Logan knew it.

Smiling at him, Logan said, "What are friends for? It's what we do." And with that, he left him alone with Tori.

Closing his eyes, he rested his head against the back of the chair. Letting out a deep breath, he focused on feeling Tori against him. Having her safe again. He used the time Tori rested to come up with a plan, to find somewhere he could take her to make sure Damien couldn't get to her or Lexi. When the idea came to him, he called Gillian. She answered immediately, "Hey there, how are you?"

"Hey Gilly, she's good. Better than I could've hoped for," he said with a smile as he looked down at her.

"I already know that, Jay. I've been riding Logan's ass for information since you got there. I asked how *you* were?" Gillian clarified.

Jason sighed. "I'm fine now. But I need some help; can you make some reservations for me? Or am out of line to ask?"

"Don't make me sick Allie on you, Jason Michaels. Just tell me what you need."

Jason smiled. It was his first real smile since the dead weight residing in his stomach dissolved. "Okay, okay. Don't rat me out." He then proceeded to tell her what he needed her to set up for him. By the time the doctor returned with discharge papers some time later, Jason had everything ready to go. He wasn't going to bring Tori back to San Diego to be hunted by her ex. No, she deserved a little bit of paradise to erase the hell she'd just endured. To help her forget that he was still out there and most likely looking for her.

~*~*~*~

TORI sighed as she relaxed against the back of the huge tub. Jason had booked a room for them, and her first order of business was soaking in a warm bath to soothe her aching muscles. After being discharged, she'd assumed they were going straight home. Everyone had lives to live, despite the interruptions her kidnapping caused. But Jason surprised her by saying they weren't leaving until tomorrow, and that they weren't going home. Her immediate concern was for Lexi, because she had to get back to her. But Jason anticipated this and added that Lexi would be going with them, too. Wherever it was they were going.

She honestly couldn't care where; so long as she had Lexi and Jason, she would be happy. When they arrived at the hotel, Jason handed her the phone and told her to let Allie know what necessities she would need from home. For both her and Lexi. She tried to be as cooperative as possible, but she felt like she was putting these people out. Then again, being difficult would be rude considering all they were doing for her. Once done with that, Jason took the phone and sent her to the bathroom, where she currently rested in the luxury of warm bubbles, in complete bliss. She sighed again.

The door opened a few moments later. With her eyes remaining closed, she heard Jason moving around the bathroom. So she was startled a bit when she felt him move her body forward in the tub. Looking up, she watched as his naked form slid in behind hers, before pulling her to rest snugly against him. Okay, so maybe the bubbles weren't as blissful as she thought. Leaning her head on his shoulder, she closed her eyes and rested her nose against the side of his neck. The smell of him was far more potent than the fragrance of bubbles that filled the air. The scent of car exhaust and spare tire that had filled her nose earlier was long gone now.

Relaxing further into him, they sat silently, his arms wrapped around her. His lips pressed against her forehead, he would periodically kiss her. When the water began to cool, Jason turned on the hot water. After reaching for a washcloth, he leaned her forward and proceeded to wash her skin. At first it hadn't occurred to her, but when he slowly used the washcloth to go over each one of her fingers, clear to the tip, she wondered if he was only washing her. Their silence, though comfortable, might be telling her more than she realized. Turning toward him, she saw his intense eyes roaming her skin as he caressed, wiping away the soap.

The power of his stare confirmed he was doing more than just cleaning her, he was checking to make sure she was okay. Just as he'd done with her scars. She reached for his hand, stilling it against her skin. When he looked at her in question, she smiled for him and said, "I'm okay Jason, I promise."

Jason blinked, and a frown formed on his face, but no more than a second later, it was gone. He nodded. "I know that's what you said ... I just need to make sure myself."

It had skipped her mind how this might have affected him. But she understood now. The love she felt for him exploded in her chest, sending warmth throughout her body. Worry for what he must have gone through, not knowing what had happened ... she couldn't imagine what that would be like if the positions were reversed.

She knew what he needed, not only because it was his way, but because it would be what she needed, too. Placing her hand on his cheek, she nodded her understanding before adding, "I love you."

"I love you, too," he whispered in a shaky voice. Then he continued to wash every part of Tori's body he could reach, until he was satisfied with her answer—that she was fine.

CHAPTER THIRTY-TWO

JASON was pleased the trip to Long Beach wasn't extended by the usual Southern California traffic. Considering it was a work day, they'd planned their drive around those heavy traffic times. Since they were meeting Allie and Mike there, with Lexi, he wanted to get there sooner rather than later. And that wasn't just for Tori's benefit; he wanted his eyes on Lexi, too. Tori had never gone that long without seeing her daughter, and it was clearly causing her some anxiety. This was her first trip from Las Vegas to Long Beach, so she had no idea how long it would take, and the fact that she asked several times during the trip how much longer it would be, proved she was suffering.

When Logan parked the car they all got out, and Jason grabbed the one bag he had with them. Taking Tori's hand, they walked toward the dock where Allie and Mike were supposed to meet them. Jason didn't think it was possible for Damien to be nearby, but he found himself looking around anyway. And when Tori caught sight of Allie holding Lexi, he reluctantly let go of her hand and watched her jog over to them. Her long, vibrant hair trailed behind her, picked up by the wind, and he found himself mesmerized by the beauty of it—once again, of her.

The sounds of Lexi's laughter broke his trance, and he watched as her chubby hands found their way around Tori's neck, and straight into her hair. He understood the compulsion to touch it, but Lexi gravitated to it every time, entwining her little fingers into it. Jason smiled at the sight of his girls together, just as they should be. Then Allie wrapped her arms around Tori in an overenthusiastic hug, pulling a laugh from everyone as she said, "I'm so excited to see you, I almost peed my pants!"

Tori pulled her face out of Lexi's hair and kissed Allie on the cheek. "I know the feeling."

After a few moments, Allie finally let go of his girls, and he was able to get close. Hugging both of them, he kissed Lexi on the head. "Hi there, baby girl. I missed you."

And he did. Both Tori and Lexi had become an important part of his life in such a short period of time. Remembering the pain from only twenty-fours ago confirmed just how important. He quickly shook off the residual pain lingering in his chest; they needed to get a move on. Taking a look at the large volume of luggage surrounding Allie and Mike, he asked, "Did you bring both of our closets with you?"

Allie said, "Not all of them are yours. Mike and I are going to Catalina with you guys."

Shocked, Jason looked to Mike for confirmation. Mike shrugged. "She thinks you might need us around to help with Lexi, but don't worry, we rented our own villa. Besides, I think Allie's a little attached." The two of them looked to Allie, who was playing peek-a-boo with Lexi.

Jason snorted a laugh. "Doesn't surprise me." He shook Mike's hand and added, "Thanks for getting Lexi up here. I appreciate your help."

Mike said, "You'd do the same for me." Jason nodded in agreement. With his friends, once you were brought into the fold, you had no choice but to accept the help.

Picking up one of the suitcases, he asked, "Allie, did you bring all the papers we need?"

Allie broke away from Lexi and grabbed her purse, pulling out their boat tickets and handing Jason the ones he needed. Then she handed Tori her own purse and said, "You're gonna need this."

Tori shouldered it and said thanks. They were all busy gathering their stuff when Logan spoke up, "Don't worry about me here on the mainland. I'll be fine. I'm just gonna jump in the rental and drive back to San Diego all by myself. Some of us have to hold down the fort and all ..."

Jason laughed, and Allie snorted, "Oh, please." While Mike just smiled.

But Tori, she walked to Logan and hugged him tightly. Logan looked surprised by the action, and it took him a few seconds to return the hug. When she pulled away, she kissed his cheek. "Thank you."

Logan winked at her and said, "Anytime. But just for the record, I'd be happy to accept enchiladas in lieu of a thank you in the future."

Tori giggled. "I'll have to keep that in mind."

"Tori, don't fall for his crap! He's just desperate for a home-cooked meal since he's on his own now," Allie chided as she passed by.

TORI watched a wave of sadness pass over Logan's face before he schooled his features. She didn't know the details of his divorce from Gillian, but he had a front row seat to her new life. Tori felt bad for him, and she didn't like how Allie's comment saddened him. It made her want to defend him, but it wasn't her place. So she decided to be his friend. Winking back at him, she said, "I have no problem making you a home-cooked meal, anytime." Logan smiled back, the bit of sadness she saw there now gone. She knew what it was like to live with mistakes, but it had to be even worse when it was thrown in your face repeatedly.

With a nod, Logan stepped away before Jason gave him a hug. They spoke quietly to each other, about what she didn't know, but it was a moment she didn't want to interrupt. So she moved around and took her daughter back from Allie. Then, as a group, they gathered the rest of their stuff. Tori was surprised to see a running stroller mixed in with everything. She hadn't noticed it before, and Jason must have missed it, too. He rested his arm on her shoulder and said, "I guess I should know better when it comes to Gillian and Allie. I didn't think about telling them where your stroller was, but should've known they'd make sure you had one." Jason shook his head as he took Lexi from her arms. With a quick kiss to her head, he placed her in the stroller.

Then they were all boarding the boat. Or was it a ship? She wasn't sure what distinguished the difference, but she was excited regardless. She'd never been on either. Hell, she'd never seen the beach before last year, let alone visit an island. Excitement coursed through her veins at the new adventure. All thoughts of *why* they weren't going home were pushed to the back of her mind.

~*~*~*~

Tori discovered on the boat ride to Catalina that she gets motion sickness. Her mom had the issue, but Tori had never had a problem. Then again, she'd never been on a boat before. But the thought of having another similarity to her mother brought a smile to her face. In spite of the lingering queasiness.

Once on the island, she let Jason take the lead. She had no idea where they were going, so she just followed and took in the sights around her. Catalina was crowded, probably since it was summer, but the island was magnificent. Everywhere they went, there was something beautiful to stare at.

She'd been told they were staying at a villa, and while she wasn't really sure what a villa was, she didn't want to ask and sound ignorant. *Guess it was going to be a learning trip,* she thought as they made their way through town. When they arrived at their location, she let out a small laugh. "So apparently a *villa* is another word for condo?"

It was beautiful, but it was basically a condo. The old, Spanish-style building was done in white and topped off with heavy terracotta shingles. There were shutters on the visible windows and planters beneath each one, boasting a bouquet of colors. The building was narrow and on one of the higher points of the island. Or so she assumed since they drove up a hill to get there, but she had no viewpoint from where they stood. Allie came around from the other side of the car and said, “On an island like Catalina, people can call their shoe box a villa if they want. So long as it has a view, people will rent it.”

And with that, Allie and Mike grabbed their bags and made their way to the villa next door. Jason had opened the door to theirs and stood there waiting. “Are you coming or what?”

She nodded with a smile and grabbed her bag. Making her way inside, she was surprised by the elegance of the interior. It had obviously been remodeled and decked out in high-end appliances, complete with marble countertops, but she felt it didn’t match the front of the building. Then when Jason opened the double doors leading to a balcony, her entire vocabulary fled her brain, leaving her speechless.

The view was breathtaking. She now knew that they were on the top of a hill, and from where she was, she could see virtually everything. If she could choose to, she would stay in that spot the entire time they were there. Taking in a deep breath of ocean air, she let it out and smiled at Jason, who was apparently waiting for her reaction.

She snorted a laugh and asked, “Are you seriously worried I wouldn’t like this place?”

Shoving his hands in his pockets, he shrugged and looked out at the ocean. “No, I hoped you’d love it.”

Moving to him, she quickly wrapped her arms around his waist and hugged him tightly. She kissed his chest then looked back out at the view. “It’s the most beautiful thing I’ve ever seen.”

His hand lifted to her hair, sweeping it off her face. The breeze blew it right back, but it didn’t block her view when he said, “It sure is.”

She blushed at his implication. “You are quite the sweet talker, you know that?”

He shrugged. “I call ‘em like I see ‘em.”

Resting her head against his chest, she stared out at the water again, the serenity of the view soaking into her bones. Between the view, and being in Jason’s arms, she was beyond content. Sighing, she said, “I could stay right here forever.”

Jason kissed to top of her head and held her tighter. “We’ll stay as long as we need.”

He couldn’t be serious, she thought. Pulling back to look at him, his expression told her he most certainly was. “Jason, you know you can’t hide me away in a cliffside villa to protect me forever, right? It might be paradise, but it’s very public.” Her hands motioned toward the view and the crowds lingering the streets in the distance, like he needed it pointed out to him.

Scowling, he retorted, “I’m not locking you away. I’m *hiding* you in paradise in hopes to distract you enough that you forget about *him*.”

She gave him a sad smile. “I know you are, and you should know it’s working. But it’s not because of where I am; it’s because of who I’m with. You have a life to get back to, and I won't let you put it on hold for too long on account of me."

"That's not what's happening here, Tori, and I'll do what's necessary to protect you," he said firmly. She noticed the slight bit of anxiety in his voice.

Nodding, she rubbed her hand on his chest, not meaning to upset him. She recalled his actions and how he looked in the bathtub the night before. He was still battling his demons over what happened, and she didn't want to dismiss them. So she changed the subject—for now. "How long do we have the *villa* for?"

"Ten days. I paid to have the kitchen stocked, so we don't have to venture out to eat with the crowds. Plus, I know you love to cook. There are two bedrooms, and I made sure Allie packed the baby monitor for us so we can have some privacy but still give you peace of mind. It can be a lot like everyday life, but with a beautiful view. We can look at it as a vacation, yes?" he said with enthusiasm. His nervous rambling was clearly done in an effort to convince her. Like she really needed convincing.

Tori smiled. "Then it's perfect timing, because I'm in desperate need of a vacation."

He picked her up and kissed her hard. Since Lexi had fallen asleep on the car ride over and was resting quietly in the living room, Tori took full advantage of having Jason's lips on her again. The night before he just wanted to hold her. But tonight, she was having none of that holding back crap. When her hands found his hair, she gripped it tightly and was about to tell him just that when a voice interrupted them.

“I’m posing a rule of no sex on the balcony! I have no desire to see Jason’s bare ass, thank you very much,” Allie said from a few feet away. Their balcony apparently butted up against theirs, and the wall separating them only reached waist height and was topped off with a rod iron decoration of some sort. It was clearly not designed for privacy.

Jason huffed. “Then I’d stay off the balcony if I were you, half-pint.”

Tori giggled into Jason’s chest, embarrassed that he basically announced they would be having sex on the balcony. Not that she didn’t want to, but she just didn’t want everyone to know.

Tori laughed when Allie responded. “How about we draw up a schedule? That way I can avoid seeing your ass, and you can avoid seeing me go all *rodeo style* on Mike.”

“Aahh! For the love of God, Allie, I can’t *not* hear those words! What the hell is wrong with you?” Jason exclaimed as he covered his ears and walked inside.

Tori laughed even as she blushed. Shaking her head, she asked, “You love to torture him, don’t you?”

Allie winked. “I’ve been very good for the past two days, so I was ready to burst. There was nothing I could do to stop that from coming out.”

Shaking her head, Tori turned to walk inside, but first said, "I'm going to check out the food situation for dinner. Are you eating with us?"

"If you're cooking, I'm eating," Allie said enthusiastically.

"Well, if I'm feeding you, then you should minimize the torturing. Yes?" Tori said with humor as she walked inside.

As she did, she heard Allie mumble a curse and say, "Well played, Tori, well played."

CHAPTER THIRTY-THREE

JASON tried not to laugh at the face Lexi was making, but it was too funny. After fending off her attacks, Tori said he should just let her have the lemon wedge on his plate. So he did, and they were all rewarded with the face she continued to make after each attempt to eat it. It was like she thought it wouldn't be sour the next time. Making a face to mimic hers, he found himself on the receiving end of a mangled lemon wedge. Sitting up straight in mock anger, he scowled at Lexi, hoping to make her laugh. But, instead, she started to cry.

Jason couldn't get out of his seat fast enough. He was standing and lifting her quickly into his arms before the first wail left her lungs. He turned to face the table, expecting to find shock or anger in everyone's expressions. What he found was Mike smiling, Tori trying to conceal her laughter behind her hand, and Allie actually pointing and laughing at him. He could only imagine what he looked like, because he felt completely freaked by her reaction.

He scowled at his friends and gave Tori a pleading look as he bounced a crying Lexi, trying to soothe her. Tori put her hands up in surrender. "I got nothing. She has you wrapped so tightly around her little finger you don't even realize it. Just keep doing what you're doing, big guy, and I'm sure she'll stop ... eventually." Then both Tori and Allie laughed louder.

Shaking his head, he faced Lexi. "Hey, baby girl, I'm sorry I upset you. I was only playing around." Then the funniest thing happened; she stopped crying. Before Jason could even register it had happened, she already had her hands on his beard, playing with the bristles. Astonished at how quickly things had changed, he sat back down and watched as Lexi acted as if nothing was wrong. When he looked back over to Tori he asked, "Did I just get played? Or was she just easily distracted?"

Tori laughed and said, "Let's go with a little of both."

"I think it's a lot of both!" Allie said.

Kissing her on her head, he placed her back in the highchair and went about eating his dinner. Across from him, he caught Tori's eye, and she gave him a perfect smile, before she winked at him. Damn, how he loved it when she winked at him. One might argue that Tori, too, had Jason wrapped around her little finger. Yeah, he was whipped for sure.

They'd been on the island for a week, and he knew that Tori was feeling bad about both of them missing work. Jason had made sure to offer whatever assistance he could in hopes that she would relax more, but she refused it, saying it wasn't about the money. Allie and Mike offered to keep Lexi with them in their villa that night, and Jason was quick to accept their generosity. Looking forward to the night ahead of them, he found himself eating faster than necessary.

With only three days left at the villa, he knew they would need to come up with a new game plan for Tori's safety. Taking her anxiety and concern to work into consideration, he decided they would talk about it and make whatever plans needed—together.

When finished with dinner, the group walked together toward their villas. It was a warm summer evening, but the ocean breeze blowing in made the temperature tolerable. Walking with her hand in his, while pushing the stroller, they were just outside their doors when Jason's phone rang. Pulling it out, he saw it was Mack calling. Since there was only one reason he'd call him, Jason was concerned. "Hey Mack, what's going on?"

"Hey Jason, sorry to bother you, but I just came home from work and there's all kinds of activity going on across the street," Mack offered.

"Like what kind of activity?"

"It appears as if the house caught fire today. The whole back half of it is gone, and there are people milling about in the wooded area behind the house. I tried to get some information, but they just shut me down and told me to stay behind the tape." Mack sounded irritated, and Jason understood the notion.

Pulling the phone away from his ear, he looked to everyone. They knew something was going on, and they were anxiously awaiting instructions. He looked at Allie. "Call Sean, and ask him to call Idaho and find out what's going on. There was a fire at Damien's house."

Allie nodded and dialed her phone. Beside him, Tori clutched his arm and waited for him to tell her more. He kissed her before putting the phone back to his ear.

"Thanks for letting me know. I'm going to have my friend call the PD there and see if they know anything," Jason said.

"Good idea. Let me know what you find out," Mack requested. Jason agreed, and they said their goodbyes.

Ending the call, he turned his attention to Tori. He rubbed his hands up and down her arms as he said, "All Mack knows is that there was a fire at the house. Let's go inside and wait to find out what Sean can tell us."

Tori's face was tense as she nodded and moved past him into the villa. Allie and Mike followed, obviously not saying goodnight until they, too, knew what was going on. Fortunately, they didn't have to wait too long. Within minutes, Jason's phone was ringing.

"Hey Sean, were you able to find anything out?" Jason asked. His voice was thick with hope. It had been a long week, and with every passing day, Jason's own anxiety grew. He found himself intently staring at all the strangers they came in contact with. It was borderline obsessive, so they needed to find Damien soon. Sean sighed into the phone then told Jason what he knew.

TORI watched as Jason listened intently to whatever Sean was saying. Occasionally he would nod, but he didn't say anything. Allie had perched herself on the arm of the couch next to her and rested her hand on Tori's back. The support she had from her new friends was humbling. She knew she would never be able to repay them for it, but she would try somehow. As she waited for Jason to finish his call, she noted every expression he made. Even as the anxiety of the situation rose, she took comfort in him.

When Jason finally ended the call, the silence in the room was deafening. It may have only been a few seconds, but it stretched out as they waited for him to tell them. When his shoulders lifted in a deep breath, she prepared herself, keeping the hope at bay.

"Sean said they think Damien is dead," Jason said. The look on his face was devoid of emotion as he gazed at Tori. *Dead?*

Tori asked the first thing that came to mind, "How? Are they sure?"

Jason scooted across the couch to her, Allie moved over to another seat, and Mike stood behind the couch holding Lexi. "According to the police, the house caught fire mid-morning. Since there was a patrol out front watching the house, firefighters were on scene quickly. But it was fast moving, and it took them a few hours to put it out. When investigators went in, they found a body."

Tori sat still as a rock, waiting for Jason to finish. The emotions that rolled around her insides ranged from sorrow to fear, then to relief and excitement. Could it be over?

When Jason continued, she hung on every word. "He said they still need to confirm it with DNA since the body was burned badly, but the height and size is consistent with Damien's."

Damien was dead? Relief was heavy and overwhelming as it washed over her. Her eyes filled with tears and spilled over at the thought of her nightmare being over. Thoughts of what that meant passed through her mind on fast forward. They could go home now. She could really move on. Lexi was safe now.

Jason pulled her against him, mumbling, "I'm sorry."

She wondered if he mistook her tears as anything other than just emotions coming out. They weren't because she was sad. Pulling back, she looked at him and said sternly, "I'm not sorry."

He gave her a questioning look. She cupped his face in her hands and repeated herself, "I'm not sorry at all ... I'm relieved." Her body sagged with the admission. "Does that make me a bad person to feel almost giddy knowing he probably suffered pain when he died?"

Jason's face relaxed and a small smile formed, "No baby, it doesn't make you a bad person at all. It makes you human."

Tori threw her arms around Jason's neck and held on tightly as she let the information sink in further. *Damien couldn't hurt her anymore*. Jason's hand rubbed up and down her back as he held her. Only a noise from Lexi brought Tori's attention away from the thoughts in her head. Turning, she found Mike and Allie standing nearby with Lexi. Allie motioned over her shoulder with her thumb. "We're gonna head out then; you two enjoy your night. Let us know what the plans are for going home in the morning, yeah?"

Tori stood from the couch and moved to hug Lexi, relishing in the fact that Damien would never hurt her. She kissed her goodnight before hugging Allie, as well. "Thank you for everything."

Allie only winked before looking at Jason. "No balcony sex tonight. If we're going home tomorrow, I want to enjoy the view of the ocean. So I call dibs, got it?"

Jason came up behind Tori and wrapped his arms around her before answering, "Fine, no balcony tonight." Tori sagged against Jason, feeling exhaustion set into her limbs as the anxiety she'd been wearing all week finally left her body.

They watched as Mike and Allie left with Lexi, and they just stood there silently. Tori closed her eyes and turned in Jason's arms, needing to hold him, too. Once she was settled snuggly against his chest, she sighed and absorbed the warmth of his embrace. His arms were her safe haven and she never wanted to leave them, and now she wouldn't have to.

Looking up at Jason, she asked, "Are we going home tomorrow?"

He swept her hair off her forehead and furrowed his brow. "Only if you want to. But we can stay another day or two if you'd like."

She shook her head. "No, I'm ready to go home. Let things get back to normal and move on."

"I sure hope that moving on includes me?" he asked with sarcasm, but she detected his insecurity there.

Rising up on her tiptoes, she kissed him softly before whispering, "All my plans include you."

To her surprise, he lifted her quickly, pulling a laugh from her while she rushed to wrap her legs around his waist. Now above him, she smiled as he said, "Good, because you're in all of my plans, too."

She laughed as her hands roamed through his hair. Playfully, she asked, "Oh yeah? And what plans do you have for the immediate future?"

His chest rumbled against hers, and his arms tightened his hold. Pressing his lips against hers, he nipped her bottom one as he started moving toward the bedroom. Before entering the room, he declared, "My current plans for the evening involve making you scream my name over and over until nobody on this island doubts who owns your pleasure."

A shudder ran through her body at his words, and she responded by taking his lips in a hungry kiss. She already knew the answer, but if he wanted to make sure the whole island knew, as well, there was no way she was going to stop him.

CHAPTER THIRTY-FOUR

JASON was happy he'd managed to convince Tori to stay one more day on the island. After spending all night getting lost in each other, they were able to spend all day enjoying the sites. It was the first day Jason wasn't looking over his shoulder at every turn, so all his attention was on his girls. They'd spent some time on the beach, played in the sand. Then, even though Tori advised against it, he bought Lexi her first soft-serve cone. Which promptly melted all over him before they made it to the villa. He still didn't understand how it was all over him and none was on her. He shook his head at the memory, but smiled as he recalled Tori helping him clean it all off in the shower afterward.

Now that they were home and unloading their stuff from Mike's truck, he was looking forward to some more alone time with Tori. In his house and in his bed. He wanted to call it their bed, because in his head it already was, but he figured he'd let them settle back into their lives before tackling that. Placing all the luggage inside the garage, they said their goodbyes as he lifted a sleeping Lexi from her seat. Carrying her inside, he laid her down in the playpen upstairs before returning to help Tori with the bags.

When he entered the garage, she handed him the bag of food they'd brought back from Catalina. "I'm starving; you want to light the grill and we can cook those steaks? I put the rest of that marinade on them before we left so they should be perfect now."

He kissed her and took the bag. "You feed me so good, baby."

Tori snorted. "I'm told I give good meat."

Jason laughed. "Yeah you do! I'll throw these on the grill, and I'm gonna take a quick shower. I can feel the salt from the air on my skin."

"But you taste good salty," she said with a pout as she opened the suitcases on the garage floor. "But go ahead, I'm gonna throw in a load of laundry, and then I'll meet you up there."

He laughed and headed inside. After turning on the grill just outside the patio doors, he went about putting the food away before throwing the steaks on low. He took the stairs two at a time and rushed about getting in the shower, looking forward to running his hands all over Tori's wet skin. His body responded to the image and willed it to calm down; she'd be there soon.

TORI separated their clothes directly from their suitcases. She didn't see a need to take them inside and empty them, only to bring them back out there. Throwing a load in the washing machine, she turned it on before closing the garage door and heading inside. Stepping into the kitchen she could see the grill on outside the doors and hear the shower on upstairs. Knowing they had a short window of time to enjoy their shower, she pulled the salad out to make sure it survived the trip. Pleased with it, she placed it back in the fridge and moved to the sink to wash her hands.

When she felt a body press up against hers from behind, she smiled and turned off the water. It was at the same time she turned off the water that she felt a hand stroke down the length of her hair. She stiffened at the similarity of the movement and was about to tell Jason just that when she picked up on the sound of the shower still running upstairs. Panic, confusion, and fear all welled up inside her at the possibility of what was happening.

She closed her eyes and willed the nightmare away. That's what it was—a nightmare. She had let her imagination get the best of her. When she opened her eyes, it would be gone, and she'd be standing in Jason's kitchen alone. But then the hand began to slowly wrap itself around Tori's hair, and she knew it was very much a reality. Tears began to spill from the corners of her eyes, completely unbidden. There was no reason to control herself; he knew what she was feeling.

Gasping in pain at the tight grip on her hair and subsequent yank, her eyes shot open and met the evil gaze of her own personal devil. Apparently back from the dead. She chastised herself for letting them believe he was dead. She should've know he wouldn't be gone. True evil didn't die easily. His breath was hot as he washed over her face, making her skin crawl. It felt like an eternity as she stared into those evil eyes before he spoke, "It's about time you came back, Victoria. Did you have a good time on the island?"

He said her name with disgust, which was fine with her because it wasn't her name anymore. She shivered at his reference to her being on Catalina because that meant he knew where she was the whole time. She closed her eyes at that thought, not wanting to look at him any longer. Damien responded with another yank and a sneer, "Open your fucking eyes! You don't get to hide from me any longer."

She didn't want to look at him, but she definitely didn't want him to have all the control, so she reluctantly opened her eyes. This way she knew what he was doing. Leveling her eyes on him, she waited.

"That's more like it. Did you know that you show all of your emotions in your eyes? Fear, pain, all of it plays out across your face like my own personal movie."

She did know this. While it was typically a good thing, in this case it was a death sentence. Steeling her spine, she tried to mask those emotions and not give him what he wanted. Above her, she could hear the shower still running, and it made her want to cry knowing Jason was so close, yet so far away. He was probably waiting for her to come to him and wouldn't be coming down anytime soon. Not wanting Damien to see the sadness in her eyes, since it was for Jason, not him, she blinked away the tears. Unfortunately, Damien knew just what to do to make her break.

"It appears my movie is on pause. How about I do something to get it going again? What do you say, we go upstairs and play with my daughter?" he asked in a low voice, but it had Tori's attention.

Her back became more rigid, and her hands fisted on the counter in front of her. Glaring at him, she said in a voice laced with venom, "I'll never let you touch her, you bastard."

"Ah, so that's what it takes to spark a fire in your eyes. I'm looking forward to the fight, Victoria. How about I up the stakes?" Damien said with a chuckle as she felt cold metal press up against her cheek. "Would you like a scar on this side to match your other one? We could even give one to your daughter if you'd like. It's the least I can do after what you did to *my* face."

She closed her eyes as fear and panic rose again. Her bravado lasted for only a few moments, but resolve was setting in. She would do anything to protect her daughter, and Damien had to know this. In a voice just above a whisper, she said, "Me, I'll take it. Do whatever you want to me, just leave *my* daughter alone."

Damien's laughter was malicious, his words full of intent when he said, "That's right, Victoria, I can do whatever I want to you. You're mine, and I refuse to share you. Not with my daughter and certainly not with that oversized moron upstairs."

His words angered her, but reminded her of the risk Jason and Lexi were in. She felt the blade of the knife, now warm from her skin, shift against her cheek. Damien was making his point clear. When it shifted a second time, she felt the tip pierce her skin and gasped at the pain. A moment later she felt blood trickle down her face. It mingled with the tears she couldn't control.

Damien's body shuddered and hardened against hers. Staring at the knife on her cheek, his pleasure was evident.

Being completely at his mercy was terrifying, but at least he wasn't anywhere near Lexi. And she knew she was definitely at his mercy when his eyelids lowered and his nostrils flared. She whimpered. He was getting off on what he was doing, and she saw what was coming a moment before he slid the blade across her skin, slicing it open as it went. She cried out in pain but heard the knife fall into the sink below her.

The roar of her heartbeat deafened her ears as Damien spun her around to admire his handiwork. He sighed in pleasure a second before she heard a loud thud, and Damien's body flew away from her.

JASON knew something was wrong. He'd been waiting in the shower for Tori, but a sinking feeling in his gut told him to get out. Leaving the shower running, he stepped out and slipped on the jeans he'd discarded when he got in. Forgoing a shirt, he padded barefoot down the hall. Peeking in on Lexi, he was relieved to see she was fine, but still no sign of Tori. As he exited the room, he grabbed a bat lying in the pile of toys he had for his nephews. Gripping it tightly, he rested it on his shoulder as he quietly closed the door. Cautiously he descended the stairs—prepared to swing at anything he came in contact with.

When he reached the bottom step, he listened carefully as he turned toward where he'd left Tori. As he got closer to the kitchen, he heard it. An evil chuckle followed by words that made his blood run cold. *You're mine, and I refuse to share you ...*

Not in this lifetime, asshole, he said to himself, staying quiet so Damien wouldn't know he was there. The kitchen came into view seconds later, and Jason fought the urge to run head-first into the bastard. He could see him standing behind Tori, one hand gripping her hair, and the other out of view. Because he wasn't sure if Damien had a weapon on Tori, he chose not to charge at him.

Stepping closer, he heard Tori gasp and then whimper, and he knew for sure Damien was armed. Assessing his options, he continued to get closer. He readied the bat, he thought maybe he could swing at the guy's legs, taking him by surprise. Hopefully then he'd let go of Tori long enough for Jason to do some permanent damage.

Then everything happened in slow motion. Tori cried out in obvious pain, and Jason knew he couldn't wait any longer. At the sound of metal clinging in the sink, he knew Damien had dropped something. When Damien spun Tori around, and Jason caught sight of her face, he sucked in a painful breath and swung with all the power surging through his body.

With a sickening crunch, the bat made contact with Damien's ribs, and his body flew to the side. Taking in his motionless body, Jason dropped the bat and moved to Tori. Her hand cupped her cheek and blood seeped through her fingers. Jason couldn't handle the sight of his beautiful girl covered in her own blood. Grabbing a towel, he quickly pressed it over her hand and wrapped his other around her for support, her body immediately relaxing into him. "I've got you, baby."

CHAPTER THIRTY-FIVE

JASON held his hand tightly against Tori's cheek. When she opened her eyes, he said, "I'm so sorry, baby. Did he hurt you anywhere else?"

She took in a ragged breath before shaking her head no. He kissed her forehead and sighed. "Thank God. Let me call for help." She nodded this time, closed her eyes, and rested her forehead against his chest. Holding her to him, he reached across the counter to call the police. Phone in hand, he turned it to dial when he was struck in the arm. He roared in pain as he felt his bones snap, his arm now hanging limp at his side. Bracing for another attack, he pulled Tori closer to him and turned away from Damien and his own bat.

Tori screamed, and Jason felt the second blow against his ribcage. The force pushed them forward, and Jason shoved Tori out in front of him, "Go! Get out of here." Jason wheezed as he spoke, unable to get his lungs to expand further without pain wrapping around his body.

Tori tripped and landed on the floor, but quickly recovered and was making her way around the other side of the kitchen island. Taking his free arm, Jason braced himself on the counter to turn and look at his attacker. It was the first time he'd been able to look the bastard in the eye. He wanted to look him in the eye and tell him that Tori was *his* now.

With short, shallow breaths, Jason stood as tall as he could and glared at the man in front of him. He could hear Tori's rapid breathing behind him so he knew she was still in the room. There was no way she could get out of the room and reach the stairs without passing Damien. Jason needed to find a way to make that happen, so Tori could get to Lexi and get the hell out of there.

Damien was shorter than Jason as he stood before him, slightly hunched to the side. Clearly he'd inflicted damage to the guy when he hit him. It was a small victory considering Jason's arm hung lifelessly at his side, numbness beginning to set in. He didn't care; Tori and Lexi were all he cared about in that moment. Looking in Damien's eyes, Jason could see the desperation and craziness swirling around in them. He was surprised they weren't black.

Jason smirked when his gaze landed on the scars he saw covering the right side of Damien's face. His girl did that to him, and he was damn proud of her for it. Wanting to provoke the asshole, he said, "So you're Damien. I think I pictured a bigger, more imposing beast. Not the broken, damaged weasel I see here."

It worked because Damien snarled and gripped the bat tighter. His breathing was labored like Jason's, but he didn't say anything. So Jason continued, needing to push harder, "How does a guy like you even manage to father a child? Did you have to inflict pain on her just to get it up?"

Damien chuckled. "Something tells me you don't want to hear the pleasure I got from hurting her. Do you want to hear about the time I held her down and sliced her cheek open with the top of a can?"

Jason tensed. No, he sure as fuck didn't want to hear about that.

"That's what I thought. How about two minutes ago when I sliced open the other side of her face? Do you want to know what the sound of the blade sliding across her flesh does to me?" Damien asked, visibly shuddering.

He wanted to vomit. Here, Jason was trying to provoke him, but it was being turned on him instead. If he had use of both his arms, he'd wrap them around the sicko's neck. Needing to turn the tables back around, Jason said, "I want to hear that shit about as much as you want to hear me tell you what it's like fuck her senseless."

Hitting his mark, Jason smirked as Damien bared his teeth at him like an animal. "Yeah, we could even talk about how she loves to go down on her knees and wrap that pretty mouth of hers around me."

Jason inwardly cringed at his words. It felt wrong to belittle anything he'd done with Tori, but he needed her safe. Backing up a step, in hopes Damien would step forward one, he could now see Tori in his peripheral vision. He couldn't take his eyes off Damien, but could tell she was ready to move when she saw an opening. *Good girl.*

When Jason stepped back again, Damien followed this time. Backing himself into a corner may appear to have been to Damien's advantage, but that was part of his plan. Even with his arm broken, he was confident that he'd be able to deflect a blow from the bat with the other one. So long as he gave Tori the ability to get out of the room.

Gearing up for another verbal attack, Jason took another step back until he hit the wall, and said, “Tell me, Damien, when you fucked her, did she ever scream your name like she screams mine?”

His eyes bulged, and Jason knew he was almost ready to snap, so he finished with, “Oh wait, that’s only when she orgasms … and she told me you didn’t know how to make that happen.”

With a roar, Damien raised the bat and attacked. Coming at Jason like a crazed animal with one mission: kill its prey.

TORI listened to what Jason was saying, but didn’t let it bother her. She knew he was only saying that to get at Damien. And she could see it was working. With each word and each step back, she could see Damien’s rage grow like a living thing. His posture changed, his breathing became shallower, clearly compensating for his injury.

All she needed to do was get past him so she could call for help. She didn’t know where the phone was since he’d knocked it out of Jason’s grip, but she could see the alarm pad on the wall by the garage door. If she could get to the panel, she could hit the emergency button and alert the security company. So when she heard Jason throw his next insult at Damien, she knew her window of opportunity had just opened. When Damien yelled and charged at Jason, she took off running across the room. Behind her, she could hear the grunts and groans of the two men in battle, but she had to ignore them. Reaching her destination, she promptly pressed all the emergency buttons she could see on the keypad. Seconds later, the house phone rang; the transmission was successful.

The ringing led her to the phone in the family room. Jason and Damien had now moved from the corner where Jason previously was to the other side of the kitchen island. The family room branched off the kitchen, and she could see them clearly. Dropping to her knees, she found the phone under a chair and answered it.

"Hello? Please help us!" she screamed breathlessly into the phone.

The emergency operator on the line asked for more information, and Tori yelled, "We need police and paramedics." She swallowed, her mouth dry and gritty. "Send everyone!"

Tori kept the phone to her ear as she scanned the room for a weapon. She couldn't tell who was winning, but Jason was already hurt enough. Spotting the fireplace in the corner, she grabbed the poker and lifted it with one arm, testing its weight. She'd need to put the phone down to swing it properly, so she did. Moving closer to the fight, she cringed when Jason howled in pain after Damien landed a punch to his already injured arm.

When Jason stumbled back, Tori took a swing at Damien. She hadn't realized she'd closed her eyes until she heard his below. Opening them, she could see him holding the side of his head. Apparently she'd only grazed him, but she hoped it would give Jason a moment to recover. Before Jason had fully recovered though, Damien landed a kick to Jason's ribs, and he went down on his knees.

"No!" Tori screamed as she watched him fall. Out of the corner of her eye, she saw Damien grab the bat and lift it over his head. Trying to push herself into action, she lifted the poker to swing at him. Her heart racing, blood dripped from the wound on her cheek, and she felt her stomach turn at the sensation. Ready to strike at Damien, she watched as he began to swing the bat at Jason who was completely unguarded on the floor.

In an attempt to warn him, she yelled Jason's name, just as a gunshot sounded and echoed loudly. Stunned by the sound, and not knowing where it'd come from, she looked around. The bat clanged against the tile floor as it fell from Damien's hands. Tori watched as Damien looked down at his chest, pressing his hand to it. That was when she saw the blood spreading across his shirt and trickling through his fingers. Damien had been shot?

Still looking around to see who fired the shot, Tori wasn't sure who the newcomer holding the gun was, but she'd never been more grateful to see a stranger in her life.

Tori dropped the poker and rushed to the ground next to Jason. When she cradled his head against her chest, she made eye contact with Damien as he fell to the floor. Seconds later, she watched as his eyes went blank, and he gurgled his last breath. Jason's body heaved in distress as Tori held him, his hand reaching up to touch hers. Releasing her hold on his head, she let him lift it, and he looked to the doorway where the man stood. His gun was still in hand, but now at his side. He looked to be in shock, and a moment later he mumbled, "Police, don't move."

Tori thought it was the strangest thing to hear, after the fact, but she wasn't about to question it. The man was clearly in shock. Jason's voice brought her attention back to him when he said, "Thanks, rookie."

JASON never thought he would owe his life to the rookie officer who'd thought Jason had something to do with Tori's kidnapping. But there he stood, gun in hand, shock on his face, with Damien lying dead on the floor opposite him. Jason couldn't remember the rookie's name, and when he thought to look at his nametag for it, he realized the guy was in street clothes. As odd as it seemed, he was grateful nonetheless.

"Do you think you can call for backup, officer?" Jason asked, his voice strained and fatigued.

The officer blinked and finally took his attention away from Damien's body to look at Jason and Tori. He didn't get a chance to answer before sirens filled the air. Jason sagged against Tori and waited. When his front door opened and Sean walked in followed by other officers with guns drawn, Jason wanted to laugh. *The show's over guys*, he thought.

Sean took in the scene around them before his eyes landed on the rookie in the doorway. "Officer Jennings, I'll need to confiscate your weapon. Standard procedure."

The young guy still hadn't said anything, but he nodded at Sean's request before removing the magazine from his gun and unloading the round from the chamber. Sean took it from him and handed it off to another officer who had a bag ready. Jason took the pause in activity to ask, "How did you know to come here?"

The young guy obviously had a reason other than being alerted by nine-one-one.

“I got a call from the landlord, Hal. He said someone had been snooping around his place and thought I should check it out. Then he insisted I check out your place, too. When I got here, I could see the smoke coming from the barbeque over the fence, so I thought something was wrong. That’s when I saw him aim to take your head off with the bat.”

“Then you have impeccable timing,” Jason said as he closed his eyes. The pain in his side was increasing in his current position, and he feared he’d pass out from hyperventilating. Looking up at Tori, he sighed when she smiled at him. The amount of blood on her face was frightening, but he was so happy that was her only injury.

“Hey you,” he said.

“Hey yourself,” she said in a whisper.

“I think we both have an ambulance ride in our future.”

She nodded. “I think you might be right, but you can take the bed. In fact, I insist.”

CHAPTER THIRTY-SIX

TORI parked the car and turned off the engine. Looking to the passenger seat, she couldn't help but laugh at Jason again. Shaking her head, she said, "Oh, will you stop pouting. There's nothing wrong with letting me drive you around."

Jason scowled. "You're injured, too." He tried to cross his arms over his chest to complete his pout, but grunted in pain when his casted arm landed on his broken rib.

"Are you seriously comparing my stitches to your post-surgical arm and two cracked ribs? Suck it up, big guy, and let me take care of you," Tori said in her best stern-mom-voice.

Still scowling, he grumbled, "But it's my job to take care of you."

She was about to tell him that he was being ridiculous when a stuffed animal came flying from the back seat and nailed him in the back of his head. Tori let out a laugh before quickly schooling it and looking at Lexi. As she was about to scold Lexi, she got as far as saying her name when the stuffed animal flew back and landed in Lexi's lap. Looking back at Jason, he shrugged. "What? She started it."

"How can I tell her not to do it if you do it, too?" To prove her point, the toy came up and hit Jason on top of the head again. Jason picked it up from his lap and smiled for the first time since they left the house. "She's got great aim, doesn't she?"

Shaking her head, she got out of the car, and said, "I give up."

After getting Lexi out, leaving the toy behind, she opened Jason's door for him. His scowl was back as he stood. Tori once again fought her need to laugh at his bad mood. Closing the door behind him, she said, "You know, if you're so resistant to letting me take care of you, you could've opened your door yourself."

Between his arm being casted and padded from surgery on the one side and his ribs being cracked on the other, he couldn't. But she was going to give him crap over his bad mood until it disappeared.

"Very funny," he said as they began walking. "I think you're enjoying this a bit much."

"Does anyone enjoy grumpy Jason? 'Cause I gotta tell you, he was cute at first, but now I'd like to smack him," Tori said playfully, although there might've been some truth to it. Okay, it was definitely true, but he needed to get over it and let her be there for him. After all, she was the reason for his current condition.

Jason stepped in front of her, halting her. "I'm sorry, really, I am. But I'm all sorts of pissed off because I can't even hold you. I'm broken on both sides, and I hate it. Poor Lexi will think I don't like her anymore, and it kills me."

She immediately felt bad for giving him grief. She'd hate it if she were in his position; and since she hadn't thought of it that way, she apologized. Putting a hand to his cheek, he leaned into it. She ran her thumb over his cheekbone, as she said, "I'm sorry, I didn't look at like that. In fact, you should be a lot grumpier when you put it that way. But before long, you'll be good as new, and you can hold both of us as much as you want."

"I'm counting the days," he said with determination. She smiled then kissed him as best she could with the tape restricting her facial movements. *What a pair they were*, she thought as they resumed walking. Jason had a follow up appointment with his orthopedic surgeon, and she had one with the plastic surgeon. They'd been fortunate enough to be transported to the hospital Gillian worked at after the incident. While in the emergency room, Gillian made sure to use her connections, and both of them were seeing specialists immediately. Jason said it was another perk of being part of his group, and Tori would have to agree.

When they reached the floor for orthopedics, Tori kissed Jason before he stepped off the elevator. "I'll be down as soon as I'm done, okay."

He gave her a hopeful look. "Are you sure you don't want me to come with you?"

"Don't be silly; go get your arm checked, and I'll see you in a little while." She ushered him out and let the doors close. She was a little nervous to see what her face looked like under the bandages. It had been a week, and Gillian had reassured her that the plastic surgeon she had was the best, and she trusted her. Walking into the waiting room, she found Gillian chatting with the receptionist. When she spotted Tori, Gillian promptly removed Lexi from her arms.

Tori thought she should be used to them always swooping in and snagging her daughter, but it still surprised her they didn't ask.

Giving her a one-sided smile, she teased, "Are you working on this floor now?"

Gillian leveled a stare at her. "And how do you plan to hold on to this little hellion while lying still to have sutures removed?"

She had her on that one. "Guess I hadn't thought that far. I was too busy chastising the grumpy giant."

She laughed. "I can only imagine." Gillian sat when they called Tori back, and within ten minutes she was standing in front of a mirror, looking at the newest scar added to her collection. It wasn't as bad as she thought it would be, but then again, that was probably because it was better than the other cheek. Pleased with his work, the doctor assured her that the redness of the line would go down as he placed a thin, flesh-colored tape along the length of the wound.

When she walked out of his office, she was confident with the knowledge that her man would have no problem with her new scar.

JASON hated feeling helpless. As he waited for the doctor to examine him, he tried not to focus on what he couldn't do. It only pissed him off more. And the fact that he'd needed to be saved by a cop fresh out of the academy ... he didn't even want to go there. His ego had taken a few major blows when Damien violated the sanctity of his home and harmed Tori. It didn't matter what anyone told him about it being out of his control—it was going to take time to get over that.

Sighing again, he was relieved when the doctor finally came in.

"How's the patient doing today?" the doctor asked in a much-too-cheery voice for a grown man to use. It only pissed Jason off more.

"Grouchy as hell is how the patient is doing," Jason admitted.

The doctor laughed under his breath as he washed his hands. "From the pain?"

He checked Jason's vitals as he waited for an answer. "No, because I have zero use of the repaired arm and can't lift the good one because of my ribs. I need help using the damn bathroom, and I can't even give lame, one-armed hugs like this, but I'd settle for them if I could."

There was a pause before the doctor asked with humor, "So you're a hugger?"

"Yeah, I'd like to hold my woman. In the past three weeks, she's been kidnapped, then found, then her ex came in to my house and tried to take her again. He sliced up her face that needed over thirty stitches to repair, and then left me like this. It pisses me off that even though the bastard is dead, he's preventing me from holding the woman he tried taking from me." Jason's voice had gotten louder with each word he spoke.

Apparently, he'd felt the need to take his frustration out on the doctor. He was about to apologize when the doctor said, “All right, how about we x-ray those ribs and see if we can’t get you more mobility with a good binding wrap? You’ll be getting a more condensed cast on the arm if everything looks good, but you still need a cast. Can’t do much about that one I’m afraid.”

He welcomed the relief he felt at the possibility to be more independent and actually hold his girls. After several x-rays, one cast removal and subsequent replacement, and a torture session where his ribs were bound, he was heading to the waiting room. His mission: to give Tori a lame, one-armed hug. He smiled when he found her in the hall letting Lexi walk around.

When she saw him coming, she smiled in return, and he almost missed the bandage on her face. Walking up to her, he cautiously wrapped his good arm around her waist and slowly leaned in to her. When her body rested against his and there was no pain, he relaxed. Finding her lips, he gently kissed her.

Pulling back, she smiled and said, “Look who’s not so grumpy anymore.”

He laughed. “Apparently I just needed a hug.”

She winked at him before reaching down to pick up Lexi. He gave her a cautious hug, too, and was pleased when she hugged him back. Feeling content, he walked out of the hospital with his girls.

Once in the car, Tori said, “Is it okay if we stop by my place? I need to pick up some different clothes for us. Been wearing the same things over and over and I’m getting kind sick of them.”

Since she had basically been staying with him for the past three weeks, he figured now was as good a time as any to bring up what he wanted. As it always was with Tori, he got nervous about what her response might be. Since he'd been giving it some thought recently, he'd come up with some ideas if he needed to convince her to stay.

"What if you just brought *all* of your clothes over?" he asked vaguely. She looked to him in question before turning her attention back to driving. Realizing it was a chicken shit way of asking her, he rephrased, "What I meant to say was, how about we just move all your stuff over to my place, and you can call it your place, too?"

Tori smirked at him. "Call it my place, too? That was really cute."

He shrugged, waiting for her answer. She glanced at him once more before they exited the freeway. When they stopped at a light, she turned toward him. "You really want me and Lexi to invade your space on a permanent basis? Because I understand that you need me right now, but I also know there will come a time when you won't. And I would hate it if you felt stuck with us. Maybe you should wait until you feel better ..."

Jason was grateful his arm was more mobile because he covered her mouth with his hand. "Stop right there."

She did, so he added, "This is usually where you start to babble stupid shit that pisses me off. So let's just cut to the chase. There will not come a time when I won't need you, so just give me a yes or no answer. Will you move in with me?"

Tori smiled as the light turned green, and she started driving again. "I'm not the only person in this car who babbles, you know."

"True. Now stop avoiding the question and give me your answer," Jason insisted.

They'd just pulled into her driveway, so once the car was turned off, she turned to him. "You're not just proposing this now so you can get out of lifting things, are you?"

"Okay smartass, what's a guy gotta do to get a straight answer out of you?" he asked as he kissed the back of her hand.

"A kiss is always helpful, but I can see you're getting worried, so yes. We'll move in with you." Tori finished with a smile.

"That's a great answer. How about we go inside and I can give you that kiss to help seal the deal."

"Sounds like a plan to me." Tori stepped out into the warmth of the day, smiling at the turn of events. Helping Jason out and then getting Lexi, they'd started toward her door, when a voice behind them had her stopping dead in her tracks.

"Victoria Chambers?"

CHAPTER THIRTY-SEVEN

JASON felt Tori stiffen at the sound of her former name. They turned around together and stared at the stranger. A few moments passed by before Tori took a deep breath and said, "Why say my name like a question when you know exactly who I am? Or do you not recognize me with my new scar?"

He wasn't sure who this guy was, but he didn't sense any fear from Tori, so he stood quietly next to her and offered his support.

"My apologies. I only said your name as a question, because I know you don't go by that name anymore," he confessed.

"Then how did you find my address, and why are you here? He's dead so you should have no business with me," Tori spat at him. Her anger at the man was palpable as she turned to walk to her door.

"I may not have any business with you, but I do with your daughter." At that, Jason had to say something.

"Okay, who the fuck are you, and what do you want? You have about five seconds to get to your point before I call the police and have you removed," Jason growled at the small man.

Straightening his spine, he pulled a business card from his pocket. Handing it to Jason, he said, "My name is Richard Quinn, and I'm an attorney."

Jason looked at the address and phone number on the business card and realized whose attorney he was. "I guess it'd be safe to assume that your client is the late Damien Chambers?"

"You'd be correct. And in light of his recent death, I have been appointed as the executor of his estate," Mr. Quinn stated.

"I know damn well he didn't include me in his will so I don't understand why you're here. The last time I saw you it was when you showed up at my hospital bed and informed me I was not allowed back in the house. That my belongings had been packed and could be picked up from your office. And while those might have been fun times for you, Mr. Quinn, I'd rather not revisit them. So, please leave," Tori snapped. Jason had never seen her temper flare in such a way, and he couldn't help but get a little turned on by it—no matter how inappropriate the timing. Her fiery beauty was sexy as hell when angry.

"No ma'am, you are not listed, but your daughter is."

"That's impossible! He didn't even know she existed, and he never would've put her in his will."

"If I may sit down and discuss this with you inside, I would appreciate it. Even though I'm well aware I'm not a person you like, I assure you I am not a threat," Mr. Quinn pleaded. Tori paused to consider his request and looked to Jason before answering. He gave her a nod to let her know he'd be there to back her up if needed. The man wasn't a threat as far as Jason could tell, and if he had malicious intent, he wouldn't be asking to sit down and talk it over inside.

"Fine," Tori said with irritation, "but I don't have all day." Then she marched to her door and let them all in. She set Lexi in her play area as Jason motioned for Mr. Quinn to have a seat on the couch. Jason took the chair opposite it, and Tori stood next to him, hands on hips, waiting.

Mr. Quinn opened his briefcase and pulled out some papers. Tori looked to Jason with uncertainty, her rage from a few moments ago fading. He motioned with his eyes to the arm of the chair and she took the suggestion. Sitting on it, he was able to put his arm on her leg and comfort her the only way he could. Once he'd finished pulling papers from the briefcase, Mr. Quinn set them on the table and turned them toward Tori.

TORI soon realized she wasn't too smart when it came to legal matters. She stared at the papers, afraid to touch them. Unsure what they were, she looked back to the slimy little man she hated, asking, "What part am I supposed to be looking at?"

"I marked it in the margin, but to simplify, when my client, your ex-husband, drew up his will, he made sure to exclude everyone from it." Tori knew all too well how he made sure everything was his. "The problem was that he had to name someone as his benefactor. He didn't want to donate it to anyone—no person or charity. He was quite content with the thought of dying and having his assets sit, benefiting no one."

The distaste in his voice confused Tori. "You talk as if you didn't like Damien."

Mr. Quinn shook his head. "He was my client, not my friend. I carried out tasks based on my professional obligations, but I know a selfish bastard when I see one."

Jason chuckled under his breath, and Tori was more eager to find out why he was there. "Good to know you saw the real him. Please continue."

"As I was saying, he had appointed no one as his benefactor, but a will is not complete unless one is designated. So, being the selfish bastard he was, he decided to designate his "heir" as the sole benefactor of his estate. Since he didn't plan on having any children, he figured he'd found a loophole in the system. Little did he know, you'd have the final word." He finished his statement with a smirk, and Tori found herself smiling. It was almost as if he was pleased that Damien didn't get what he wanted.

Jason interrupted her thoughts when he said, "So you're saying that when he designated a child to inherit his entire estate, he did it with belief he would never have any?" Mr. Quinn nodded and Jason continued. "And since Lexi is his only offspring, she gets his entire estate?"

"That's exactly what I'm saying."

"Well, isn't that just all kinds of funny. Talk about irony," Jason said with a laugh. Tori didn't know if she wanted to laugh or cry. She didn't want anything from Damien and didn't need anything. They should give it to charity, she thought.

"We don't want it," she blurted without thinking. Finding Jason's gaze, she added, "We don't need it."

"Of course you don't, baby," Jason offered as he rubbed his hand on her leg. She smiled, falling a little more in love right then.

"Unfortunately, since you're not listed, you can't make that decision," Mr. Quinn said.

Surprised, Tori stated sarcastically, "Well, I know the one year old can't make that kind of decision."

"No, she can't. But I can make arrangements for the assets to be sold, and the funds can be placed in an account. The account will sit there untouched, gaining interest until your daughter reaches age eighteen. Then she can make the decision herself."

Tori had no idea how much Damien's estate was worth, and she didn't want to know. She found herself looking to Jason again, not for answers but maybe guidance. He smiled. "Sounds like a good idea don't you think? Maybe she could put it toward college."

Mr. Quinn interrupted them, saying, "I assure you the funds would allow her to pay tuition at any college she chose and she could even bring a few friends with her."

As if Lexi knew they were talking about her, she picked that moment to throw her toy. It bounced off Mr. Quinn's head, and while Jason couldn't help but laugh, Tori quickly apologized before glaring at Jason. He just continued to smile and said, "She's got great aim, don't you think?"

~*~*~*~

Later that evening, back at Jason's, Tori found herself standing over Lexi as she slept in her crib. It had been a long day, and her mind was still processing all of it. Turning the baby monitor on, she left the room, in search of Jason. She found him awkwardly brushing his teeth with his left hand. Smiling, she filled a cup with water and handed it to him. Before rinsing, he gave her a grin full of toothpaste and said, "I could totally be left-handed by the time this is over."

Tori laughed and shook her head, enjoying his lighter mood. She was glad to see the grumpy giant had left the building, at least for the time being. She handed him a towel, he wiped his face before asking, "What's wrong, baby?"

He set the towel down and pulled her cautiously against him. Once she knew he wasn't in pain, she rested her head on his chest and sighed. "I'm glad you can hold me again. I missed your chest."

"I missed having you on my chest." He kissed the top of her head as they stood in silence for a little while. "You gonna tell me what's running through that head of yours?"

Tori turned and pressed her lips against the skin of his chest before saying, "I was thinking about Mr. Quinn's offer to come back with the papers for Lexi's trust."

Jason's eyebrows dropped in question. "I thought by the time he left you were okay with the thought of Lexi inheriting his estate? You gotta admit, it's some crazy poetic justice that it happened like that."

Tori let out a laugh, "Yeah. He must be throwing one hell of a tantrum in hell right now." She paused before adding, "But that's not what I'm thinking about."

"Tell me."

"Well, I was hoping that maybe I could delay signing them until you're a little better, and we could go to Idaho to take care of it."

"Of course, if that's how you want to handle it, we will," he said as his hand swept up and down her back. She really had missed being held by him.

She nodded. "Yes, I'd like to go to Idaho. There's someone there I'd really like to see."

"Then we'll make arrangements for as soon as I can fly." Jason kissed her once before saying, "Now get ready for bed, baby, I finally have use of one of my arms." He waggled his eyebrows suggestively then winked as he left the room. She smiled to herself, loving how playful he was. Facing her reflection, her eyes landed on the older scar. Her hand went to it and slowly traced its path. Then her other hand went to the bandaged side and repeated the motion.

When she let her hands drop to her sides, she grinned and thought about Damien. It was the first time she could recall smiling when thinking of her personal demon. She let her eyes travel from one side to the next, noticing the angles matched. Again, she smirked as she silently acknowledged that he at least made them symmetrical.

Turning to the side, she examined the scars over her right shoulder—the ones she had given herself and thought it funny that these were irregular and blotchy. She harrumphed and faced front again. Pulling the waistband of her shorts down, she exposed the scar low on her belly. Noticing that it, too, was a straight, even line, she let out a laugh. He definitely didn't have the last word since every attempt he had at marking her, inflicting damage, or trying to destroy her were failed. Sure, he left marks behind, both physical and emotional, but they were her badges of survival. And with that wonderful realization, she put all thoughts of Damien away and got ready for bed with her man.

CHAPTER THIRTY-EIGHT

JASON and Tori had decided—at Tori's request to see the house again—to meet Mr. Quinn at Damien's. Tori had things to do while they were there in Idaho, and he wasn't about to go sit in an office where they would be made to wait. No, this way, he showed up, Tori signed the papers, and they were done. Especially since they'd requested the papers be sent to an attorney back in San Diego look everything over already, and Jason knew there was no further discussion needed.

Now that she'd handed over the signed papers and that was behind them, they stood together looking at the remains of Damien's house. The house that Victoria had lived in. He had no idea what was going through her head, but he let her have her space. Taking hold of Lexi, he tried to keep her busy as Tori processed whatever she needed to.

It had been two months since Damien died, and all of their injuries were finally healed. Lexi was comfortable walking now, and Jason let her roam around, keeping her attention away from Tori. When she tripped on the edge of the grass, Jason picked her up and dusted her off. Once he finished, he noticed a man standing at the edge of the property, looking apprehensive but determined. He knew immediately who it was. Jason walked right over to him, extended his hand, and said, "Mack?"

Mack smiled and took Jason's hand, returning the shake, he said, "Jason. It's great to meet you. When I saw you out here, I hoped it was you guys."

Mack was in his sixties and was probably pretty imposing in his days. With a full head of salt-and-pepper hair, a mustache, and shorts paired with a Hawaiian shirt, he reminded Jason of *Magnum PI*. Concealing the humor of his thoughts behind a smile, Jason said, "Yeah, we came to town for Tori to sign some papers, and she wanted to stop here."

"This must be the little one; she's beautiful," Mack said as he reached out and touched Lexi's hand. She smiled pretty for him, showing off what baby teeth she had.

Jason kissed her and agreed, "She sure is. Looks just like Mommy."

Just then Tori walked up next to them and stood silently for a moment. Jason watched as tears formed in her eyes before she smiled and said, "Mack ... I'm so glad you're here."

Tori threw her arms around Mack and hugged him tightly. The endearing look on his face made Jason appreciate him even more. Besides the fact he helped Tori escape the evil clutches of her husband, he had taken the time to seek her out when he thought she might be in danger. They were indebted to this man forever.

A minute or so passed before Tori finally let Mack go. She stepped back and wiped the tears from her cheeks. "Sorry, I promise I have self-control, but I seem to very emotional today."

Mack smiled. “No need to apologize, sweetheart. I’m just glad I got to see you.”

She nodded, apparently still trying to compose herself. Jason wrapped his arm around her shoulder, pulling her against him. Tori leaned into him as she asked Mack, “Can we take you to lunch? I’d love to spend time with you. You only know the parts of my life that were dramatic.”

“I’d love to,” Mack said as he motioned over his shoulder, “Let me just lock the house up.”

They stood for a few moments before Mack returned and they set out to have lunch together. Jason enjoyed spending time with Mack, reminding him of his own father. As they waved goodbye to Mack and set out for their next destination, Jason made a mental note to have lunch with his dad when they returned.

TORI wasn’t sure why she was nervous; there was no reason to be. Maybe it was just anticipation, she thought as Jason passed through the rod iron gates. Taking in the scenery, she tried to remember where they needed to go. Having only been there the one time, she hoped she would recognize it when she saw it. The grass was a healthy green, cut tightly to the ground. In some areas, it just looked look like a large lawn to roll around on and play. She supposed that was their goal in those areas, to hide the stones and make it look less like a cemetery.

Jason drove slowly, asking, “Does anything look familiar yet? We could go to the office and get a map I think.”

Tori took Jason's hand and squeezed. "Just keep going please, I see some things I recognize. I'm certain I'll know it when I see it."

"Okay, just tell me when."

She nodded and turned back to the lawns. Her mother's stone wasn't a large one, but it wasn't flat. The day she'd laid her to rest, Tori was mesmerized by the large tree that stretched over her plot. Because her mother had wanted to be cremated, she was able to choose the spot under the grand tree in hopes that she would have visitors. It made Tori's heart hurt to think that she hadn't been back since that day. But deep down, she knew her mother understood. After all, she believed she was watching over her all this time. How else would she have been saved in so many ways?

When the car came over an embankment, the glorious tree came into view, and Tori's eyes filled with tears. Squeezing Jason's hand, she pointed. "It's over there, beneath the tree."

"Wow, that's some tree," Jason said in awe. Tori smiled; it was so like her mother to pick that spot. Jason parked the car on the small road in front of the tree and turned off the car. Tori stared for long moments before he asked, "Would you like me to go with you?"

Tori nodded. "Yes, please. Can you carry Lexi?"

"Of course. You ready?" he asked softly, ever thoughtful of the situation. Again she nodded through the lump in her throat, and they got out of the car.

Jason came around the back of the car with Lexi. He stood next to Tori and held her hand. Tori took a deep breath and willed herself forward. Slowly, they traversed the sunny lawn, moving around headstones and flowers. When they reached the shaded canopy of the tree, she felt a sense of peace wash over her. It was a feeling she always felt around her mother.

Stopping just before the roots started, they came upon the rose marble stone engrossed with her mother's name. The words 'Beloved mother and friend' were carved just below her name. Although she was so much more than that, those words spoke volumes to Tori. Together, they stood silently, feeling the peacefulness of their surroundings. It was almost like Lexi understood something was different about where they were because she, too, was quiet.

When Jason squeezed her hand in support, she whispered, "I'm not sure what I'm supposed to say or do."

"What would you do or say if she were standing right in front of you?" Jason asked softly.

Tori sniffled and a small laugh escaped as she said, "If Mom were standing here right now, I'd introduce you to her, and then she'd lean over and whisper something inappropriate about how handsome you are."

"And of course I would be oh-so-charming and say something like, 'I thought I was meeting your mom, not your older sister,'" Jason said with humor.

She giggled, "She would've been so charmed by that, too. I can imagine her response would've been to slip her arm in yours and tell you to take her to lunch so she could hear more."

"Then I would take her to lunch and tell her what a beautiful, strong, and amazing daughter she has. And that I love her very much," Jason said, squeezing her hand. She looked up at him, tears streaming down her face and smiled.

"I can see it all in my head," she wiped her cheeks and sniffled, "as if it really happened."

Jason kissed her hand. "In a way, it just did. You can hold on to that image and let it live in your heart."

Tori looked at him in shock, and shaking her head, she stated the obvious, "I'm so happy I found you."

"Ditto," he said before kissing her forehead and adding, "We'll give you some time alone. I'll be right over there if you need me."

She nodded and watch Jason and Lexi walk away before turning back around. Closing her eyes, she latched onto the vision she had of her mom meeting Jason and smiled. She would keep that close to her heart and pretend it was real.

"So I guess I should thank you, Mom. You know at first, when things went bad with Damien, I thought how strange it was for you to have not seen it. Since you were such a great judge in character, but now I see it." Tori laughed to herself, looking over her shoulder in the direction of the car. She took in the sight of Jason holding Lexi over his head as she giggled. Looking back at the marble stone she continued, "I know you would never have given your approval of Damien if you knew what he was capable of. But I see that it was just a step in a direction that led me to where I am now. If I hadn't been with Damien, I never would've ran to San Diego. And then I never would've found Jason."

Swallowing her tears, she continued, "He's so good to me, Mom. So good to *us*. He's everything you would've wanted for me." She smiled. "But somehow I think you already know this, don't you."

After a long moment, she dried her cheeks, and said, "I won't be by as often as I'd like to be, but I promise to come when I can. Just know that I'm happy, healthy, and loved. I have everything I could've hoped for, and I promise you're never far from thoughts."

She blew a kiss to the stone and smiled again. "Bye Mom."

Turning around, she walked toward her future with a full heart and a smile on her face.

EPILOGUE

JASON leaned back in the chair and laid her head against his chest. Dropping his face into her hair, he placed a reverent kiss there. Quietly, they sat together. He would periodically kiss her head as he rubbed her back, his body finally losing the tension from the day's events. Deciding he had a few things he wanted to tell her, he gently cleared his throat and spoke softly to match the atmosphere of the room.

"So, I was thinking. And you don't have to say anything; you can just listen and let me say what's on my mind. Unless you want to, of course. Anyway, I wanted you to know that since you've come into my world, I've thought of little else but you. On a daily basis, I worry about how you're doing and if you're okay. You should try not to hold it against me, it's just how I am. In fact, you should just embrace it and see it as a good thing."

He placed a kiss to her forehead before continuing, "I want you to know that I'll do everything in my power to make sure you are happy, and healthy, and safe. There is nothing I wouldn't do for you. All you have to do is say the word, I promise you."

She opened her eyes and he smiled. "I love you so much already; it takes my breath away. And I promise to make sure you know that every single day."

Finished with his speech, he felt the enormity of his words, the permanency of their connection. Sweeping an unruly curl on her forehead to the side, he watched as it sprang back, it's color so mesmerizing. Her eyes began to droop until they closed completely and she went to sleep. Still smiling, he said with a little humor, "That's okay, you don't need to say anything. I know you'll love me, too. I just needed to make sure you knew how important you are to me and how much I love you."

A moment later, Tori's voice, laced with exhaustion said, "Sounds like I should be jealous."

Jason stood immediately, but cautiously, as he held his daughter tightly to his chest. Moving to her bed, he sat on the edge and smiled down at her. "How are you feeling, my love? Do you need anything? Would you like me to call a nurse? Should I get you some ice chips?"

Tori lifted her finger to his lips, "Shh. Did you know you babble when you're nervous?"

He chuckled, "Yes, dear wife, I do, but only with you."

She shook her head and smirked, "Not true. I do believe there are now three women in your life who can make you babble like a nervous monkey."

Looking down at the newest addition to their little family, he asked, "Is it bad that I already want to lock her up and never let anything hurt her?"

Tori smiled before whispering, "I think it makes her one of the luckiest girls around."

Jason shook his head before kissing Tori softly and whispering back, "It's me who's the lucky one."

~THE END~

About the Author

Melanie is an amazing mother of four, an awesome and tolerant wife to one, and nurse to many. If you don't believe her, just ask anyone in her family, they know what to say. She is also a devoted chauffer, the keeper of missing socks, a genius according to a six year old, the coolest soccer uniform coordinator according to a twelve year old, and the best damn 'mac-n-cheese-with-cut-up-hot-dog maker in the whole world. Well that last title isn't really official, but it's still pretty cool to be called it.

When not being ordered around by any of the kids, you can find her with her nose in a book or on the sideline of a soccer game cheering on one team or another. But that's mostly because she has a thing for the coach. When she is not doing all of the above, you can find her obsessed with a group of fictional characters all vying for a spot on the page of whatever she's working on. It's a fun and crazy life to lead, but wouldn't have it any other way.

If you liked my book you can keep up with upcoming books, sneak peeks, and more at:

Twitter: @MelanieCodina

Good Reads: **http://tinyurl.com/d8bz7mw**

Facebook: https://www.facebook.com/MelanieCodinaAuthor

Thank you for reading. Please look for other books in this series, as well as more to come. Remember that the best compliment you can pay an author is to leave a review ... We love to read them.

The Real Love Series:

Love Realized

Love Resisted

Love Required

And coming soon...

We get to hear from the younger generation of Baxters in:

Assumptions

Expectations